To remember what you've read, write your initials in a square!

558

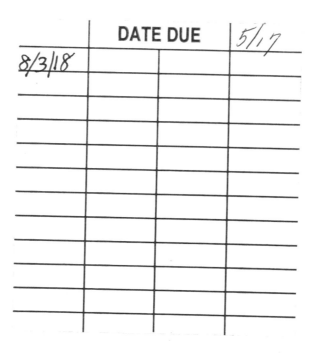

		DATE DUE	5/17
8/3/18			

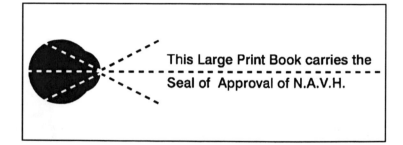

This Large Print Book carries the
Seal of Approval of N.A.V.H.

A COUNTY CORK MYSTERY

BURIED IN A BOG

SHEILA CONNOLLY

WHEELER PUBLISHING
A part of Gale, Cengage Learning

GALE
CENGAGE Learning·

Detroit • New York • San Francisco • New Haven, Conn • Waterville, Maine • London

Copyright © 2013 by Sheila Connolly.
A County Cork Mystery.
Wheeler Publishing, a part of Gale, Cengage Learning.

Wheeler Publishing Large Print Cozy Mystery.
The text of this Large Print edition is unabridged.
Other aspects of the book may vary from the original edition.
Set in 16 pt. Plantin.

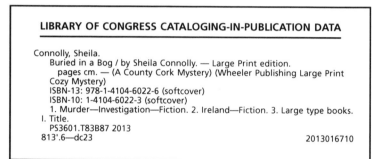

LIBRARY OF CONGRESS CATALOGING-IN-PUBLICATION DATA

Connolly, Sheila.
　Buried in a Bog / by Sheila Connolly. — Large Print edition.
　　pages cm. — (A County Cork Mystery) (Wheeler Publishing Large Print Cozy Mystery)
　ISBN-13: 978-1-4104-6022-6 (softcover)
　ISBN-10: 1-4104-6022-3 (softcover)
　1. Murder—Investigation—Fiction. 2. Ireland—Fiction. 3. Large type books.
I. Title.
　PS3601.T83B87 2013
　813'.6—dc23   2013016710

Published in 2013 by arrangement with The Berkley Publishing Group, a member of Penguin Group (USA) Inc.

Printed in the United States of America
2 3 4 5 6   21 20 19 18 17

ACKNOWLEDGMENTS

My father's father, John Connolly, was born in County Cork in 1883 and arrived in New York City in 1911. I never knew him. As an adult I thought that visiting Ireland, particularly the area where he was born, might help me understand who he was, and the result was a series of trips to Cork that I hope will go on.

My grandfather's part of Cork is known as the Wild West, about as far as you can get from Dublin. It's where Michael Collins was born, and where he was ambushed and died. It's also an area that was particularly hard-hit by the Irish Potato Famine in the mid-nineteenth century. Somehow my Connolly ancestors managed to thrive, and there are still Connollys there.

This series was inspired by my discovery of a pub called Connolly's, in the tiny village of Leap near my grandfather's even tinier townland of Knockskagh. While the

5

pub was small, it was well known for the musicians it attracted from all over Ireland. Sadly the last Connolly owner passed on a few years ago, but I had a chance to attend some memorable events there. I hope I've done right by it, in reviving it here at Sullivan's, and there may yet be music there.

I've been a genealogist for years, but Irish genealogy poses some challenges, mainly because in the past many Cork families held to traditional naming patterns — for example, a first-born son is named for his father's father, a first-born daughter for her mother's mother. You can imagine the confusion in a small community when multiple children are named for a shared grandfather! The solution has often been to add a nickname: Big Sean, Red-Haired Mick, Old Jerry, or even PatJoe (Patrick son of Joseph). I've used some of those in this book to help keep things straight. I hope I've got all the family connections right, but I won't blame you for getting a bit lost. Not to worry — it'll all come right in the end.

But this series might not have seen the light of day were it not for the several years I've spent taking classes in the Irish language. Some of the difficulties in learning Irish are due to the "improvements" in spelling imposed by the English in the middle of the last century. But when you hear it spoken, it's far more musical, more expressive. I wish I could say I could speak it well after so many classes, but I'm still stuck on basics. I can at least follow a conversation, and the credit goes to Peigí Ni Chlochartaigh, *mo mhúinteoir,* a great lady with a wicked sense of humor (in any language), and to my more fluent colleagues in those classes.

Of course I have to thank my amazing agent, Jessica Faust of BookEnds, who helped shape my protagonist's character, and to my long-suffering editor, Shannon Jamieson Vazquez, with whom I had many debates about what was "really" Irish. I also appreciate the prompt assistance of the Public Relations Office of the Garda Siochána (the Irish police force) in Dublin, which answered my questions about Irish police jurisdictions and procedures.

Sometimes I wonder if County Cork is part of the modern world, despite the satellite dishes and mobile phones and supermarkets stocked with a wealth of European foods, because it feels timeless. It's a special place, and I hope you'll see that here.

Ar scáth a chéile a mhaireann na daoine.
People live in one another's shadows.
— IRISH PROVERB

CHAPTER 1

Maura Donovan checked her watch again. If she had it right, she had been traveling for over fourteen hours; she wasn't going to reset it for the right time zone until she got where she was going, which she hoped would be any minute now. First the red-eye flight from Boston to Dublin; the cheapest she could find; then a bus from Dublin to Cork, then another, slower bus from Cork to Leap, a flyspeck on the map on the south coast of Ireland. But she was finding that in Ireland nobody ever hurried, especially on the local bus. The creaking vehicle would pull over at a location with no obvious markings, and people miraculously appeared. They greeted the driver by name; they greeted each other as well. Her they nodded at, wary of a stranger in their midst.

She tried to smile politely in return, but she was exhausted. She didn't know where she was or what she was doing. She was on this rattletrap bus only because Gran had asked her to make the trip — just before she died, worn down from half a century of scrabbling to make a living and keep a roof over her granddaughter's head in South Boston. Now that she thought about it, Gran had probably been planning this trip for her for quite a while. She had insisted that Maura get a passport, and not just any passport, but an Irish one, which was possible only because Gran had filed for an Irish Certificate of Foreign Birth for her when she was a child. What else had Gran not told her?

And what else had she been too young and too selfish to ask about? Gran had never talked much about her life in Ireland, before she had been widowed and brought her young son to Boston, and Maura had been too busy trying to be American to care. She didn't remember her father, no more than a large laughing figure. Or her mother, who after her father's death had decided that raising a child alone, with an Irish-born mother-in-law, was not for her and split. It had always been just her and Gran, in a small apartment in a shabby triple-decker in a not-so-good neighborhood in South Boston.

Which was where Irish immigrants had

12

been settling for generations, so Maura was no stranger to the Boston Irish community. Maybe her grandmother Nora Donovan had never shoved the Ould Country down her throat, but there had been many a time that Maura had come home from school or from work and found Gran deep in conversation with some new immigrant, an empty plate in front of him. Gran had taken it on herself to look out for the new ones, who'd left Ireland much as she had, hoping for a better life, or more money. The flow of immigrants had slowed for a while when the Celtic Tiger — the unexpected prosperity that had swept Ireland then disappeared again within less than a decade — was raging, but then it had picked up again in the past few years.

Maura suspected that Gran had been slipping these newcomers some extra cash, which would go a long way toward explaining why they'd never had the money to move out of the one-bedroom apartment they'd lived in as long as Maura could remember. Why Gran had worked more than one job, and why Maura had started working as early as the law would let her. Why Gran had died, riddled with cancer after waiting too long to see a doctor, and had left a bank account with barely enough to cover the last bills. Then the landlord had announced he was converting the building to condominiums, now that Southie was becoming gentrified, and Maura was left with no home and no one.

It was only when she was packing up Gran's pitifully few things that she'd found the envelope with the money. In one of their last conversations in the hospital, Gran had made her promise to go to Ireland, Maura to say a Mass in the old church in Leap, where she'd been married. "Say my farewells for me, darlin'," she'd said, and Maura had agreed to her face, although she had thought it was no more than the ramblings of a sick old woman. How was she supposed to fly to Ireland, when she wasn't sure she could make the next rent payment?

The envelope, tucked in the back of Gran's battered dresser alongside Maura's passport, held the answer. It had contained just enough cash to buy a plane ticket from Boston to Dublin, and to pay for a short stay, if Maura was frugal. Since Gran had taught her well, she didn't think she'd have any trouble doing that. How Gran had managed to set aside that much, Maura would never know.

She'd buried Gran, with only a few of her Irish immigrant friends in attendance, and a week later she'd found herself on a plane. And here she was. Maura was surprised to feel the sting of tears. She was cold, damp, jet-lagged, and — if she was honest with herself — depressed. It had been a long few weeks, but at least staying busy had allowed her to keep her sadness at bay. Gran had been her only relative, her only tie to any place, and with Gran gone Maura was no longer sure where she belonged. She was free, if broke. She could go anywhere she wanted, and with her work experience tending bar and waitressing, she could pick up a short-term job almost anywhere. The problem was, she didn't know where she wanted to go. There was nothing to hold her in Boston, but there was no point in leaving either.

Maura looked out through the rain streaming down the windows. She'd always heard that Ireland was green, but at the moment all she could see was grey. What had Gran wanted her to find in Ireland?

Since Gran had never really mentioned any people "back home" to Maura, she'd been surprised to find a bundle of letters and photographs stashed next to the envelope with the money, where Gran must have been sure that Maura would find them. Sorting through them after Gran's death, she had found that the few photographs were ones she had seen no more than once or twice in her life, but luckily Gran had written names on the back; most of the letters had come from a Bridget Nolan, with only the skimpiest of return addresses — not even a street listing. Taking a chance — and wanting to believe that someone in Ireland would still care — Maura had written to the woman about her old friend Nora's death and her wish that Maura make the trip to Ireland to pay her respects there. Mrs. Nolan had written back immediately and urged her to come over. Her spidery handwriting hinted at her advanced age and suggested that Maura shouldn't delay, and it was barely two weeks later that Maura had found herself on the plane. And then on a bus, which passed through small towns, cheerfully painted in bright colors, as if to fight the gloom of the rain. Most often it took no more than a couple of minutes to go from one end of the town to the other, and between there was a lot of open land, dotted with cattle and sheep and the occasional ruined castle to remind Maura that she was definitely somewhere that wasn't Boston. The towns listed on the road signs meant nothing to her. She was afraid of dozing off and missing her stop.

16

Mrs. Nolan had given Maura sketchy instructions to get off the bus in front of Sullivan's Pub in a village called Leap, and they would "see to her," whatever that meant. The bus lurched and belched fumes as it rumbled along the main highway on the south coast, though "highway" was a rather grand description: it was two lanes wide. More than once the bus had found itself behind a truck lumbering along at a brisk twenty miles per hour, but nobody had seemed anxious about it; no one was hurrying.

Finally, through the murk of the late March afternoon, Maura could make out a large painted sign by the road: Sullivan's of Leap, with a dashing highwayman riding a horse straight out of the sign. It was no more than a minute later that the bus driver called out "Leap" (which he pronounced "Lep," as in "leper"), and Maura gathered her belongings — which consisted of a battered duffel bag with her clothes plus an old school backpack with everything else — and waited while a few other women climbed down. The women appeared to be regular riders; they exchanged farewells and vanished quickly in different directions, leaving Maura standing alone in the rain looking at the dilapidated facade of Sullivan's.

Despite the rain she took a moment to study the town and get her bearings. Actually "town" was probably not the right term, since she could see most of it from where she stood on the main road. There was a string of brightly painted houses along each side of the road, with a glimpse of the occasional cow grazing on the hill behind. Two churches — one Catholic, one Church of Ireland — faced off across the road from each other. One school, next to the Catholic church. A small hotel, and a couple of shops. And she counted three pubs, including Sullivan's, huddling together where the road widened.

From what little she'd read online at the local library in Southie, Leap's population had been hovering around two hundred people for more than a century. Once the ladies from the bus had vanished, there was no one in sight, though she spied a few lights on here and there, including one inside Sullivan's. Gran had always said that making a good first impression was important, but Maura didn't have a lot of options: she hadn't brought much with her, and she'd left even less behind. Now she was wet and rumpled. She ran her fingers through her hair, then hoisted the straps of the two bags up on her shoulder, approached the door, and pulled it open.

Inside it seemed barely brighter than the dusk outside. A black-and-white dog lay sprawled on the floor near the entrance. It lifted its head as Maura approached, then decided she wasn't worth bothering about and went back to sleep. There was a small, smoke-stained fireplace at one end, surrounded by shabby upholstered chairs, and what Maura guessed was a peat fire glowed dimly. The smell of the peat smoke helped to conceal the other, less pleasant odors: a mix of stale beer, staler cigarette smoke, unwashed bodies, and just a hint of urine. As her eyes adjusted to the light, she took in the bar that occupied half of the back wall and the complete absence of customers, except for a bulky figure slumped in the chair nearest the fire. Maura wasn't sure he was breathing.

A young girl was swabbing the top of the bar with a damp grey rag, her eyes on whatever sitcom with laugh track was playing on the television mounted over the end of the bar. Her hair was carelessly tied up in a ponytail, with a few curls escaping, and her delicate face was lightly sprinkled with freckles. She looked up eagerly when Maura came in, and said, "How can I help you, ma'am?"

Maura would bet that she was no more than ten years older than the girl, who looked about fifteen — when had she become a "ma'am"? And why wasn't the girl home doing her schoolwork on a weekday in March? Not that it was any of her business. But at least the girl was polite and welcoming, and Maura was cold and tired and hungry. She couldn't even remember when she had eaten last. "I'm Maura Donovan," she said. "Bridget Nolan said I should stop by here?"

The girl looked perplexed for a moment, then recognition dawned. "Ah, you'd be the American, come to visit. She left a note for you — I know it's here somewhere." The girl turned and shuffled through odds and ends on a shelf behind the bar. "Here it is." She smoothed the slightly crumpled folded piece of paper before handing it to Maura. "Would you care for a cup of tea? Or coffee? Americans do like their coffee, don't they?"

To Maura's experienced eye, the coffee she spotted on a hot plate behind the bar would probably be suitable only for sealing asphalt. "Tea would be fine, thank you." How far wrong could she go with a tea bag and hot water?

As the girl hunted up the cup, the bag,

20

sugar, milk, a spoon, and a napkin, Maura took a seat on a creaking bar stool and read the note Mrs. Nolan had left for her. She apologized for not being able to come out and meet her right away, and instructed her to cross the street and talk to Ellen Keohane, who would fix her up just fine. Maura shook her head, trying to decipher what Mrs. Nolan could mean by that.

The girl proudly set a steaming mug in front of Maura, with a tea bag tail dangling. At least it was Barry's tea, which her gran had loved — Maura couldn't fathom crossing an ocean just to get a cup of Lipton's. "Thank you. What do I owe you?" She'd gotten some euros from what she'd finally identified as an ATM at the airport, after a bit of wrangling with numbers — at least her debit card had worked, not that there was a lot in her bank account. It was funny, putting in the card and getting out a handful of bills with pretty pictures on them — it was like play money. Just to reassure herself, she had broken a few bills, buying something to drink and a bun, to have coins on hand, but after paying for the bus ticket she wasn't sure how much she had — or how long it would need to last. She'd seen neither a bank nor an ATM in Leap so far.

"Seeing as you're a friend of Mrs. Nolan's,

21

it's on the house," the girl said, flashing a dimple. "By the way, my name's Rose Sweeney."

"Nice to meet you," Maura said. "I can't say that I exactly know Mrs. Nolan, but my grandmother did."

"No matter, Mrs. Nolan said that we should be looking for you. At least Mick, her grandson, did — he'd be the one who brought the note here for you. We didn't know when you'd be coming."

"I wasn't sure myself — I kind of had to grab the first cheap plane ticket I could get, and there wasn't time to let anyone know. Is it a problem?"

"Mrs. Nolan knew you'd be here soon, and she let Ellen know. Don't worry yourself.

"So, who is this Ellen Keohane I'm supposed to find?" Maura asked.

"She takes in a few visitors now and then, in the house over by the harbor there." Rose gestured vaguely across the road. "It's a small place, she only rents out the two rooms, but it's nice. Quiet, and the views are pretty."

"That was nice of her. Tell me, does Ellen charge much?"

"It's off-season, and Ellen Keohane's a fair woman, or so me da says. And cheaper

22

than the hotel, not that there's any space there. Full of fishermen, it is. Will you be staying long, or are you just stopping for a bit?"

Maura dunked her tea bag a few times, then pulled it out of the water. "I . . . really don't know. A week, maybe?" She'd booked a return flight for a week later, but only because it was cheaper that way. She looked around the room, darkening by the minute. The clock above the bar said it was only four o'clock. How could it be so dark, so early? "Does this place get busier?" She was the only customer, although the old man sleeping by the fire had a half-full pint glass in front of him. She didn't remember seeing anyone pass by on the street outside in the time she'd been in the pub.

Rose looked momentarily confused, then smiled. "It's Tuesday, and it's early yet. Come Friday, you'll see the place more lively. Where're you from, then?"

"Boston, in the States. I guess I'm used to having more people around."

"I've never been farther away than Cork City," Rose said wistfully. "Is Boston much bigger than Cork?"

"I think so," Maura said. "It's more than half a million, I know."

Rose's eyes widened. "We've only about

four million in Ireland, all in. Cork City's got little more than a hundred thousand and some, but I'm told Dublin is over a million. So your Boston would be more crowded than Cork, but not as big as Dublin."

"I didn't get a chance to see Dublin, just the airport." Which had seemed smaller than Boston's to Maura. "But yes, it's pretty crowded, at least in parts. How big is Leap?"

"A couple of hundred, no more."

"And you've lived here all your life? Are you finished with school?"

"I've done my Leaving Certificate." When Maura looked blankly at her, Rose went on to explain what that meant.

Maura tried hard to follow Rose's explanation of the Irish educational system. She didn't mean to be rude, but the long trip was catching up with her, and she quickly lost the thread. She thought she understood that Rose had finished with her secondary education, but apparently had no plans to go on. "Listen, I'd better go see this place of Ellen's," Maura finally said. "Is there someplace to eat around here?"

"We're not doing food here at the moment, unless just crisps will do, and they're none too fresh," Rose said dubiously. "There's the hotel," she added. "And maybe the café's open, though they do mostly lunches. You'd be better off in Skibbereen."

"I don't have a car. How often do the buses run?"

"Ah," Rose said. "Well, maybe you should ask Mrs. Keohane. She'd know better."

"Good idea. Thanks for the tea, Rose." Maura slid off the bar stool and almost fell over — her muscles had stiffened up, not that she'd been sitting long. She really needed to get some food and some rest, preferably but not necessarily in that order. "I'll go over there now. Just across the road, you said?"

"Well, across and down a bit. You'll see the drive off to your right, and then you go down the hill, kinda. You can't miss it."

Maura wasn't so sure, especially now that it was getting darker by the minute — the heavy clouds showed no sign of thinning. At least there wasn't much traffic. "I'm sure I'll be seeing you again. Bye for now."

The straps of her bags were digging into her shoulder — how had they gotten heavier since she had arrived? Outside the pub Maura stopped a moment to get her bearings. She looked both ways — and then looked again, reminding herself that the cars would be driving on the left here — and then headed across the road. Rose had been right: there weren't many chances to get lost. She followed the graveled drive down and discovered a house with its front door facing the drive. Nowhere did it indicate that there were rooms to let, but at least there were lights on inside. She found the doorbell and pushed it. She could hear it ringing somewhere inside the house, and the bell seemed to precipitate a clamor of childish voices, followed by footsteps. The door was opened by a thirty-something woman wearing an apron; the noise of clamoring children grew louder. The woman pushed her hair out of her face and said warily, "Can I help you?"

"I'm Maura Donovan. Are you Ellen Keohane? Bridget Nolan said I should talk to you."

"Ah, of course — you're the American. She mentioned you'd be coming soon. Welcome! I'm just giving the kids their dinner, but come in."

Maura willingly followed her in, dropping her bags on the hall floor.

"Come on through — I'll only be a minute," Ellen said, striding back toward the brightly lit kitchen at the end of the hallway. Maura hesitated, then followed.

In the kitchen, Ellen said, "The three of you, eat up now. This is Maura, come all the way from America. Maura, this is Kevin,

Sean, and Patrick, and the baby's Gráinne. Kevin's ten, Sean eight, Patrick seven, and Gráinne's not yet two." The children looked up briefly, then returned their attention to their fish sticks. Maura guessed that strangers held no particular interest for them: if Ellen welcomed a succession of guests, no doubt they'd seen their fair share.

"Gráinne?" Maura asked, confused. It sounded like "grawn-ya," and she'd never heard it before.

Ellen laughed. "Of course, you wouldn't know it. It's a girl's name here, and Gráinne's my little darling. I'm so glad she turned out to be a girl, after this lot." She smiled affectionately at the children around the table. "Boys, I'll be showing Miss Donovan here the room, below. I'll only be a minute. Kevin, you keep an eye on the little ones." Ellen turned back to Maura. "It's downstairs, at the back. Kevin's the only one sleeps down there, but he'll be no trouble. He's a quiet one. Shall I show you now?"

"Please," Maura said. The idea of a space of her own — with a bed — was becoming more and more appealing with every passing moment. She snagged her bags from the hall and followed her hostess down a flight of stairs and around a corner. Ellen pulled a key out of her pocket and opened the hall door, ushering Maura into a midsized room with one double bed and one single tucked in the other corner.

"The bath's at the back," Ellen said, "and you can hang your clothes in the cabinet there. I'll push the heat up a bit, now you're here. Do you know how long you'll be needing the room?"

"I . . . don't really know. A week? And I guess I have to ask how much you'll be charging?"

Ellen cocked her head at Maura. "The off-season rate is 250 euros a week. Does that suit you?"

Maura tried to translate euros to dollars and thought that came out to something like forty-five dollars a night — if she was right, that certainly sounded reasonable. She could work it out later. She desperately craved food and sleep. "Sure, that's fine. Listen, I'll let you get back to your kids. But is there someplace I can get something to eat?"

"There's the hotel — it's the closest. You look dead on your feet. Why not get a bite there tonight, and I'll tell you about some other places in the morning. You'll be wanting the full breakfast?"

"What's that?" Maura asked.

Ellen laughed. "And you a good Irish girl! It's everything you can fit on a plate — eggs, streaky bacon, good Clonakilty sausage, beans, mushrooms, and more. It comes with the price of the room."

"It sounds wonderful," Maura said, overwhelmed. Maybe with a breakfast like that she wouldn't need to eat the rest of the day. She should try it, at least once, on her first day. "Thank you."

"Grand." Ellen handed her a set of keys for the room and the front door, and hurried back up the way they'd come, where the sounds from the kitchen had increased in volume. Once Ellen was gone, Maura carefully closed the door and surveyed her temporary home. It was clean and tidy, more practical than elegant. She checked out the tiny bathroom and splashed water on her face, then sat down on the bed: it felt comfortable, and there were plenty of pillows and blankets. She lay down, just for a moment . . .

Maura woke some time later to pitch dark. Real dark; cut-it-with-a-knife dark. And there was no noise: no cars passing, no airplanes overhead, no distant sirens. Where was she? Oh, right: Ireland. She was in a small town her grandmother had never said a word about. All her life Gran had kept

29

quiet about where she had come from, yet in the end she had wanted to send Maura here. *Well, Gran, you wanted me to be here, and here I am. What now?*

As she lay in the dark listening, she realized she *could* hear something — the rhythmic lapping of water against the shore. Hadn't Rose said there was a harbor? She hadn't seen it, but now she could hear it, and in the end it soothed her back to sleep.

CHAPTER 2

Maura woke again when light began to filter around the floor-length curtains opposite the bed. The clock on the table by the bed had been unplugged at some point, probably because the room didn't get much use, and she hadn't remembered to reset her watch. What was the time difference? Five hours? Six? Still, if it was light outside, she must have slept nearly twelve hours, a rare luxury in her life. She swung her legs over the edge of the bed and stood up, pulling her shirt down, trying in vain to smooth out the wrinkles. Her bag still sat on the smaller bed across the room, unopened, and the clothes she had packed would be equally wrinkled after being crammed in there for a couple of days.

Now what? The long drapes at the end of the ground-floor room must cover a door. Maura pulled them back, then stopped, transfixed. Last night the weather had been cold and wet, but today the sun had broken through. Outside her door lay the harbor, an inlet maybe a mile wide, with tall pines clustered on the right and open fields rising up the low hills beyond. There were sheep grazing on the hillside and swans floating on the water nearby. It looked like every tourist picture of Ireland that Maura had ever seen, and for the second time in two days she wanted to cry, this time because it was so lovely.

From upstairs she could hear sounds of activity — mostly the thuds of children's feet, then Ellen's voice as she shooed them out the door. To school? What day was this? She had to think for a moment before confirming that it was Wednesday, which meant it was a school day. With the kids out of the way, Ellen would be looking for her for breakfast, and Maura reluctantly tore herself away from the view to take a quick shower before she faced . . . what? She had no idea what her plans were for the day. But a shower and breakfast would be a good start, and she was starving.

But the shower baffled her. She hadn't done more than the bare minimum in the bathroom the night before, but now she was faced with plumbing she didn't recognize. Shower stall, relatively modern fiberglass, check. Handles, although left and right were switched. Hot water? She ran it for a minute or so but it stayed cold. She examined a small rectangular box set on the wall outside the stall, and after a couple of minutes she realized she was looking at a point-of-use water heater, something she'd heard about but never seen. It had a button, and when she pushed it, hot water miraculously came out of the showerhead. She felt ridiculously proud of herself for having figured it out, and stepped into the shower.

Ten minutes later she headed up the stairs in search of Ellen — and food. She found her landlady in the kitchen, with her youngest child in a high chair at the table. "Good morning," Maura said tentatively.

"Ah, there you are. I hope the children didn't disturb you?"

"Not at all. I didn't hear a thing. I hadn't realized how tired I was. Something smells good."

"You said you'd be wanting the full breakfast, right?" Ellen grinned a challenge at Maura. "Do you prefer coffee or tea?"

"Either's fine, if you have it made."

"Coffee, then. Go settle yourself in the parlor and I'll bring it out to you."

"I don't want you to go to any trouble." And the idea of this nice woman serving her made her uncomfortable. "Do you mind if I just stay here, or would I be in your way?"

Ellen laughed. "With four kids I'm often doing at least six things at a time! If you don't mind the mess, you're welcome to stay." She busied herself with a frying pan at the stove. "So this is your first trip to Ireland?"

"Yeah. My grandmother was born somewhere around here, but she never told me much about the place. Before she died recently, she made me promise I'd visit."

"That'd be Nora Sullivan?" As she talked, Ellen handed Gráinne a piece of bread with butter.

"That's right, before she married. Bridget Nolan told you about her?" Ellen was nowhere near old enough to have known her grandmother personally.

"She did indeed — her grandson brings her by now and then, seeing as she doesn't drive anymore."

"How old is she? If she knew my gran, she can't be young."

"Eighty-some? But she still lives on her own, bless her. Mrs. Nolan told me she knew not only your gran, but your grandfather and father too, come to that."

Maura realized with a shock that she had

never considered that. People who had known her father as a child? And his father, the grandfather she had never met? But Gran had said so little about the losses of her husband and her son, and Maura hadn't wanted to upset her by prying. "Hers was the only name I could find in Gran's things. I'm looking forward to meeting her. But how do I find her? When I wrote her, the address was kind of vague, although the letter must have gotten here." Worse, Maura knew that even when she found out where to find Mrs. Nolan, she had no idea how she was supposed to get there. Would there be a bus? Maybe someone would lend her a bicycle . . .

Ellen must have read her mind. "Mick'll be coming by to give you a ride out. That's Michael Nolan, her grandson. He looks out for her."

Maura hated to have to impose on anyone else, particularly someone she didn't know. "I can get there on my own."

Ellen laughed. "Not unless you know your way around the townlands. Mick's back and forth between the pub and his gran's in any case, so it's no problem."

Maura didn't recall seeing any man at the pub the day before, other than the old one in front of the fire. "He works at the pub?"

"Manages it, him and Jimmy Sweeney. That'd be Rose's father."

"Does Rose actually work at the pub?"

"She does. She's done with school. Her ma passed on a couple of years back, and she's living with her da."

And working at a dead-end job in a dead-end town, Maura thought. Surely a smart and nice-looking girl would have better options? Then a sharp voice in her head reminded her, *Like you, Maura?* But she'd had Gran to think about, and she owed her. Maybe she should find out what Rose's story was. "So Mrs. Nolan has lived around here for a long time?"

Ellen did some mental math. "She's lived in that cottage in Knockskagh since she married, and she's not about to give it up. Mick brings her groceries and keeps the place in good shape." Ellen set a plate heaped with food in front of Maura.

"Oh my. What's this?" She poked a round slice of something the color of tar.

"Blood sausage — Clonakilty's famous for it. You don't need to eat it if you don't want to."

"It really is made from blood?"

"That it is, among other things. Give it a try."

Nothing ventured, nothing gained, as

36

Gran had often said. As Ellen watched, Maura quartered the piece, speared a quarter with her fork, and stuck it in her mouth. She chewed thoughtfully. Not bad, as long as you avoided thinking about what it was made from. There were a lot of chopped oats in the mix somewhere, and a touch of seasoning. Definitely not American sausage. "Interesting. Where's Clonakilty?"

"It's along the main road, to the east. You must have come near it on the bus. So tell me, other than calling on Bridget Nolan, what are you planning for your visit?"

Maura chewed slowly on some of Ellen's bacon, which was closer to ham than what she was used to. "I . . . really don't know. It was Gran who wanted me to come, and she made me promise. She even left enough money to pay for it, although I don't know how she managed to put that much away. I haven't really had time to think about any touristy stuff. Heck, I've never been out of the country before." Maura had never even given traveling much thought. She and Gran had never taken anything like a vacation, unless a quick excursion out to Cape Cod with a friend counted. "I found the letters Mrs. Nolan had written to Gran, for years. I wrote to tell her that Gran had passed and that I wanted to meet her, and she answered right away. So here I am. Would anyone else remember Gran?"

"Surely they do." Ellen sat down across the table from Maura with a cup of coffee. "Your gran was born in Knockskagh — that's a townland only a few miles from here. Bridget Nolan was a neighbor."

"What's a townland?"

"Ah, do you not know the term? It's a land division. Leap here is a village, but the townlands are smaller. Now, Skibbereen is a town — there's maybe two thousand souls there. That's five miles down the road. You came from the Cork side?"

"Yes, I flew into Dublin, and then I took buses from there."

"Well, then, you've not seen Skibbereen. Why don't you talk to Mrs. Nolan and see how much time you'll want with her, and then you can plan?"

"Sounds good to me," said Maura. "Where am I supposed to meet this Mick?"

"He'll be stopping by here in a bit. No doubt Rose has told him you've arrived."

"Who owns the pub? Is there a Sullivan there?" Maura asked.

"That's a bit up in the air. Mick'd like to take over the place, but old Mick Sullivan died a week ago, and nobody's figured out who inherits."

38

Maura swabbed her plate with the last of the coarse brown bread. "I don't mean to be rude, but from what I saw of it yesterday, it's kind of a dump."

Ellen laughed. "You're right. Old Mick was ninety-odd, and he didn't much like change. He ran the place to suit himself."

"Does the place still do any business? It looked pretty quiet yesterday."

"It does. You'll have to go back in the evening. The locals, they don't mind a bit of dirt in the corners, and there are regulars who stop by, and the tourists think it's charming — they come mostly in the summer — although they usually leave after one drink, thinking they've seen the real Ireland." Ellen made a face before going on. "It's the people around here who keep it alive. Old habits die hard."

Someone rapped firmly on the front door, and Ellen stood up. "That'd be Mick. You finish up, and I'll bring him back. No need to hurry."

Ellen disappeared down the hall and returned a moment later followed by a tall man in his early thirties, Maura guessed. He was casually dressed in corduroys and a knit sweater, with heavy and slightly muddy shoes, and he needed a haircut. "Mick, this is Maura Donovan."

39

"Mick Nolan. Good to meet you." Maura had stood when he entered the room, and took the hand he offered. She noticed that he didn't smile.

"Thank you. Ellen tells me you're my ride out to . . . the townlands, is it?"

"Yes. My grannie, Mrs. Nolan, still likes living out there. Are you ready to go? She's sharpest in the mornings. I know she's looking forward to seeing you."

"Let me get my things," Maura said.

Downstairs she looked in the mirror. Her clothes looked as bad as she had feared, and her hair had dried every which way. But Mrs. Nolan would have to take her as she was. She sighed and picked up her bag and went up to meet Mick.

CHAPTER 3

Mick was waiting outside the front door when Maura came up the stairs. Ellen saw them off. "I'll be in and out today, Maura," she said. "But you've a key to the door at the back, so you can come and go as you like. Mick, say hello to your grannie for me."

"I will," he said, then fell silent again. He guided Maura to a car parked halfway up the drive, waited until she was settled in the passenger seat, then followed the drive to the road at the top. On the main road they turned right, then left almost immediately onto a small country road. Maura watched the countryside roll by. In today's nice weather, she could see that spring was further along here than back home: there were cheery clumps of daffodils blooming along the road and in the fields, as well as yellow flowering bushes she couldn't identify.

After a couple of miles of silence, Maura

realized Mick hadn't said anything. She was the visitor, the guest. Where was the Irish charm she'd heard about? Wasn't he supposed to be entertaining her? Had she done something to offend him? "So, where exactly are we going?" she asked, in an attempt to make conversation.

"Knockskagh."

Maura waited for him to add something, anything, more, but he didn't. "Ellen tells me that's a townland? What does that mean?"

He glanced briefly at her. "It's the smallest geographic subdivision. Townlands have been around for nearly a millennium. They're usually small, no more than twenty or thirty families. Knockskagh's where your grandmother was born, and where she lived when she first married."

"Well, she never told me word one about it. And your grandmother?"

"She lives in a house her husband's family built, maybe a hundred and fifty years ago." He glanced briefly at Maura before going on, "Look, just remember that my grannie is old and she tires quickly. But she's kept in touch with your grandmother all these years and she wants to see you. Just go easy, will you? Don't wear her out."

What did he think she was planning to

do, grill the old woman? Maura wondered. What made him assume she'd be rude and thoughtless? Didn't he like Americans? "I'll do my best," she said a bit stiffly. "I don't know how long I'll be around. Will I be able to see her again? Or do I have to fit everything into this one visit?"

"Let's see how it goes, will we?" He turned left and his car labored up the hill, along a fairly steep one-lane road. He stopped for a moment just short of the crest. "This is Knockskagh, what there is of it."

Maura had a quick impression of a cluster of houses, some of which seemed to be abandoned. Behind them lay green fields dotted with grazing sheep and an occasional cow. "How far does it go?"

"All in, it's about a hundred and fifty acres."

Maura didn't bother to tell him that she had no clue how large an acre was; she really only knew how to measure space in city blocks.

Mick released the brake and drove on to a little yellow cottage, set perpendicular to the lane and surrounded by a handsome stone wall culminating in a pair of stone posts. The posts were closely set, meant for a cart rather than a modern car, but he turned with practiced skill into the minuscule yard in front of the house and parked. He hadn't even turned off the engine when the brightly painted green door opened and an old woman stepped out. She couldn't have been more than five feet tall, even allowing for the curve of her back, and her face was a network of fine wrinkles, like an old kid glove. But her blue eyes were bright and curious.

"Ah, Michael, you've brought her, then. Come in, please, and welcome."

Ignoring her taciturn driver, Maura clambered out of the passenger side and approached. "Mrs. Nolan? Yes, I'm Maura Donovan, and I'm delighted to meet you." She followed her diminutive hostess from the bright sunlight into the home's shadowed interior, and waited for her eyes to adjust. It was a tiny place, two rooms downstairs, with a large fireplace dominating one end of the room they were in, a stove planted in the middle of it. It was like nothing she'd ever seen in Boston — a true Irish cottage.

When Mick started to follow, Mrs. Nolan stopped him with a raised hand. "We'd just bore you with our talk of old times, darlin'. Why don't you come back in a couple of hours?"

"You sure you'll be all right, Grannie?"

"I think I can handle one nice young American girl on my own. Go on, then."

She watched as Mick headed out the door and pulled away in the car, before turning back to Maura. "Will we sit in the parlor?" Mrs. Nolan gestured toward the smaller room, where Maura could see upholstered chairs. "And can I get you something? Tea? A biscuit?"

Maura hated to put her to any trouble, but she didn't want to insult her hospitality. "That would be lovely. Can I help you with anything?"

"No, dear, I've got the kettle on the boil. I just need to set the tea to brewing. Go on, sit."

Maura went through the doorway and into the parlor, which boasted a smaller and more elegant fireplace with a coal grate. The shallow mantel above it held a collection of photographs, of children, grandchildren, and quite possibly great-grandchildren, interspersed with china knickknacks that Maura guessed were at least a century old. There were other, earlier pictures on the walls, as well as a religious print of the Virgin Mary in a prominent central spot. The sole window in the front of the room let in a flood of spring sunshine. Maura listened to the clink of cups and cutlery as Mrs. Nolan pottered around in the other room, and while she waited she studied the faces in the pictures, trying to find resemblances among them.

Finally Mrs. Nolan made her careful way into the room, carrying a tray laden with quaking tea things. Maura made a move to help her, but Mrs. Nolan nodded her off. "Ah, don't worry yourself — I'm slow but steady. I do all right, most days. Better now that spring's coming." Maura watched with trepidation until the tray was safely settled on a table. "But you could pour for me, there's a dear? I can't manage the big pot so well these days, and it's hot."

Maura busied herself with filling the lovely bone china cups. She wondered if they were brought out only for special events. Did her visit qualify? She handed one to her hostess, then took the other and settled herself in an overstuffed chair. It gave off a faint musty sigh as she sank into it, and the pattern, to Maura's unskilled eye, could have dated from the 1950s. She looked up to see Mrs. Nolan beaming at her.

"I'm so glad you've come. It gets lonely a bit here — so many of you young girls are off to work these days. Not like the old days, when there were lots of people around, kids

46

calling after each other. Like when your grandmother Nora was young. What did she tell you of us here?"

"Very little, I'm sorry to say. I know she came to Boston after my grandfather died, with her son — my father. But I didn't even know my father very well. He died when I was young."

"I know, I'm so sorry — I knew him when he was only a lad, and he was a lovely boy, smart as a whip, and with a bit of sass to him."

"And you know about . . . my mother?"

"That she ran off and left you in your gran's care? I do — Nora wrote me regularly over the years. I know life was hard for all of you. Did your mother never come back?"

"No, and I haven't looked for her either," Maura said, uncomfortable talking about her mother.

Mrs. Nolan seemed to sense her discomfort and smoothly changed the subject. "Look here, I found some of the letters your gran sent me. I thought you might like to see them." She rummaged among the bric-a-brac on the small table next to her chair and handed Maura a packet of papers and photos tied up with a faded ribbon. Maura recognized her grandmother's hand on the envelopes and felt a stab of sadness. Why

47

couldn't they have made this trip together? But she knew the answer: they could never have afforded it, or taken the time off from work. "May I?" she asked Mrs. Nolan.

"Go on, dear."

Maura untied the fragile ribbon and leafed through the stack. She pulled out the photos first. Some she recognized from her grandmother's slim photo album; others she had never seen.

The photos were neatly labeled on the back in her grandmother's handwriting. Most were of her, and she watched herself progress from a chubby baby to a sulky teenager, ending with her high school picture. Interspersed were a few pictures of her father, and one of her father and mother together, apparently taken shortly after their wedding. Some Maura remembered, and she carried a few in her bag now, but others she had never seen. It was startling to see her mother, especially looking so young and happy. Her parents made a handsome couple. What would their marriage have been like if her father hadn't died?

A clipping with her father's brief obituary. Gran had never been much for picture taking, and after those early days they were few and far between. She looked up to see Mrs. Nolan watching her sympathetically.

"You have the look of her, you know."

"Of Gran? I suppose," Maura said. She'd never given it much thought. Gran had looked like a grandmother should look, kind of soft and warm, even though she had always seemed tired. Her hair had gone grey early. But Maura shared her bright blue eyes. "So tell me, what was it like here, when my grandmother was young?"

"Ah, we had little money, but we counted ourselves lucky . . ." And Bridget Nolan was off and running. The next time Maura checked her watch, over two hours had passed, and she could tell that Mrs. Nolan was running out of steam. Maura saw an opening in the flow of words and seized it. "Is Mick your only relative around here now?"

Mrs. Nolan settled back into her chair. "There's his sister, Bridget, over at Clonakilty — Mick's dad, my son, is gone, sad to say, and his mother lives with Bridget and her husband. But so many of the children in the country, they're off to school, or the city, or even overseas. No one wants to stay here — they say it's dull, and too quiet for them. And there's no work for them anymore." She paused for a moment, then looked at Maura with a birdlike tilt of her head. "Mick's a good boy, stops in near every day, and sees to the place for me. His sister keeps saying, 'Gran, why don't you come in with us? We'd love to have you.' But I like my own space, and I know where everything goes here." Mrs. Nolan pulled herself up in her chair. "Well, my dear, it's been a joy to talk with you, but I think it's time for my nap now."

Clearly she was being dismissed. Maura didn't want to overstay her welcome, so she stood up. "Thank you so much for talking with me. I hope I haven't worn you out."

"Nonsense. Everyone's in such a hurry now — no one seems to care about the past, the families. I'm so glad you came by today. Will you be stopping by again?" The small, wrinkled face peered up with eager hope.

"I'd like that very much. I'll be around for a week, and I'd love to see you again, if it's no trouble. It's been a real pleasure to meet you, Mrs. Nolan."

"Can you make your way out? Mick should be back shortly to collect you."

"Of course. And thank you for the lovely tea."

Maura carefully gathered up the teacups, put them on the tray, and carried the tray back to the main room. It seemed the least that she could do. She gave one last look at Mrs. Nolan, who was already nodding off in her chair — not for the first time, from the look of the chair, and the way the small body nestled into its curves — then went into the courtyard, closing the heavy door quietly behind her. No sign of Mick, but the air was pleasantly warm, at least in the sun. She wandered over to the lane that ran alongside the Nolan cottage and stood still, looking at the view, trying to imagine it filled with the sound of childish voices, women calling. Right now all she could hear was the lowing of a flock of sheep a couple of fields over, the swish of a single car down on a road below. It was likely quieter now than it would've been a century before. Pure country, as far as she could see. She crossed the paved road and then followed an unpaved lane until it petered out in the midst of three old houses. The houses all looked abandoned, although in different eras. One was no more than a roofless stone shell, while the others showed more recent use. Maura leaned against a wire fence to greet the sheep in the field. The ones closest to her looked blankly at her for a few moments, then returned to cropping the grass beneath their feet.

She heard the sound of a car coming up the hill, and made her way back just as Mick parked and got out. "She's gone to sleep, has she?" he called out as Maura approached.

"How'd you guess? I forgot to thank her for fixing things with Ellen, and for sending you to get me."

"She's glad for the company. I come by as much as I can, but it can be lonely here. The old families are gone. I've got her a telly, and she's on the phone" — he waved at a satellite dish on the far side of the building that Maura hadn't noticed — "but she's never got in the habit of using them. She prefers the old ways."

"She did ask if I could come back and see her again, but I don't want to impose on you — is there any other way to get here?"

He quirked an eyebrow at her. "So she didn't mention . . . No mind. She's seen to that. Follow me." Mick led her around the back of the cottage, and Maura saw there was a small shed there, far newer than the cottage itself. He pulled open the double doors to reveal a small but highly polished car. "She wanted you to have the use of this, while you're here."

She turned to gape at him. "What? She wants to lend me a car? I can't take that."

"And why not? It's not new. In fact, it was my grandfather's, not that he used it much, and he's been gone some twenty years. Can you manage a stick manual transmission?"

"Uh, I guess." In fact Maura hadn't driven much at all in her life. In Boston it was simply too expensive to own and insure a car, and besides, there had always been buses or the T. She had a license, but mainly as an ID — she'd cadged the bare minimum of lessons from the older brother of a friend, and once she'd passed the test she hadn't had much opportunity or need to drive anywhere. And here she'd have to drive on the left, with a stick shift, for God's sake. This was not a good idea. Was it?

"You'll do fine. The keys are in it, and I made sure it still runs and filled the tank. And that way you can visit when you like. But like I said, she tires easily."

Like I can't tell when she's tired? she thought. "Uh, could you at least back it out of the shed for me?"

He gave her a critical look, then wordlessly climbed into the car, started the engine, and swung the car out of the shed, pulling to a stop only inches from his own car. "There you go. Can you find your way back?" Without waiting for an answer, he said, "Down the hill, turn right at the T, then follow the road. It's easy." He handed her the keys, then turned and got into his own car.

"Thanks!" Maura called out to his re-

53

treated back. He raised a backward hand and pulled out onto the lane, leaving Maura standing in the small courtyard with the keys in her hand.

Things were happening much too fast. It had been kind of Mrs. Nolan to set her up with a place to stay at Ellen's, but to hand her a car? Not even knowing whether she could drive it? *Could* she drive it? Well, she'd better find out, since Mick had disappeared and left her stranded out here in the middle of nowhere, and she wasn't even sure how to find her way back to Leap, despite his directions. This Irish "welcome" business was a mixed blessing.

CHAPTER 4

Maura squared her shoulders. If she couldn't handle the car, then she'd just have to find a phone. Or walk. Or wait a day for Mick to come back, to see if she was still hanging around annoying his grannie. Why was he so protective of Mrs. Nolan? She'd been the one to invite Maura. Maura hadn't just showed up and imposed herself on a stranger. She had every right to be here.

The car was no model she recognized. It was small, probably European, its color faded to a tired grey. Maura walked around it, jiggling the key ring in her hand. Its tires seemed to be in good shape, and it had a license plate, so she wouldn't be breaking any local laws. She hoped. Was it insured? Or was she? She had no idea who to ask, although Mick seemed like a law-abiding type, based on her extremely brief interaction with him. She opened the door and slid into the driver's seat, its upholstery cracked with age. She spent a moment locating all the relevant parts, then stuck the key into the ignition, planted one foot on the brake, pushed down on what she hoped was the clutch, and turned the key. To her surprise the engine started up on the first try, and it did have a full tank of gas, as Mick had said. She grinned to herself, almost against her will: she had wheels!

Now what? Sitting still was fine, but she was supposed to move, starting with getting out of the woefully small enclosure and through that narrow gap between the posts. And then navigate what amounted to a one-lane road lined with either towering hedges or more stone walls close to either side.

At least the gear pattern was stamped on the gearshift. How did it go? Shift into the gear you wanted, slowly release the clutch, and keep one foot on the brake at all times. Maura shifted into reverse and let out the clutch slowly — and stalled. She tried again, raising her foot at a snail's pace, until the car actually began to move — which startled her, and she stalled again. She cursed and tried again, and this time she moved backward by a few feet, at which point she was afraid she was going to crash through the hedgerow and jammed both feet on the pedals.

This was ridiculous!

Fifteen minutes later Maura had managed to maneuver the car so that at least it was facing the direction she wanted to go. If she turned right, at least it was downhill, and then she should turn . . . right at the bottom? Inch by inch she moved forward and managed to slide through the stone posts without scraping anything. She made the turn, then slowly went down the hill, braking all the way. Thank goodness there were no other cars coming up the road, though at the bottom she discovered a police car blocking the way to her left. Not that she wanted to go that direction, but the mere presence of a cop made her stall out again. She sat at the bottom of the hill and pounded the steering wheel in frustration. The cop walked over, and she rolled down the window.

"Having a bit of trouble?" he asked politely.

She looked carefully at him: he appeared younger than she was, and he hadn't quite grown into his uniform, which looked almost new. But he didn't seem to be making fun of her. "Yes, I guess I am. I don't drive much, and I've never driven on the left, and I've never driven this car before. Sorry, am I in the way?" That seemed unlikely, since there were no moving cars in sight.

"Not at all. That'd be Bridget Nolan's car, right?"

"Yes. She's letting me borrow it." Maura tried not to sound defensive, and hoped the nice young policeman wouldn't ask for proof, because she didn't have anything like documentation. Would he think she had stolen it?

Her worries were answered quickly but raised another question when he asked, "So you'd be Maura Donovan?"

He knew who she was? "Yes, I am. How did you know that? And you are?"

"Sean Murphy. Mrs. Nolan's been talking of nothing else but your visit for days now. She wanted to be sure we'd all look out for you, in case you got lost. If it's Leap you're looking for, it's that way." He pointed down the road Maura had planned to take.

Had Mrs. Nolan talked to the whole village? "Thank you. I can use all the help I can get." She looked behind him and for the first time noticed other vehicles, and several official-looking men moving around the field. "What's going on here?"

His expression turned somber. "They've found a body in the old bog." At Maura's horrified expression, he hastened to add,

"No way yet to tell how long he's been there. Could be a year, could be a century."

That made her feel slightly better; a hundred-year-old body felt less like crime and more like history. She'd been happy to leave violence behind her in Boston. "Well, I'd better be heading back. At the rate I'm going it may take a while."

He nodded. "Good luck to you. And drive safely!"

After half an hour of driving — or more accurately, lurching and stalling, hands clenched on the steering wheel — Maura arrived back at Leap. She carefully pulled into the driveway at the bed and breakfast and parked behind the building. After turning off the engine, she sat and shook for a minute. Part of her wanted to say "never again" and abandon the car where it sat; another part reasoned that if she was going to go anywhere and see anyone, particularly Bridget Nolan, she needed to get over herself and drive the damn car. At least the roads were mostly empty, although she wasn't sure what she would do if she encountered someone coming the opposite way on some of those tiny lanes. Were there rules for things like that?

When her hands finally stopped shaking, Maura struggled out of the small car and looked around. It was midafternoon, and there was no sign of Ellen or the children. She could take a walk, explore the land around the harbor — she could see some buildings from where she stood. But she was keyed up and wanted to celebrate . . . what? Surviving a five-mile drive? Well, yes, in fact. Call it surviving a challenge, or finding a solution, or at least grabbing the one that had been handed to her. She wanted a drink. Since Sullivan's was the only pub she knew, Sullivan's it was, then.

It was clear the moment she walked into the place that there was something going on. For one thing, there were people there — lots of people, unlike the day before — and they were all talking at once. Rose was the only person serving, and she looked overwhelmed, dealing with shouted orders from all corners as well as at the bar. Maura waded through the crowd toward her, and when she finally reached the bar, she waited to catch the young girl's eye. Poor Rose looked like a cornered rabbit. "Need some help, Rose?" she shouted.

"I need three hands! It's never been so busy in the middle of the day."

"There's nobody else working today?"

"Da's gone off to Bantry to get supplies, so it's just me. He left before all of this."

Rose waved her hand at the crowd. "I've tried calling Mick on his cell, but it's off, and he wasn't due to come in for a couple of hours yet."

"I've tended bar in Boston — I can work the taps if you want."

Rose looked as though she'd been handed a Christmas present. "Oh, could you? I'd be so grateful. At the very least I've got to get some glasses washed or we'll have nothing to drink from. Can you handle the Guinness tap?"

"I know the routine, no problem." Maura made her way around the bar and slid in behind it. She took a moment to familiarize herself with the layout, but she'd worked in plenty of bars, and they were all pretty much the same. Especially the Irish ones all over Boston. She looked out at the crowd, still growing as more people came in the door. Several of them stopped talking long enough to look back at her, as though she were some exotic creature dropped in their midst. Maura smiled. "What can I get you?"

"American, are you?" the nearest man said. "A pint, please. You'd be Bridget Nolan's visitor, then. Do you know, have they cleared away the body in the bog yet?"

Chapter 5

Maura laughed to herself at her earlier impression that Sullivan's was short of business. At the moment the small pub was filled to capacity, which she estimated at maybe thirty if a few didn't want a seat, with a few people even spilling out the door onto the sidewalk beyond. For all she knew, the entire population of the town was there, men and women alike — and they were all talking about the body pulled from the bog. Word had spread fast, probably by mobile phone, but apparently people wanted face-to-face conversation about something this big.

Maura could tell that people were curious about her — it looked as though all the people in the room knew each other well, while she was the stranger — but she and Rose were madly busy filling pints, finally helped out by Rose's father, Jimmy, when he returned empty-handed from his excursion of the day. Maura smiled when she saw his expression at finding a stranger behind the bar, but when he realized she knew what she was doing, he joined in the fray.

"You'd be Maura Donovan, eh? Rosie said you'd arrived."

"I am."

"You've pulled a few pints in your day, haven't you?" He smiled, even as his hands were busy filling yet more pints.

"Enough. Hope you don't mind, but Rose was swamped."

"We're glad of the help." He turned away to a waiting patron. "What'll it be, Con?"

Maura kept working at a steady pace. When those few people who took the time to talk to her found she had been on the scene when the body was found, they were disappointed at how little she could tell them. No, the policeman hadn't told her anything, nor had she seen the body, and she wasn't about to guess about its age or condition. She didn't even know enough of the local landmarks to explain just where the bog site was, but when she admitted that, people were happy to fill her in about its entire history, going back to who had owned it in the 1800s.

Maura fell into the familiar rhythm of pulling pints from the taps at the bar and opening the occasional bottle of hard cider, while Rose collected the empty glasses and washed them so they could be used again. Thank goodness Maura knew how to handle Guinness properly, else she might have been faced by a riot. When there was a lull, she allowed herself a brief break, first heading for the restroom at the back (and shutting her eyes to the filth there), then making her way into the thick of the crowd, just listening to fragments of conversations, in accents both familiar and different at the same time. The main topic seemed to be the identity of the body, although as far as Maura knew it still hadn't been established how long it had been in the bog. Twenty years, two hundred, two thousand? Apparently it wasn't uncommon for ancient bodies to be pulled from bogs in Ireland, often sliced up by the mechanical turf-cutters or other industrial-strength equipment that had exposed them in the first place.

If she'd thought the crowd would thin out as the evening wore on, she was wrong. "Where's Mick?" she shouted at Jimmy at some point. "We need help!"

"No idea. We'll manage," was Jimmy's unhelpful reply.

Maura was beginning to feel exhausted as the clock approached midnight, but the crowd hadn't budged. She shoved her way back to the bar, where Jimmy was in place.

"Don't you have some kind of closing time here?" she shouted over the din.

"Sometimes." He winked at her, without pausing in pouring the next pint. "You aren't sayin' we should turn away a roomful of customers?"

"Won't you get in trouble?" Maura asked.

"I'd wager the gardaí have enough on their hands, what with this body turning up. They're based in Skibbereen and they don't pass by often, so don't worry yourself about it." He set the current glass aside to settle as he topped up the one he'd started before.

She assumed "gardaí" meant the police. "If you say so," Maura mumbled to herself. It wasn't up to her to work out the legal issues. "Did Rose go home?"

"She did. It's just the two of us, darlin'."

Mick was still AWOL, although if it was past regular closing time it seemed unlikely he'd show up now. "So, still need me?"

"Indeed I do, if you're willin'. You're an angel dropped from heaven."

"If I can stay awake." She started yet another glass, while eager hands reached out for the finished ones.

At midnight Jimmy turned out the lights in the front, but no one budged from their place in the bar. Maura didn't think that would fool any passing policeman, but at least Jimmy was acknowledging the law, sort of. The room in the back, where other people had drifted, was still lit and noisy. *These people must be starved for excitement,* Maura thought. *Half the town is still here, and they're all talking about the body from the bog.* How long would it take the police to figure out who it was? Would they ever?

It was well past one when the last customer straggled out into the cool night air. Maura had been so busy doling out drinks and collecting the empties that she hadn't noticed when Michael Nolan had come in. He finally shut the door and pulled down the shades in the front.

"You've missed all the fun, Mick," Jimmy said, bouncing nervously behind the bar, a dirty towel in his hand. "Grand evening, wasn't it? Wish we could order up more of them."

Mick slouched against the bar. "I doubt there'll be a body all that often."

Maura perched on a stool to rest her feet, noting that he hadn't explained his absence. Again, none of her business — he and Jimmy could work that out. "Not that many suspicious deaths around here?"

Both men shook their heads. "It's a rare

66

thing," Mick said. "Not like Boston, I wager."

Maura debated about how to answer that. "Last year Boston had, like, sixty homicides."

Mick's mouth twitched. "Ireland had about that for the entire country. What're you having?"

It took Maura a moment to realize that he was talking about drinks. "I don't need anything. I should be going — I'm beat."

"Come on," Jimmy chimed in. "Surely you need to taste Guinness on its home turf. To celebrate your arrival, kinda."

"All right, I guess. Thank you." Maura hated to appear ungracious, but it was late, she was tired, and she really didn't drink much — she'd seen too many barroom regulars reeling home after late nights, sloppy and stupid. Still, she thought she should be polite.

As Jimmy poured her a Guinness, she sat silently, mesmerized as always by the cascading bubbles of the dark stout. It was almost a religious ritual, when done properly — there was no rushing a Guinness. When it was finally judged ready by the men, Mick reached for it and handed it to her with a flourish. *"Sláinte!"*

Maura raised her glass and nodded, then

took a sip. Dark, bitter, yet not heavy. Maybe it *was* better over here, closer to the source. Or maybe she was wiped out. Had she even eaten dinner? No, or lunch — her last food had been tea and cookies at Mrs. Nolan's, a long time ago.

Jimmy and Mick exchanged complicated glances, involving eyebrows and nods, and Maura wondered what they were trying to communicate to each other, or if they'd had some earlier conversation. Finally Jimmy said, "You did a grand job here today — don't know how we would have managed without you. I said it — like an angel, you were, dropping in like that." He hesitated for a moment, then said, "I don't suppose you'd be wanting a job?"

It took Maura a moment to digest what he'd said. A job, tending bar — here? In Ireland? "What?"

"You know, working regular like, here. It's clear you've done it before," Jimmy said.

Maura couldn't make sense of his offer. "But I hadn't planned to stay here long. Shouldn't you be looking for someone more permanent?"

Another exchange of cryptic glances. This time Maura was watching for it.

"I didn't come to Ireland to spend my time cleaning up after drunken old men, you know," she snapped, more rudely than she had intended. "I've got a flight home next week. And I can't afford to buy another ticket. I've got no money."

"We'd pay you, of course," Mick said carefully.

"Enough to live on here, even for only a while?" Maura shot back.

Mick cocked his head at her. "What do you need? I'll venture Ellen will give you a good rate for a longer stay–she doesn't see much business herself, this time of year. You've got my grannie's car, and you'll be needing a bit of gas for that, to get around. That leaves you with food to worry about. We can manage enough for you to get by on."

"How many other employees are there?" Maura said.

"There's my Rose," Jimmy began.

Maura cut him off quickly. "Is she even old enough to be serving here, legally? What about you, Jimmy — do you take your turn?"

Jimmy managed to look hurt. "Now and then — I watch over the business side." He ignored Mick's short laugh. "Ordering and the like. But it was Old Mick who covered the bar, most days, and we're still adjusting to him being gone. When it was slow, he'd sit by the fire there, but when we got busy, he'd be behind the bar, telling stories and having a grand time. We always thought that was what kept him going so long."

"So do you two own this place now?"

"No, we just manage it," Mick answered. "Old Mick only died last week. He was ninety-four when he passed, and he'd never married and had no children. He'd outlived most of the rest of his family, or they're long gone from Ireland. It'll take a bit to sort out what'll happen with the place now. We're just keeping it running until then."

"I'm sorry to hear about his passing," Maura said. Not that she was, particularly — after all, she'd never known him — but it was the polite thing to say. "So who does the pub go to now?"

Both men shook their heads. "We don't know. Old Mick, he didn't say much about his affairs. There might be a will, or not."

"Apart from tonight, are there ever many customers here?"

"Ah, you've just seen it at a slow time," Jimmy said jovially. "Come the weekend, there's lots more going on. And summer! We're right along the main road here, and there's many a tourist who stops by for a quick glass. It's a solid business, isn't it, Mick?"

"It could be," he agreed. "If Old Mick had done anything with the place, it could have been better."

Maura yawned. "Listen, guys, I'm about to fall over. Look, I'm glad I could help out today, but that doesn't mean I want to keep doing it, okay? Let me think about it. Good night."

She gathered up her bag and jacket and walked quickly out the door, to end any discussion. The road was deserted, and nothing moved. Quiet: something she wasn't used to. There wasn't any real quiet back where she came from, or any real dark. She crossed the road slowly, marveling at the unexpected emptiness. Gravel crunched under her feet as she walked down the drive that passed in front of the now-dark Keohane house and found her way to the back door leading to her room.

But before going in, she sought out a plastic chair on the small patio and dropped into it. She was exhausted, but she was also confused and bewildered by what she had seen and done that day. She'd spent time with what was probably her grandmother's oldest surviving friend; she'd acquired a car, if temporarily; she'd been offered a job. Before she'd left Boston, she'd thought about what she might say to Mrs. Nolan,

71

once she'd learned of her existence, but the car and Jimmy's offer had come as a complete surprise. And as for that last, she needed to think. Now, when she was wiped out? Heck, maybe that was the best time — her first reaction might be the truest one. If she had a job, even short term, she could stay around as long as it lasted. Did she want that?

Maybe — and she was startled to find herself thinking that. Of course, that would give her more time to get to know Bridget Nolan, and her last chance to learn anything about her gran's life before she went to Boston. That would be good. And maybe, just maybe, she should learn something more about Ireland — the real Ireland, not the shoddy caricatures. She knew that it wasn't all shamrocks and rainbows, but what was it really? And wasn't she Irish herself? She had a passport that said so, but she'd never really felt it, inside.

And there was nothing waiting for her at home. In fact, there was no home. She had no ties, here or there. So why not stay awhile?

Maura stood up, slid the door open as silently as she could, and slipped inside, stopping only to brush her teeth before she fell onto the bed.

And still couldn't sleep. She had come to Ireland because her promise had made Gran happy, and she wanted to honor her memory. She had planned to spend at most a week doing her duty to Gran. She'd been so caught up in burying Gran — next to her father — and then clearing out what little there was in their apartment, that she hadn't had time to think about what she wanted to do next.

But now she had freedom, and an unexpected opportunity. She didn't have to rush, and if she could make enough money to cover her simple needs, she would have some breathing room to decide about her future. And it wasn't like she was making a long-term commitment; she would be helping out, just for a bit, while she got to know the area better. Got to know people who had known her gran and her father, as a child. This would probably be her only chance, so why not take it?

Feeling obscurely reassured, she turned over and fell asleep.

CHAPTER 6

The next morning Maura was awakened by the tapping of rain against the glass sliding doors. It came as a surprise, but Maura realized it shouldn't have: it must rain all the time in Ireland, to keep all those fields so green. Still, she was glad she'd had a day of sunshine first. If it had stayed cold and grey, like the day she'd arrived, she might have turned tail and run. She lay listening to the sounds: the rain, of course, but also the clinking of pans and plates in the kitchen above, and the young voices as the Keohane children pounded down the hall and out the door. She thought she heard the rumble of a male voice as well — Ellen's husband? She didn't want to move, but she knew Ellen would probably be waiting breakfast on her, and surely her landlady had other things to do today.

She checked the clock: 8:00. That meant she'd had no more than six hours of sleep, after a long day yesterday. The night before, Jimmy and Mick had offered her a job at the pub. And by the light of day she still thought she wanted it. She could stay longer. It wouldn't be much of a vacation, working all the time, but she'd never had any vacations anyway, so nothing new there. She wouldn't be seeing much of Ireland, but she'd never been a fan of touristy things back home in Boston, and she didn't plan to join groups of gawping tourists here. And she'd get to know some real people.

But there were a lot of things that were murky, starting with how long Jimmy and Mick might expect her to stick around, and how much money she'd actually see from the job. She'd served in enough bars to know that it was hard work, hard on the feet and back. In Boston she'd had to fend off her share of randy drunks who thought she was an easy target. Would it be like that here?

Maybe she should talk to Mrs. Nolan about it. Maybe she should take another look at the pub: if it stood up to her inspection on a gloomy day like today, maybe there was hope.

Maybe she should get out of bed.

She swung her legs to the floor, then stood and crossed to the door to pull the curtains back. No one for miles to see her standing there in the ratty old T-shirt she slept in, unless she counted some curious sheep a few miles away. The sky hung low with grey clouds, and sheets of rain swept across the harbor, obscuring and then revealing the hills beyond. In the nearest pasture the cows were huddled together in one corner. The land on the right was filled with dark pines, closely packed, with no visible buildings. A few birds she couldn't identify swooped low over the water, then sped away.

She shook herself. *Take a shower, put some clothes on, and go eat breakfast. Then visit Mrs. Nolan. Then come back and take a long hard look at Sullivan's.* She showered, dressed in her last clean pair of jeans, and shoved her feet, sockless, into her shoes. After running a comb through her hair, she declared herself ready to attack breakfast.

"Ah, there you are," Ellen said cheerfully as Maura walked into the kitchen. "Will you be wanting the full breakfast again?"

"Don't go to any trouble, please. You can give me whatever's easy."

"If you don't mind what the children have left, there's plenty. Always late for school, they are. Except Gráinne here." Ellen reached down to tousle the curls of the little girl that had been hiding behind her legs.

"Come on, darlin', let Mummy do breakfast for the nice lady." Gráinne didn't budge, but stuck her thumb in her mouth and stared at Maura. "Shall I bring it out to you?"

"Do you mind if I sit in here with you again?" Maura asked. "I like having someone to talk to, and besides, I've got some questions for you."

Ellen cocked her head at Maura curiously. "I'd be glad of the company — it's a treat to talk with someone older than ten, and I have few guests this time of year. Gráinne, will you sit down at the table now?"

Reluctantly Gráinne sidled up to a chair across from Maura and climbed into it.

"Coffee, Maura?" Ellen asked.

"I'll take tea, if you've got it made. I should get used to it, shouldn't I?"

"Sure." Ellen filled a mug and set it in front of Maura. "My husband, Thomas, tells me there's a strange car out back — would that be yours?"

"Yes and no, I guess. Bridget Nolan offered to let me use it while I'm here, I think mostly to be sure I'd be able to come back and see her again."

"I'd been wondering how you'd get around — Mick's not always handy to give rides."

"What the heck does Mick do? I gather he's supposed to be working at the pub, but he's not there much. Does he have another job?"

"He does a bit of this and that. When he's away he's usually in Cork City. He used to work for one of the big foreign companies that set up here, but then the economy fell apart and so did his job. You'll hear a lot of tales like that, mostly from men sitting in the pub in the middle of the afternoon." She took a swallow of her tea and handed Gráinne a toy. "Do you know, I've been thinking of your gran. Nora, she married a Donovan, did she not? I knew some Donovans back when I was in school, but that would've been after she went to Boston, I'd guess. When was that?"

"She left here not long after my grandfather died, more than forty years ago, I think. She managed all right while my dad was growing up, and I guess things looked up after he got married and they had me. But then he died in an accident at work."

"Did you have the chance to know him?" Ellen asked as she dished up scrambled eggs from a pan on the stove. "Go on, finish them up for me. I never know what my lot is going to want to eat in the morning, so I make plenty."

78

Maura obediently forked up some eggs. "I barely remember him — he's more like a big shape to me than a person, if you know what I mean. Anyway, according to Gran, my mother couldn't take it, living with an Irish mother-in-law and taking care of a squalling kid. She just packed up and left one day."

"And she never returned? In all these years? Never called or wrote to see how you were?"

"No. Or at least, if she did, Gran never told me. She really believed in family loyalty, and when my mother ran out on us, she was as good as dead to Gran. Heck, I turned eighteen a few years ago — if my mother had wanted to find me, she could have. Gran raised me on her own."

"It was a hard life, then?" Ellen pushed a plate of toast toward Maura.

Maura took a piece and buttered it. "I guess, but we managed. I've been working since I was sixteen, but Gran told me that I had to finish high school. Then I started working full-time. Just like Rose at the pub. Didn't she ever want to see more of the world than this small town?"

"She's a good girl, and she's stuck by her dad. As you said, family comes first."

Maura resolved to have a chat with Rose

when they had a bit of quiet time together. But talking about Rose had reminded her of what she wanted to ask Ellen. "Can you sit for a moment?"

Ellen checked to see that her stove was turned off, then took a chair next to Maura, pulling the still-silent Gráinne into her lap. "Nice to have a few minutes of my own. You said you wanted to talk?"

Maura fumbled for a way to ask politely but in the end just blurted out, "Jimmy and Mick asked me if I want to work at the pub while they figure out who the new owner will be. I hadn't planned to stay around long, and I've got a ticket back next week. I'm not sure what to do."

Ellen tilted her head at Maura. "What is it you're asking me?"

"I'm not sure." Maura considered. "Probably a couple of things. I mean, I've been here, what, not even two days? First Bridget Nolan hands me the keys to her car, and then these guys offer me a job. They said you'd give me a deal on my room if I stayed. Sorry, that sounds kind of pushy, but they're the ones who brought it up. I don't even know if they talked to you about this. And I really can't afford much."

Ellen sat back in her chair and laughed heartily, and Gráinne in her lap looked up at her curiously. "Ah, that'd be Jimmy, I'll wager. No harm done. But is that what *you* want? Why'd you come to Ireland at all?"

"Because Gran wanted me to come — I'm doing it for her sake. I think she wanted to come back herself, but we never had the money. When she got sick, she went fast — she was only seventy. I think she wore herself down, between worrying about me and working, and sometimes she even took on extra jobs just to make ends meet. I helped as much as I could, but it wasn't a lot, until I finished high school. So before she went, I promised her that I'd come over and at least tell Bridget Nolan face-to-face." Maura looked down at her plate, her eyes blurred with tears. "I never even knew until after she'd died that she kept in touch with Mrs. Nolan — Gran never talked about her life in Ireland. I only found out when I was clearing out her things."

"I'm so sorry — she must have been a good woman. Sounds like you've had a hard time of it. So you've no place to go back to? No one who's waiting for you back home?"

"No," Maura said, then added, "Jeez, that makes me sound pathetic. No home, nobody in my life, and here I am dumping on you, when I only met you the day before yesterday. It's not your problem."

81

Ellen was silent for a few moments, thinking. Then she said slowly, "But you came to me, asking what to do. Since you asked, let me tell you this: I think you need to give yourself some time. You've had a lot to worry you, for a long time, and maybe now you should just step back and not decide anything for a bit. If you go back now, you'd have to deal with finding a place and a job and all that. You need to give yourself time to grieve for your gran. If you stay here, you can get by on little while you figure out what it is you want. There's no need to hurry. Do you see that?"

"You mean, sort of put my life on hold and just be?"

Ellen smile. "Maybe. Have you ever done that?"

Maura shook her head. "I never had the chance. But I guess you're right. If I can switch that plane ticket, I suppose there's no reason I can't just hang out here in Leap until I figure out what comes next."

"Exactly. And I'll see to it that Jimmy and Mick pay you enough to cover your room."

"You can do that?"

"Sure. I know Mick's sister, and my cousin taught Jimmy's girl Rose in school. We go back a ways."

"I'm not asking for charity, you know,"

Maura said dubiously.

"It's not charity — it's helping each other out."

She was talking about simple kindness, which had been all too rare in Maura's life. That was going to take thinking about. "Should I talk to Mrs. Nolan about it?"

"You're off to see her again?"

"I'm planning on it, and I think she'd enjoy another visit. Look, about this car of hers — I feel funny just taking it like this."

"She wouldn't have offered if she didn't want you to have the use of it. She hasn't driven in years, and it can't be worth much. Just enjoy it, will you?"

Enjoy. Relax. Have fun. These were concepts Maura was having trouble wrapping her head around. And the fact that people wanted to do things for her, make her life easier, took getting used to. Was it that the people here were extraordinarily nice, or were the people in Southie, or even Boston, just less friendly in general?

"Thank you for being frank with me."

"So you'll be staying on?"

Maura smiled at her. "Maybe. I need to have another talk with the guys at the pub. That place is a pigsty, and I don't know if I want to be spending a lot of time there."

Ellen waved a hand at her. "Ah, it's got

good bones. Old Mick, he was used to the dirt. But the place has some life in it yet."

"Hey, I'm just a temporary bartender who can't stand dirt. Well, I should go get ready for the day. I'll let you know what I decide after I speak to Mrs. Nolan and drop by the pub for a chat, if that's all right with you."

"No problem. I'll be here."

Maura stood up, then waved at the child in Ellen's lap. "Bye-bye, Gráinne."

Gráinne looked silently at her, then raised one starfish hand and waved back.

CHAPTER 7

Maura collected her bag and her car keys. Dressing had proved challenging, since everything she had squashed into her one bag was still as hopelessly wrinkled as it had been the day before. She could almost hear her gran's voice: *Ah, Maura, sure and you're not in such a hurry that you can't tidy up?* She put the bag down again, shook out the rumpled clothes on the bed, and put them one by one on hangers. She was not happy with the results. If — still an "if" — she chose to stay around longer, she'd have to do some wash. Worse, she'd need more clothes: she was not going to make it working at the pub with only two pairs of jeans. She wondered briefly whether she should ask Ellen where to shop for inexpensive clothes, but that could wait, along with the "where to do laundry" question. She'd make it through one more day with the clothes on her back, and right now she wanted to get to Mrs. Nolan's house.

She slid the house door shut behind her and wrapped her jacket around her against the rain, hurrying to the car. She climbed in quickly, then sat, taking it in. "Hello, car," she whispered, feeling foolish. "Are you going to be nice to me? Because I don't know a whole lot about manual shifts, you know." The car did not answer.

Maura inserted the key in the ignition, checked to see if the parking brake was on, depressed the clutch and the brake pedals, sent up a brief prayer, and turned the key; the car started immediately. *Oh, yeah!* Next, she located the controls for the windshield wipers — essential today — and then the headlights. Both worked. Now she was supposed to tackle the driveway, which both curved and slanted up to the road some forty feet above her. Somehow it had looked less intimidating when she had parked the night before, but even she knew clutches were tricky going uphill. Why couldn't she be staying in a nice, flat place? But there was only one way to the road. Maura gritted her teeth and engaged the clutch.

Multiple lurches and heart-stopping stalls later, Maura found herself at the top of the rise, looking at the two lanes of the main south coastal road. At least there was little traffic. She had to turn right to get onto the road, therefore to the far side, then turn left almost immediately, where the smaller road ran between a high rock face on the left and the trickling river on the right. And then she had to hope that she recognized the road she'd taken yesterday. *You can do this, Maura. You did it yesterday. It will get easier.* She inched out onto the road, then made the turn and followed the road as it wound past a few newer houses close to the village, then older houses farther away, then a few abandoned construction sites and fields clotted with brambles. She kept going until she recognized the intersection where the policeman had spoken to her yesterday. Since there were no moving vehicles in sight, she stopped for a moment, but there was no sign of the police activity of the day before, not even any tire tracks. A trio of incurious horses contemplated her car as they munched on whatever grass they could find around the bog.

With a sigh, Maura turned and drove up the hill until she came to the Nolan house on the left. She debated with herself for a moment: try to maneuver into the small area in front of the house, enclosed by a wall, or take the easy way and park next to the abandoned stone houses opposite, where there was more room? The second option, she decided: she'd rather get wet than risk scratching her borrowed car. She turned right and stopped, carefully pulling on the parking brake before turning off the engine. The rain continued to fall in sheets around her, and an unhappy cow bellowed in a nearby barn, setting off an unseen dog behind another wall.

Maura got out of the car and debated about locking it. Back in Boston it wouldn't have been a question: even if a car there was locked, the owner might still come back to find its tires gone. On a hill in Ireland, Maura couldn't see another living soul, human or animal. What were the odds that a car thief would stumble on her car? She slipped the keys in her pocket, leaving the car unlocked, and headed toward Mrs. Nolan's house.

The door was closed when she came to it, so she knocked firmly, recalling that the older woman was hard of hearing. Inside there was the sound of shuffling, and a voice called out, "I'm on the way." After thirty seconds or so, Bridget Nolan pulled open the door and beamed up at Maura. "Ah, it is you, after all. *Dia duit, a Mhaire.* I've been hoping you'd come by. Come in, come in, and dry yourself off."

"Thank you. It's definitely wet today. Is it usually like this?"

"Oh, no. Usually we have a hard rain," Mrs. Nolan replied.

It took Maura a moment to realize that she was joking. "I'm glad I know how to swim!"

Mrs. Nolan nodded her approval at her reply. "Come in and sit by the fire. Maybe I'm old-fashioned, but I still love a good peat fire."

"Where do you get peat these days?" Maura asked.

"The real thing, not those sad blocks you find in stores? I've a few friends who still cut their own."

Maura could see more or less rectangular pieces of what must be peat, half-burnt but still glowing in the small fireplace. They gave off a peculiar but distinctive smell, one that she'd noticed at the pub, the first day she was there.

"It's nice and warm in here, isn't it?" Mrs. Nolan said. "I'll just put the kettle on for the tea. Sit, will you?"

Maura sat obediently. "By the way, I really appreciate you letting me use your car. I'd never realized that there was no way to get around once you leave the main roads."

"So Michael sorted that out for you? It

slipped my mind yesterday. Ah, you young lot — you don't walk places the way we used to. Impatient, aren't you?"

"I guess so. What was it you said when I came in? Was that Irish?"

Mrs. Nolan toddled back. "*Dia duit,* you mean?" When Maura nodded, she explained, "It's a greeting — it means 'God be with you,' but you may think of it as 'hello.'"

"You said something after it too. Ah why-ra?"

"But that's your name, dearie. I won't trouble you with learning the language — not many people speak it anymore, although our government does keep trying to keep it going, more credit to them. But your name is Maire, which is Mary."

What, now they'd given her a new name? "But I'm Maura," she protested. "And you called your grandson 'mee-hawl'?"

"Yes, that's how it's said in Irish. As for your name, your grandmother and I wrote back and forth about it, when your parents were expecting you. She wanted you to have an Irish name, but she thought that Maire with the 'a-i' would be hard for you in school, and Maura with the 'a-u' is closer to the Irish sound of it anyway, and less old-fashioned than 'o-i' Moira. Better than

Mary, don't you think? Now, if your father had wanted to follow the old naming patterns, you should have been Nora, after his mother, but she thought that might be too out of date for a girl. What was your mother's name, again? It seems to have slipped my mind."

"Helen."

"Ah, that's right. Now, had you been a boy, you should have been James, after your grandfather, Nora's husband. If you like, I can tell you where he's buried, so you could pay your respects."

She'd forgotten to ask Mrs. Nolan about that, although it had been in the back of her mind. Her Irish grandfather had never been a very real figure to her. Gran had rarely mentioned him, though she wasn't sure why. "Were he and Gran happy together?" Maura asked. She'd sometimes thought that maybe it had been an unhappy marriage, which was why Gran had wanted to put that whole time in Ireland behind her.

Mrs. Nolan's next words quickly erased that idea. "Indeed they were. He was a fine man, tall, hardworking. And he adored your gran — you could see it in the way he looked at her, when he thought she didn't see. It near broke her heart when he died. He shouldn't have, wouldn't, if he'd gotten to hospital in time. He'd cut himself haying, but he said it was nothing to worry about until it was too late and it had gone septic, and no doctor near."

"Was that why she left here?"

"In part. It made her sad, being here without him, even though she had friends and family all around. She hoped she'd have better opportunities in America. She knew some people there, and she found work, and someone to look after her son. He grew up to be a fine man, didn't he?"

Maura wasn't sure if it was a question or a statement, but she had no reason to disagree. "As far as I know. His only mistake was marrying the wrong woman. The less said about her, the better. I don't know where she is, and I don't really care."

They both sat in silence for a few moments. Then Mrs. Nolan said, "A sad thing, that poor man in the bog."

"You've heard about that?" Maura asked, surprised. How had she found out?

"Oh, yes. Mick came by yesterday and told me, and another friend or two stopped in as well. Michael insists I have a phone here, but I keep it only to please him, and I don't use it much — I don't hear near as well as I once did. My friends know to come directly rather than phone, bless them. They told me all about it."

"Do they know who it was yet?"

"No one's gone missing around here, that we remember. Could have been a traveler, although we don't see many of them around here. And why would someone from away find himself dead in our bog?"

Maura found herself getting lost in the Irish terms again. "Wait a moment — 'gardaí' means police, right?"

"It does, if there's more than one of them. It's a 'garda' if he's alone. Or she, these days. But the place they work from is a garda station."

"Okay. So what's a traveler?" Maura said.

"Ah, you don't know the term? A traveler, a tinker. They're the *Lucht Siúil,* meaning 'the walking people' — they wander about and do odd jobs."

Maura still wasn't sure she understood the term — something like a gypsy, maybe? "So you're saying that someone just passing through might have thought the bog was a good place to dump a body?"

"I don't think so, dear. More likely it was someone who didn't know the land well, who stumbled off the path after dark. Might be that he'd had a bit too much to drink — there's a pub not far along the road, at the Killinga crossroad."

"A pub? Out here?"

Mrs. Nolan nodded. "Not so long ago when people didn't have cars and such, they'd welcome a place they could walk to when their work was done. It's still there — I'm sure you'll be going by it sometime."

But one small question nagged at her: if everybody knew everybody else, shouldn't someone know the dead man in the bog? Assuming, of course, that he wasn't one of those prehistoric mummies she'd heard about. Was it a mummy if it had been preserved in a wet bog rather than a dry desert? She had no idea.

"That bog where they found the . . . remains . . . right down the hill from here — the gardaí haven't figured out how long it was there?"

"Ah, now, there's a question. A bog can hold many secrets, and it's hard to say for how long. Seems hardly a day goes by without someone digging up an ancient crock of butter or a nice bundle of old silver or the like. Sometimes it's hard to tell where a thing's been left, and they do tend to shift around over time."

"Are there experts to talk to?" Maura asked.

"Oh, certainly. No doubt we'll be seeing some high muckety-muck from the National

Museum poking around down there. Seems like the government always wants to stick its nose in our business."

The last thing Maura wanted was to get involved in a political discussion, especially since she knew nothing about the Irish government and was happy to leave it that way. Local regulations might apply to her, though. It struck her that if she wanted to stay on and work at the pub for more than a day or two, there might be paperwork to consider — or to ignore. Maura had seen more than one bar back home run afoul of regulations: were things more casual here? From what little she'd seen of Jimmy and Mick, they didn't seem like the types to bother with details like that. Maybe it would be simpler to close the place down, now that Old Mick was gone.

"Mrs. Nolan, did Mick tell you he'd asked me to stick around and help out at the pub for now?"

Mrs. Nolan beamed at her. "He did that. I think it would be grand — I'd have more time to spend with you. There's so much I can tell you about your gran and the families, but as you can see, I'm not as strong as I once was, and my memory isn't as good as I'd like. But I'd be happy if you'd take him up on that."

"I'm still thinking about it, but I'd love to be able to spend more time with you too. I wish Gran had said more, but she was always so tired in the evenings, and didn't always have the energy to talk." And Maura herself had been too young and self-absorbed to ask. She regretted that now.

"Ah, you're a kind girl to humor an old woman. The young people now, they don't want to listen to the old stories, or try to save the old language. Don't worry yourself, dearie, and don't feel you have to spend all your time with me. But if you want to listen, I'm happy to talk."

"I'd like that," Maura said. "Where was it Gran lived? Or she was born? If she ever told me, I've forgotten the names."

"She was one of the Ballyriree Sullivans, a mile or so to the west. Now, your grandfather, James, he came from up toward Drinagh. He's buried in the old cemetery there; not the one by the new church, but the one up the hill a ways from it, where the old church used to be. With his people."

"I'll have to see if I can find it."

"I'd go with you, dear, but I'm afraid my old bones aren't up to it, this early in the spring. Maybe when the weather turns warm. Heavens, what am I thinking? I near forgot about the tea!"

"Can I help?" Maura offered.

"No, I'm good. Don't trouble yourself." She stood up and went to the kitchen, where Maura could hear the clink of china as Mrs. Nolan filled the teapot and arranged cups and sugar and milk.

Gran hadn't talked much about her early life in Ireland, or her marriage, Maura reflected. As a result, Maura hadn't given much thought to the people her gran had left behind. After all, it had been decades, and somehow Maura had assumed that those people were either dead or scattered. Now her shadowy grandfather was taking shape in her mind, and she had a sneaking suspicion there were other people, living or dead, who were somehow connected to her. In Boston she couldn't have named all her neighbors who lived in the triple-deckers on either side of her. Yet here there were any number of people who knew her, or at least knew of her. She wasn't sure how she felt about that. Mrs. Nolan emerged from the kitchen carrying a tray and walking carefully. She set it down on the table. "There you go. I baked the bread fresh this morning." She sat down with a small sigh of relief. "Milk and sugar?"

Maura accepted her cup from Mrs. Nolan's unsteady hand. "Gran sent you a lot of letters over the years?" Maura asked.

"She did." Mrs. Nolan nodded. "She told me when your father married and when he died, but after that it was a dark time for her. She only started up again after a year or two had passed."

"She must have had her hands full, working and taking care of me."

"Ah, but you were the light of her life! Her very words. She wanted to do right by you, but it wasn't easy. She was sorry that you didn't go to university." Mrs. Nolan looked at her as if asking for an explanation.

"There was no money. Oh, I know, there were community colleges, and I did take some classes, but I was lousy at useful things like accounting or computer classes, and mainly I had to work to help out. Boston's an expensive place to live."

"She told me. She was so grateful that you wanted to help, but it still made her sad that you ended your schooling. She said you were a bright girl."

Maura found herself fighting tears — again. Why did that keep happening? She had always felt that she'd let Gran down by not going to college, but the money just hadn't been there. They'd never really sat down and talked about it, but they both knew the cold realities. Apparently she had fallen into the same pattern as her grandmother: don't look back, just keep moving forward and hope that things improve. Was that any way to live a life? Her grandmother had died alone, except for Maura, leaving barely enough money to bury her. She'd been only seventy, and if things had been different, she could have looked forward to more healthy years ahead of her. Instead she'd worn herself out, sacrificed her health just to keep her head above water and take care of Maura. It wasn't fair.

"She loved you very much," Mrs. Nolan said softly. "She wrote far more about you than about herself. She was so proud of you."

"Thank you," Maura said, then took a swallow of the dark tea to cover the lump in her throat. She'd done as much as she could for her grandmother, but it hadn't been enough. And she hadn't done enough for herself either, which left her with a blank future. Sure, she was young, and smart, if not book smart, and she'd proven she was tough. But what did she want to do?

CHAPTER 8

Maura straightened up in her chair. She was pleased that she could make Bridget Nolan happy, merely by agreeing to listen to her spin tales of the old days. But her problems were not for Mrs. Nolan to worry about, and it would be a shame to waste the opportunity to learn more about her grandmother's and father's early lives here in Ireland.

Just then, however, Mrs. Nolan looked up and said brightly, "Shouldn't you be off now, to see to the pub? You can find your way back all right?"

Was she being dismissed now? Maybe an hour or two was all that Mrs. Nolan could manage at one time. "I think so." Maura stood up. "Thank you for the tea. I'll see you tomorrow."

Before leaving, Maura carried the tea fixings back to the kitchen, and when she returned to the big room, she once again saw that Mrs. Nolan had dozed off. She slid out the front door and pulled it shut quietly behind her. Outside the rain had slackened, but it was still misting. The cow had finally stopped protesting, and the mist dulled sounds. Puddles punctuated the graveled courtyard in front of Bridget Nolan's house, and Maura wondered if she should try to borrow a pair of rubber boots if she did any local exploring. Perhaps more important, she had better familiarize herself with the location of the bogs so she didn't accidentally fall into one.

This time she had less trouble maneuvering the car from where she had parked it, and managed to get it pointed in the right direction without running into a hedgerow on one side or falling into the ditch on the other. Before heading down the hill, she stopped for a moment to look at the view. Mrs. Nolan's house stood a few hundred feet below the crest of the hill, sheltered from the wind and surrounded by mature pines on one side, but below the house Maura could see the road junction where the police car had stood and, beyond that, what she now knew was a bog, at least in part. The horses clustered in a corner of a pasture set off by wire fencing. To the left loomed tall pines. Everything she could see could have been there for a hundred years.

There seemed to be few people living nearby — the houses were widely scattered. Had it been any more populated a hundred years ago? Or a thousand? Could the Bog Man be that ancient, or like Mrs. Nolan said, was he just someone who had gotten lost and fallen to his death after a bit too much to drink one night? Silly to try to guess, though Maura's mouth twitched in a smile: Southie's notorious gangster Whitey Bulger and his gang back home would have found this an ideal place to get rid of a body, but it was a bit far to go from Boston, and it might be hard to explain carrying a body on a plane. It was too late anyway, now that he'd been captured, although hadn't there been rumors that he'd been seen in County Cork before that?

She released the brake and made her way carefully down the hill and back to the village, without seeing a single car on the road. Where was everybody? If they were at work, she couldn't see where. Back in Leap she parked the car behind the bed and breakfast and considered her options. Mrs. Nolan had hinted that she had more to share, and there might be others still around who also could tell her about her grandmother's early years. It was hard now to imagine Gran as a happy woman her own age, with a husband and a child, living on a farm somewhere nearby. Maura would like to see the house, if it was still standing — she'd have to ask Mrs. Nolan which one it was — as well as the cemetery she'd mentioned, where her grandfather and presumably other relatives were buried. She felt she owed them at least an acknowledgment. Ellen had said, kind of indirectly, that she'd give Maura a good rate if she stayed longer. But could she see herself working at the pub? Maybe. It was no worse than other bars she had worked in.

Maura walked up the steep grade of the driveway to the main road, grateful that the rain had finally stopped. She followed the sidewalk along the harbor side of the road, studying the town. When she'd arrived, she hadn't been paying attention to details — not that there was much to see. She dimly remembered passing churches, and a school on the left. As far as she could tell, the entire town consisted of the one main street, its single row of buildings backed by low hills behind and, to her left, the harbor. She could make out signs for a furniture store and a hardware store, but not much more. The only place to buy food was apparently the quick mart attached to the gas station, across from the Catholic church. Opposite where she stood, the clutch of pubs huddled: Sullivan's, then the road to the north, then two others, that she hadn't explored yet. And that was the entire town. Even in the persistent drizzle, Maura could tell that the buildings were well tended, painted in bright, cheery colors, with no trash to be seen. There were few cars parked along the road. How did anyone stay in business?

Maura turned her attention to Sullivan's. The pub was located in a low two-story stuccoed structure with a chimney at the nearer end, which Maura recognized as connected to the fireplace in the pub. The building resembled most of the others on the street, but this one was painted white, and sported dark painted frames around the windows and doors, and the doors were all painted red. The pub itself occupied one end, with its door flanked by two wide, plate-glass windows. There were two more doors and a couple of windows on the ground floor, but Maura had no clue what lay behind them. She looked carefully both ways, then crossed the road.

Inside the pub she paused for a moment to let her eyes adjust to the dim interior; when they did, the only person she saw was the old man seated in the well-worn stuffed chair to the right of the fireplace, warming his bones in front of the glowing peat fire. No sign of Mick, Jimmy, or Rose — did any of these people keep a regular schedule?

She realized the old man was looking at her, a small smile on his face. He could have been anywhere from sixty to a hundred; he hadn't shaved anytime recently, and his thinning white hair straggled over his collar. He was wearing an old wool jacket that had been carefully patched more than once, a tweed cap with a brim, and stout if scuffed shoes. His eyes were bright with curiosity.

"You'd be Nora Donovan's girl, Nora Sullivan that was — you've the look of her," he said.

"Granddaughter, actually. I'm Maura Donovan. And you are?"

"William Sheahan, pleased to be of service to you."

"Nice to meet you," Maura said absently. What was this man doing here, when there was no one else around? "Have you seen Jimmy or Mick?" she asked.

"Jimmy'll be here in a bit, but Mick doesn't come in until the evening, most days. I'm keeping an eye on the place for 'em. Will you sit a keep an old man company for a bit?"

"Sure," Maura said. After all, there was nowhere else she had to be, and she couldn't be rude to a nice old man who seemed to be the pub's most consistent customer.

"Could I trouble you for a cup of tea, before you settle yourself?"

The only place in the room that tea-making equipment could be located would be behind the bar, so that's where she headed. "I'll see what I can do. How do you like your tea, uh, Mr. Sheahan?" she called out. She'd guessed right, as she quickly found the electric kettle and tea bags.

"White, with sugar, love. You can call me Billy — Mr. Sheahan was me da, and he's long gone."

"White" presumably meant with milk? Maura opened the little fridge and was pleased to find a small carton of milk. She smelled it and decided it would do. She found tea bags in a jar on an adjacent shelf, and there were clean mugs lined up on another shelf. As she filled the kettle, she surveyed the bar area: the taps worked, as she knew, but she had no idea where the kegs were kept. In a cellar? A limited selection of liquors, with a big bottle of Paddy's Irish Whiskey set up in the dispenser. A standing display of assorted chips, although Maura had no idea how long they'd been

106

there. And that was it. Not much to work with.

Today she had time to take a good hard look at the place. The first day she hadn't been in any shape to take in details, and yesterday the pub had been buried under customers. There were the two armchairs flanking the fireplace, six stools in front of the bar, a couple of tables with chairs tucked in corners around the room, and a row of chairs lined up along the big windows in the front, where the wide sills served as a countertop. The place could hold maybe twenty-five people, seated. If customers were willing to stand, as they had the night before, that could easily rise to fifty or beyond.

The kettle boiled, and she poured water over tea bags in two mugs. She waited a minute or two, then fished out the tea bags, added sugar and milk to both, and carried them over to the fireplace.

"Ah, that's grand. Will you be joinin' me?" Billy said.

"Sure." Maura settled herself in the chair opposite him, noting that the springs under the seat had seen better days — in some other century. "Were you a friend of the old owner?"

"Indeed I was, from when we were lads

together at the school down the road — the old school, not the one they put up thirty years ago. We gave the nuns a time, let me tell you." He sipped his tea. "Yer from America?"

As if it wasn't obvious as soon as she opened her mouth. "Yes, Boston. Did you know my grandmother?"

"That I did, and her husband Jimmy. Sad thing about him."

Maura did a quick calculation: her grandfather James had died over forty years earlier. "Why do you say that?"

"He shouldn't have gone so young. He was a hard worker, a good man. He cut himself one day and didn't take care of it — said he was too busy. And we didn't have the clinic in the village then. So it went septic on him, and by the time he saw a doctor, there was nothing to be done. Your grandmother, she was heartbroken, her left with a young son, and no way to support herself. Jimmy'd been farming the land, raising some cattle, but he didn't own it, and she couldn't handle it herself."

"That was when she went to America?" Maura prompted.

"It was. She had friends in Boston, people from hereabouts who said there were jobs to be had there, and they'd help her get settled. So she left with Tommy. Sweet boy, he was. Your da, wasn't he?"

Maura shook her head. "Barely. He died not long after I was born. It was a construction accident." How different her life might have been if her father had lived. Or if her mother hadn't decided to dump her baby on her mother-in-law and disappear.

"Your gran, now — we always hoped she'd come back, at least for a visit."

"I think she wanted to, but she never had the chance." Was it rude to talk about the fact that they'd been lucky to keep a roof over their heads and food on the table? "But she told me that she wanted me to visit, to get to know something about where she — we came from. So here I am."

"Are yeh going ta stay long?"

"I . . . haven't decided. I was only planning on a week — I hadn't realized how much there was to see."

Billy waved a hand gnarled with arthritis. "Ah, a week's no good at all. What's your hurry?"

What *was* her hurry? Maura wondered. She'd been here all of three days, and already she'd been supplied with a place to stay, a car, an array of people who had known her grandmother — and a possible job that would support her for a time.

"None at all, I guess. So tell me, what else should I see around here?"

That was enough to get Billy started, and Maura settled back in her chair with her tea and listened.

CHAPTER 9

The next time Maura looked at her watch, more than two hours had passed. She'd refilled their mugs with more tea, but even that interruption hadn't stemmed the flow of Billy's words. Maybe it was because he was thrilled to have an audience, Maura thought; most of his stories referred to people and places from a half century ago, and no doubt all of the pub's patrons had heard them all before. Or maybe Old Mick had let him hang around to entertain the tourists with a bit of local color — or maybe simply because they were old friends. It would have kept them buying pints, and Billy had probably garnered his share.

Stop being so cynical, Maura! Billy was a lonely old man who'd outlived most of his generation and was happy for someone to talk to. And she could learn a lot by listening to him.

They were interrupted by the sound of

someone moving around the back of the building; then Jimmy came in through the door next to the bar. "Ah, Maura. How are ya?"

"Just fine, Jimmy. Is it opening time?"

"No hurry. You haven't been turning them away at the door, have you?" He grinned.

"Not exactly. Billy here's been entertaining me with his stories."

"Good man, Billy! Maura, could I have a word with you?"

"Sure. Billy, you need anything else?" When he didn't answer, Maura looked at him and realized that he'd fallen asleep. She stood up and joined Jimmy at the bar. "What's up?"

"Have you given any thought to what we talked about?" he asked.

"You mean, working here for a bit?"

Jimmy nodded. "Mick says his grandma is over the moon to have someone to share her stories with — she was always close to yours. You'd be making an old lady happy."

So Jimmy had talked to Mick about her. Mick apparently hadn't changed his mind about the job offer. "She's a lovely lady, but are you trying to push me into doing what *you* want?"

Jimmy contrived to appear hurt. "Now, why would I be doing that?"

Maura looked him in the eye. "You're playing the 'poor old lady' card to get cheap help, is why. Not that I mind — I just want to be clear from the start about why I'm doing this."

Jimmy cocked his head at her. "Would you rather I pulled the 'poor lonely daughter' card instead? Do it for Rose, then — she'd be glad of a woman's company here."

Did the guy have no shame? "Rose is a smart kid, and she shouldn't be stuck here. So be warned: if I stay around, I may fill her head with plans to escape this place."

"Ah, she'd never leave her da here all by his lonesome. She's a good girl."

And Jimmy should be looking out for his daughter, not himself. Rose deserved better — the kid deserved a chance to see what the rest of the world was like, if only within Ireland — but didn't a lot of Irish kids get jobs in other parts of Europe? Maybe she herself hadn't had many options, but she could try to see that Rose knew she had some. "So what's the deal?"

Jimmy sighed dramatically. "You Americans — always in such a hurry. You aren't giving me half a chance to work my charms on you."

Maura ignored his attempt to divert her. "How long are we talking about?"

113

"Until we know what's happening to the pub, I'd say."

"When will that be?"

"It's for the courts to sort out," Jimmy said. "Old Mick never married nor had children, but there's still lots of his family around. Too complicated for me."

"How long do Irish courts usually take to sort things out?"

"It depends," Jimmy said.

That was no help. Her temporary job might last a week or six months, for all she could tell. "Any chance you'll end up with the place, or Mick?" Maura asked.

"We'll see. But that doesn't concern you. All I can say is, the travel season will be upon us by June, say, and it'll get busier, and we can use your help. You need more than a week's time to pay your calls on folk, and there's nothing that's drawing you back to Boston. We all win, right?"

So he was figuring months rather than weeks. Surely the Irish legal system wouldn't take that long? More to the point, would that work for her? Maura had to admit that what he said made sense, though she was beginning to resent being constantly reminded that she had no life of her own. Of course, staying here didn't move her life forward much, but it was marginally more

114

tempting than going back to Boston and trying to pick up the pieces and start something new. Why not? Maura squared her chin and again looked him in the eye. "All right, here's the deal. First, I need to figure out if I can swap my airplane ticket, and how much that'll cost me. Second, I need to be paid enough to cover my room, feed myself, and put gas in the car, like Mick said, with maybe a little extra thrown in. Tell me straight — can this place afford to pay me that much?"

"We can make it work, if that's what you want. I'm hoping it won't be long. Much like yourself, I'd like to know which way the wind is blowing so I can make me own plans."

"All right. You make the numbers work, and I'll stay. But I've got one condition: we clean up this place. It looks like some of the dirt is older than I am, and don't get me started on the bathrooms."

Jimmy grinned. "Yeah, Old Mick slowed down in his later years, and I don't think he could see so well anymore — or smell. But the customers don't come here for the shiny bar top, yeh know. They're here to see friends and talk and relax."

"They can't do that in a clean place?"

"I suppose. Just no tarty bits like flowers

in the window or new curtains and the like."

"Deal. Should I start now?"

Jimmy looked startled for a moment. "Grand. No doubt people will be coming in to see if there's any news about the body."

"Is there?"

"Not that I've heard, not yet anyways. But who knows? They'll be coming in either way."

Maura took a deep breath. "Then I'll do it. Until you get things settled." She leaned closer to Jimmy and said in a low voice, "What's the story with Billy, there? Do we charge him, or is whatever he gets on the house?"

"Mick gave him a free pass for life. I'd hate to be the one to change that."

"That's fine — I was just checking. Now, where can I find some cleaning supplies? Because I'm betting there aren't any here."

"The quick mart up the street'll have what you want. You can't miss it — it's across from the church. Oh, and I'll send Rosie over here to help you out."

"What, you're not planning to help? Only women can clean?"

Jimmy held up both hands in protest. "Nothing like that! Only I've got to talk to our distributors and such."

Maura had to wonder how much time he

116

spent on business calls and how much hanging out with his buddies somewhere else. "Then while you're at it, get some more snacks, preferably some whose expiration date is in this century, not the last."

"Right, I'll take care of it. See yeh later!" He escaped out the back before Maura could make any more demands.

"You hold him to it, young lady," Billy suddenly volunteered.

So he hadn't been asleep. "You heard?" Maura came around the bar and sat opposite him again.

"Enough. He's not a bad man, just likes to take the easy road, if you know what I mean. So you'll be staying on, at least for a while?"

"Looks like it. But you probably heard that the first thing I'm doing is cleaning this place up. Gran would be horrified by the state it's in."

"As long as you don't think I'm part of the rubbish and throw me out as well."

"I wouldn't do that, Billy. I have a feeling you have a lot more stories I should hear."

"Ah, you're a good girl, you are. Your gran would be proud."

Maura hoped she wasn't blushing. "I'm going to go get some cleaning stuff, pick up a sandwich. Can I bring you anything?"

"No, I'll be fine. I'll pop into me own place, where I've got the fixings."

"You live far from here?" Maura asked.

"Just the other end of the building, the last door on the right. I've two rooms on the ground floor."

"Did Old Mick own the whole building?"

"He did. Some of it's empty, now — he couldn't be bothered to find lodgers, the last few years. But he didn't need to, he said."

"You have any idea what's going to happen to the place, once it gets sorted out? Did he say anything to you?"

"It's not coming to me, I know that much, but Mick never said more." Billy began to extricate himself from the depths of the chair, and Maura hesitated over whether to offer him a hand. Still, he managed well enough, and once he was upright she found that he was shorter than she was.

"Will you see me out?"

"I'll even see you to your door — I'm going that way."

"Ah, yer too kind."

Maura gave a brief thought to whether the place should be locked up when no one was in it, but she couldn't imagine there was anything worth stealing, and it wasn't like she had a key anyway. She made a mental note to ask Mick or Jimmy about their policy for locking up — and their ideas about opening and closing times, since they'd been all over the map so far. She dropped Billy off at his door — which, she noted, wasn't locked either — then proceeded up the street toward where she remembered seeing a gas station. On the same side of the street, she came upon the Catholic church. It seemed surprisingly large, with a spacious parking lot. It must have been built when there was greater allegiance to the Catholic Church. A cemetery climbed up the steep hill behind. Maura wondered how anyone could manage a burial there. The mourners would have to be mountain goats, though maybe those difficulties kept the burial part of the funeral short. Was Old Mick buried there? She marked both the church and the cemetery for later exploration; right now she had more pressing things to do, like see what was under the grime in the pub, and if anything could overcome the stench of generations of drunken guys missing the mark in the loo.

She found the small market easily enough, and to her surprise it looked much like any mini market back in the States. Even the packages looked familiar — until she read them more closely. Apparently international companies picked different names for different markets. She stifled a giggle: no way Fairy Liquid would sell in the U.S., but here it seemed to be an ordinary dish soap. The sandwiches were a bit boggling as well. Did she want to eat something labeled "fish paste"? Since she was in no hurry to get back to clean, she took her time, going up and down the couple of aisles and reading labels. The sugar bore the title *siúcra* in addition to "caster sugar," and there was some bottled drink called "barley water" that looked positively nasty. Despite the unfamiliar brand names, she was able to collect the basic cleaning materials she needed, including rubber gloves. It cost her much of her remaining cash, and she wondered if the pub would reimburse her. Well, duh, if she was working there, she could take the money she needed from the till — if there was enough there. What kind of bookkeeping did the place use? Silly question: the most likely answer was, none at all, no matter what Jimmy said. Well, that wasn't her problem. She'd take what she needed first and let Mick and Jimmy worry about the rest of it. And if they couldn't manage to pay her, she'd be out the door.

When she returned to the pub, laden with

two full carrier bags plus a packaged sandwich, Rose was already there. She looked up and smiled happily.

"Da says you'll be staying on for a bit?"

"Looks that way," Maura replied.

"Well, I'll be glad of the company. I don't often have anyone to talk to behind the bar here. Well, there are plenty who come in to chat, but it's not personal, like. Some days it's so dull I watch the American shows on the telly."

"I know what you mean. Listen, I told your father that the first thing I wanted to do was give this place a good cleaning. Maybe he thinks it's not important, but I refuse to work in a filthy dump. Are you okay with that?"

"Of course. I'd've done it myself, but I didn't know where to start, it's that bad. What's your plan?"

"I'm starting with a sandwich. Let me eat my lunch, and then we can dig in. Can you hand me a Coke? And do I have to keep a record of what I eat or drink?" Usually in Boston no one had cared if the bar staff helped themselves, as long as it wasn't the expensive stuff, but she wanted to start off on the right foot here.

"Sure, go ahead, and don't worry about it. Just tell me what to do with the cleaning bit," Rose said cheerfully.

"I'll take the toilets. I wouldn't ask anyone else to do something even I hate to do."

"You'll hear no complaints from me," Rose said, smiling.

CHAPTER 10

Three hours later Maura declared herself finished. No customer had even poked a head in, and Maura didn't know if she was worried or relieved. She wouldn't call the bathrooms clean, exactly, but they were substantially less filthy than they had been when she started. They were also stocked with paper towels and toilet paper, although she'd exhausted the pitiful supply she'd found. She'd have to tell Jimmy to order more. And some more lightbulbs.

She washed her hands one last time, noting the poor water pressure. Was that due to the plumbing? For that matter, how old was the plumbing — or the building? From what she'd seen around here, construction styles in the village hadn't changed much in a century or so, which made it hard to tell. Rose had scrubbed the top of the bar, and Maura could see the grain of the wood for the first time. A quick glance around the room told her that Rose had been diligent while Maura had been busy in the back; most of the surfaces gleamed, and the windows sparkled.

"Great job, Rose! This place looks a whole lot better," Maura said sincerely.

"All I did was clean the tops a bit — I saved the floor to tackle later."

"I'll bet your father will be impressed."

Rose waved a hand dismissively. "Ah, he wouldn't notice. My ma showed me how to clean, and I've been keeping our place up since she . . . passed."

"I'm sorry — has it been long?"

"Going on two years." Rose swallowed. "I miss her still. My da tells me you never knew your own mother?"

"No," Maura said without elaborating. She'd already told that story more often in the last day then she'd done in years. She turned the conversation back to Rose. "So, do you have any brothers and sisters?"

Rose shook her head. "No, there's only me. And yourself?"

"Same here. I don't know how Gran would have coped if there'd been more than me."

The door opened, and Maura was surprised to see two twenty-something men shamble in. One nodded to a table in the back corner and headed in that direction; the other came over to the bar and said, "Two pints," then turned away to join his friend.

"Friendly sorts," Maura said in a low voice. Most people she'd served so far had at least greeted her, and they often chatted while waiting for their pints to settle. "Local?"

Rose studied them briefly. "I don't know them." When the pints were ready, she took them over to the men, who looked up and nodded without smiling. When she came back to the bar, she changed the subject. She reached under the bar and pulled out a pile of letters, pushing them toward Maura. "I found these under the bar here while I was cleaning up. Should I give them to Da?"

Maura sorted through them. Mostly bills — presumably those should go to Jimmy or Mick, whichever was handling the books for the pub. They hadn't been opened, though the dates on them were fairly recent. But there was one personal letter, handwritten, whose envelope had been slit open. Maura pulled it from the stack and was startled to see an Australian return address. She looked up at Rose. "Australia! Did Old Mick know anyone there?"

Rose craned her neck to look. "Nice

stamp. No, I can't say as he did. Wonder why the letter came here instead of to his home? I'm surprised Old Mick left it here — he was real private. But maybe he was feeling poorly and forgot to take it home with him."

"How did he die?" Maura asked, hoping she wasn't about to learn that he'd dropped dead in the pub.

"He went easy. He didn't come in one morning, and when Mick went looking for him, he found him in his bed, gone. Old Mick was well into his nineties, anyways."

"How long ago was this?" Maura asked. She wondered briefly what local regulations might be for burying someone; she was more familiar than she wanted to be with the American customs.

"Ten days, is it now?" Rose calculated in her head. "There was talk of waiting to put him in the ground until a next of kin was found, but nobody was sure where to look, since most of his family's long gone. The Sullivans have a plot behind the church, so they put him there. The funeral filled the church — everyone knew Old Mick."

No wonder things were so unsettled about the pub. "Maybe we should look at the letter. If it's personal, someone might be hoping for an answer, and at the very least they should be told that Old Mick is gone."

"Go on, then — read it. It's already open," Rose said.

Feeling vaguely guilty, Maura pulled two sheets of paper from the envelope and scanned them quickly. They were covered with dense script, and it took her a moment to decipher what the writer, Denis Flaherty, was saying. Denis wrote that he was in his eighties and working on his own family history and thought that Old Mick might know something about the local McCarthys, from his mother's side. It appeared to be an out-of-the-blue letter, and the first that Denis had written to Mick, because he took the time to introduce himself as the son of Bridget McCarthy, and he wondered if she was the sister of Ellen McCarthy, Old Mick's mother, but he couldn't be sure because he'd only learned bits and pieces from his family in Australia. Genealogy, then. Something Maura had had no particular interest in, and that Gran hadn't encouraged — indeed, she'd often said that she'd made her choice to find a new life in America and looking backward was useless. And what was it with all these Denises and Bridgets and whatever? Mrs. Nolan had mentioned something about traditional naming patterns, but this was ridiculous.

How did anybody keep straight who was who, and who was related to whom? Of course, they'd probably known all their lives, unlike her.

"What's it about?" Rose asked.

"It's a letter from some guy in Australia who's looking for some of his relatives or ancestors around here. He thought Old Mick might be able to help, because he might be related."

"Who's he looking for, then?"

"His name's Denis Flaherty, but he's looking for his mother's people. Her name was Bridget McCarthy. Do you know of any McCarthys around here?"

Rose giggled. "At least a dozen. I was at school with a few."

"Should I ask people at the pub if they can help this Denis? I hate to just send the letter back, and I don't know who's who around here or where to find them."

"You can ask, but it may not help you much."

Maura looked down at the letter in her hand. Poor Denis probably didn't have many years left to him, and she hated to leave him in the dark, if there was anything she could do. "Still, I think I should do something. If you see a McCarthy walk in the door today, point him out to me, will

128

you? I'll hang on to the letter for now. And maybe I'll ask Bridget Nolan if she has any ideas — she's probably around the right age to know. Oh, and thanks a lot for helping with the cleaning, Rose."

The door opened, ushering in a few customers, who found their way to seats. Maura tucked the letter deep in her bag. If Old Mick had read and saved the letter, he must have had some reason, and it occurred to her that it might help give some clue as to who his relations might be.

"I'll give these others to me da, when he comes in, shall I?" Rose asked.

"Sure. He's the one that pays the bills, right? You want to take care of those two?" Maura nodded toward the latest arrivals. "And when we have a moment, maybe we should go over the staffing schedule."

"Right," Rose said, then went to take the newcomers' order. She chatted for a moment, then came back and started pulling two pints.

Maura began again, "Your dad said that the place doesn't usually open until mid-afternoon this time of year?"

"That's right, or later, especially in the middle of the week. No point in wasting the electric, now, is there? Of course, Old Mick was usually here, and if business was slow, he and Billy would sit by the fire and swap lies. He might have been old, but he stayed on until nearly closing, most nights. Da and Mick Nolan kind of shared the evening hours, but there was nothing like a plan — they just worked it out day to day. I cover afternoons mostly, and I help at night when things are busy. What're you thinking?"

"I can be flexible, but I want a little time to look around the area. Mick's grandmother knew my grandmother, so I want to spend some time with her, and I want to go see where my grandfather is buried. It's kind of hard to plan when I don't know how long I'll be staying." She slid off the bar stool and came around to the back of the bar. "Okay, walk me through what we've got here — you know, what's popular, where everything is." She noted that Rose had done a good job cleaning and tidying behind the bar as well.

After that there was a steady trickle of customers. Closer to six, another man came in and made a beeline for the bar. "Rosie, you're looking grand, my love. And who's this?" he asked, catching sight of Maura. "A new face for the old place?" He extended his hand. "The name's Bart Hayes."

Maura shook his hand. "I'm Maura Donovan."

"American, are you? How did you find yourself behind the bar in this old dump?" He said it with a smile, so Maura had to assume he knew the place well.

"My grandmother came from around here. What can I get you?"

The one-line explanation seemed to satisfy the man. "A pint, of course." He looked around the all but empty pub. "I'd offer to buy a round, but that seems an empty gesture. Will you join me, Maura Donovan? Rosie here's too young to raise a toast."

"You seem in a happy mood, Mr. Hayes," Rose commented.

"That I am. I've just landed a big order — that's a rare thing these days, and cause to celebrate."

Maura slid his pint across the bar and poured herself a soda. "Congratulations. What is it you do?"

"I work for one of those pharmaceutical companies, over toward Cork. One of them that arrived under the Celtic Tiger and managed to make a go of it. Business has been slow for a while, let me tell you, but maybe now things are looking up. *Sláinte!*"

After a while, Bart Hayes recognized a newcomer and went over to talk with him. It was only her second night, but Maura fell easily into the rhythm of serving. The patrons seemed to enjoy the chance to chat her up. Many were curious to meet the American girl they'd somehow already heard about. The first question was usually, "So, you're from America?" most often followed by some variation on "Why are you here?" although usually phrased more politely than that. Maura felt a bit embarrassed to be the center of attention, but from what she could see it was meant kindly. Funny — the bartending part she could handle, because she'd had plenty of experience, but she'd never been good at making small talk, much less flirting, with patrons. They all seemed to know each other, and she was the odd one out, but she was welcomed warmly. Her stock answer quickly became, "Because my grandmother came from near here," as she had told Bart, which usually led to an exchange of stories about relatives near and far, and Maura was soon lost in the maze of surnames: there were few names, but many families with the same names, widely scattered, and it was not something that her brain was ready to sort out. Hearing that she was a Donovan often prompted more questions that she couldn't answer. Sometimes that segued into stories of other relatives who had gone to America — and almost everyone could name one or two.

Luckily she could take advantage of such a conversation with a question about local McCarthys, although the answers were just as confusing. But, she rationalized, if Aussie Denis Flaherty had waited this long, a couple of days couldn't hurt, and maybe she could produce some sort of answer for him.

Some twenty minutes later Maura saw Bart Hayes head out the door, with a wave directed at her. It wasn't long after that the two dour young men who'd been hogging the corner table and nursing their first and only pints made their exit, which opened up that table, occupied quickly. Business remained brisk.

The other main topic of conversation, of course, was the body in the bog.

"They've had the man from the museum down, to take a look at him," one man volunteered.

"What does that mean?" Maura asked.

"Oh, these days whenever you find such a thing, the history folk have to make sure it isn't a national treasure. That means all work stops until it's been checked out. They've made a big thing of it, this last decade or so. There's a whole bunch at the National Museum who're working on it."

133

"And what did the museum man say?"

"Seems the poor guy isn't a thousand years old, so they're not interested. Now it's back in the hands of the gardaí."

"So how old is he? Or maybe I mean, how long has he been in the bog?"

"Fifty to a hundred years, like. Can I get another?" He held up his empty pint glass, which Maura refilled.

When the first man drifted away, another took his place at the bar, also talking about the Bog Man.

"What happens now?" Maura asked him as she presented him with the pint glass of Murphy's he'd requested.

"Well, once a doctor declared the man dead, which any one of us could have done, he was shipped off to the University Hospital in Cork for an autopsy. The gardaí'll want to know how he died."

"What if he just got lost and fell into the bog and drowned?" That had been Bridget Nolan's suggestion.

The man shrugged. "I only know what I see on the telly. Them shows — they'd have you think that the scientists can tell you what time of day the deceased met his fate, and what his last meal was. Wonder if that's still true if his last meal was a century ago? Good entertainment, but I don't believe the half of it." He slid a few coins across the bar and went to join friends on the other side of the room.

Jimmy breezed in about eight and sent Rose home — Maura hoped it wasn't far, because it was full dark and rather wet outside — although maybe she was projecting her own anxieties about walking home late in Boston, which wasn't always a good idea. Were there muggers in Leap? Drug dealers? On the face of it, it seemed unlikely, but there was crime everywhere these days, even in quiet Ireland. Better to be safe than sorry, she thought.

Jimmy was greeted enthusiastically by several people in the room, and Maura watched him make the circuit. Pulling pints did not seem to be his first priority, but generating goodwill had to count for something. Did he see himself carrying on Old Mick's tradition, as master of the place? He finally came over to talk to her.

"How's it goin'?" he asked, his eyes watching the room.

"Fine. Did you get more chips — crisps?" Maura responded.

"Ah, forgot. Tomorrow'll do. Hey, you did a grand job with the loos — I didn't even know that floor had a pattern to it."

"You owe me for the cleaning supplies. I

135

couldn't find any here."

"Take it from the till, and we'll sort things out later."

People drifted in over the next several hours, most with a comment about the man from the bog. By ten Maura was falling asleep standing upright. The crowd had dwindled to three or four regulars, who looked like they weren't going anywhere soon. Maura gestured Jimmy over. "You mind if I call it a day?"

"You look done in. Not a problem — I think I can manage this crew. You'll be back tomorrow?"

"I will. Early afternoon, I guess, if that works for you."

"Grand. Thanks, Maura — I'm glad you're here."

"Night, Jimmy." Maura found her jacket and her bag and stepped outside, glad of the cool, damp air. The street was quiet again, or maybe as always. She crossed over and walked down the drive to the back of the bed and breakfast, trying to keep the gravel from crunching too loudly, since the upstairs windows were dark. Back in her room, she pulled off her clothes, shook them out, and draped them over a chair. She'd have to decide by daylight whether she could wear them another day or if she'd have to ask Ellen if she could do some laundry.

But once she was tucked into bed, Maura realized she wanted to take another look at Denis Flaherty's letter, which she'd only skimmed before. Maybe in the morning Ellen could tell her something about Old Mick's relatives. Reluctantly she left the warm blankets and fished the letter out of her bag. It took her a few minutes to work her way through the closely packed script, written by a clearly aged hand. What she learned was that Denis Flaherty had been born in County Cork but had emigrated to Australia with his parents as a young child, and was now in his eighties. He was anxious to fill out his family tree while he could, and was finding it difficult so far removed. He hadn't known the townland, only the county, although he'd somehow deduced that Leap was the nearest village to whatever townland it was. Much like her grandmother, Maura mused: the emigrants didn't dwell on what they had left behind, and Denis had been a young child when his parents left Ireland, so he had appealed to Old Mick for help, although he didn't explain how he had come by Mick's name. According to the brief family tree he had sent, Denis's father, Thomas Flaherty, had been born in 1880, his mother, Bridget McCarthy, a few years later. Bridget's father — Aussie Denis's grandfather — was also named Denis, and he had been born in 1837.

Maura was about to give up, as her eyelids were drooping, when she read that Denis Flaherty said his uncle Denis McCarthy — another Denis! — had disappeared in 1931. That was the term Aussie Denis used: not died, but "disappeared," and as far as he knew, no one had ever found or heard from his uncle again. One day Uncle Denis was there, the next he was gone, with no explanation to the family he left behind — a wife and three daughters. One line in the letter seemed particularly sad: apparently Uncle Denis had gone missing "with no more than a few pennies and his favorite pipe in his pocket." Nothing was taken from his possessions at home.

Maura wondered . . . hadn't the man in the pub said that the body in the bog had been there less than a hundred years? And wouldn't it be an extraordinary coincidence if the body in the bog was the missing uncle?

She made a mental note to ask Ellen about it in the morning. And . . . she drifted off to sleep.

CHAPTER 11

Maura woke earlier the next morning than she had the day before, and lay listening to the sounds of the children over her head. The sight of Denis Flaherty's letter propped up on her nightstand reminded her of what she'd read the night before. It was absurd to think that she could've so easily found the identity of a man who had died some eighty years earlier. But then again, what was she supposed to do with the information she had? It seemed wrong to ignore it.

Her impressions of the Boston police had been kind of mixed. She'd never been in trouble herself, but she'd known plenty of classmates who had. On the other hand, even now a lot of Boston cops were of Irish descent, and they'd sometimes give a helping hand or look the other way when the newcomers were involved in minor incidents. She had no information at all about Irish police, beyond her encounter two days before with the friendly young Officer Murphy. Did she want to get involved with them, even in a positive way? She wasn't sure.

She dressed quickly and made her way to the kitchen above. Gráinne was sitting in a chair with a booster seat of some sort; she smiled at Maura when she walked in. That was progress.

This time there was a man at the table, handing Gráinne what looked like Cheerios, a few at a time. "Hi, Ellen," Maura said. "Are you Ellen's husband? I'm Maura Donovan."

"I am that. Thomas Keohane. I'd shake your hand but I'm a bit sticky, thanks to the little one here. So you'll be staying on for a while?"

"Looks like it. You've got a nice place here — the view is amazing."

"You can tell the house is kinda new, and the bit where you're staying was added later still. Time was it was nothing but old cottages around the cove here. The Keohanes have been on this spot for generations." He stood up. "I'll be off, Ellen. Nice to meet you, Maura. I hope you enjoy your visit."

"I expect to," Maura said.

When Thomas Keohane had left, Ellen said, "You're up a bit earlier today."

140

"I think I'm adjusting to local time, and I got in before eleven last night. By the way, I've said I'd stay on until the ownership of the pub is settled, just to help out. Is it all right with you if I keep the room?"

"Sure. I'm glad you'll be staying around — you'll have a chance to get to know the place better. Full breakfast?"

"I guess I'd better. I seem to keep missing dinner, so I'd better fill up while I can, right?"

"Full breakfast it is. Although" — Ellen leaned closer to Maura and dropped her voice — "we only serve it to tourists. We natives eat regular food."

Maura laughed. "I'm not surprised. And don't worry about me — I eat anything. Maybe tomorrow you can just give me what you'd eat anyway? Like yesterday?"

"Was your gran a good cook?" Ellen asked, placing what Maura guessed was a local kind of bacon in a frying pan.

"She was a good plain cook — nothing fancy. She taught me enough to stay alive if I have a stove."

"So we shouldn't be expecting gourmet dinners out of Sullivan's any time soon?"

"Don't think so." Maura laughed. "But who knows what the next owner will want? There's room behind the bar for a decent

141

kitchen."

"True, and he'll be sitting on a gold mine — quaint-looking place, right on the main road," Ellen said, setting butter and several jars of jam in front of Maura.

"Listen, can I ask you something?"

Ellen sat down with a full cup of coffee. "Sure."

"Yesterday Rose found a letter at the pub that was addressed to Mick Sullivan, and it looks like he'd read it before he died. It's from someone in Australia who's been doing some family research — he and Mick might be cousins, because their mothers were both McCarthys from around here. Anyway, he mentioned an uncle of his who disappeared in the 1930s. I know it would be a huge coincidence, but I was wondering — maybe that's the man in the bog?"

Ellen looked thoughtful. "No shortage of McCarthys around here. Still, it's possible, I guess."

"I'm wondering if I should tell someone about it. Like the police."

"Ah, well, but you'll have to know that in those days, a lot of people kind of . . . went away. There was no work to be had, and some of the men were ashamed that they couldn't support their families. Could be some left thinking they'd send money back,

142

maybe enough to bring the families along to wherever they'd gone. But when they couldn't . . ." Ellen didn't finish her thought. She stood and went back to the stove to turn the bacon.

"I can see that, but shouldn't I tell someone official, just in case? If they tell me it's a dead end, at least I'll know I tried."

"If it worries you, you should do it," Ellen said.

"Okay, but who do I talk to?"

"The gardaí over at Skibbereen." When Maura looked blankly at her, Ellen laughed. "Haven't you been to Skibbereen yet? It's easy. You follow the road up there until you come to a little roundabout. Go left there and it'll take you straight into town. Go left in the center; the police station will be on your left. There's a big car park for the markets just across the way."

"Thanks, that helps. Do you think they're going to think I'm crazy, just walking in with a story like this?"

"Just tell them that you've information that might be important to the investigation of the man they pulled out of the bog in Leap. They'll either take your details and thank you nicely, or they'll pass you up the line to someone who will. Easy." Ellen filled a plate with bacon and brown bread, then glanced at her watch. "Oh, look at the time. Gráinne, we've got to get you over to the creche now, and Mum's got lots to do. You take your time, Maura — eat up." She placed the plate in front of Maura. "Help yourself to more coffee if you like." Ellen hauled her daughter out of her seat and disappeared toward the other end of the house.

Ellen was out the door before Maura remembered that she had wanted to ask about doing some laundry. It would keep. She sat for a few minutes longer, sipping her coffee, and enjoying the brown bread with a healthy dose of butter, and turning over options in her mind. First, she should see what Mrs. Nolan had to say about what to do with the letter. Then, she wanted to see Skibbereen anyway, so she might as well drive over there. She didn't have to make up her mind about going to the police until she got there, did she? Energized, she stood and carried her cup and empty plate over to the sink, then went downstairs to gather her bag and keys.

The drive to Mrs. Nolan's house seemed shorter and easier each time she made it — Maura was getting the hang of shifting gears, driving on the left, and navigating winding back roads, all at once. When she parked in the same place as the day before, she saw Mick emerging from the house and crossed to meet him.

"Everything all right?"

"Sure, I was just stopping by. Grannie said she expected you'd be back."

"I like talking with her. She makes me realize how little I know about my own gran's early life. So talking to your gran is the next best thing."

"I'll let you two visit, and I'll see you later, won't I?"

"You will. Hey, can you make sure Jimmy stocks up? I left a list of things that are getting kind of low. And I was thinking, if you had more snacks around, maybe people would order more drinks."

Mick looked pained. "I'll remind him. Ta."

He climbed into his car and adroitly steered it out of the enclosure, heading back the way Maura had come. What did he do with himself most of the time? Maura wondered. He showed up kind of on and off, and the pub didn't seem like full-time employment; she had to wonder if its income could support one person, much less several. Maybe they made it all up in the summer and coasted the rest of the year.

She knocked on Mrs. Nolan's door and it opened quickly. "Ah, there you are. I was hoping you'd be by. You saw Michael, then?"

"I did. Is this a good time?"

"Oh, of course it is. Please, come in. I made sure Mick set out the tea things for us."

Maura was touched. How many relatives and friends could Mrs. Nolan have left, at her age? Despite what she'd said about liking her independence, did she get lonely, up here on a windswept hill, with more cattle than people as neighbors?

After Maura filled her in on the plan to stay on in Leap and help out at the pub for a bit (which had pleased Mrs. Nolan no end), Maura said cautiously, "Do you remember any McCarthy families around here?"

Mrs. Nolan seized on the subject and gave Maura a ten-minute summary of all the McCarthy families within twenty miles — and there were plenty. From what bits and pieces she had managed to grasp out of the torrent of facts, it was clear that there was no shortage of Denises and Ellens, Patricks and Bridgets. Goodness, Maura thought, how would she ever keep them all straight? When Mrs. Nolan paused briefly to take a sip of tea, Maura broke in.

"Do you recall a Denis McCarthy who went missing sometime after 1930?"

Mrs. Nolan laughed. "You must think I'm

as old as the hills, dearie. I was only a few years old then, and I didn't pay a lot of mind. Still, let me think . . ."

Maura waited patiently while Mrs. Nolan mined her memories. Finally she said, "I can't recall . . . But I wasn't raised right around here, you know — I came here only when I married. I grew up north of here, in a different parish, so I wouldn't be of much help with the old families. I've told you of the ones I knew after I came here with my husband. Why do you ask?"

"I found a letter at the pub yesterday — a Denis McCarthy from Australia wanted to know if Old Mick could tell him anything about McCarthys from around here. I have no idea how he found Mick's name, but he knew that Mick's mother was a McCarthy. In the letter he mentioned an uncle who had disappeared in the 1930s, and I'm wondering if the man they found in the bog is connected somehow."

"You're wondering if the poor man in the bog was this letter writer's lost uncle?"

"It's just a wild guess."

Mrs. Nolan seemed to shrink into herself just a bit. "What an awful thing that would be, that he might of been lying down there all these years and his family never knew."

"I'm sorry, I didn't mean to upset you.

Ellen Keohane told me there were plenty of cases of people who upped and left back then, when times were bad, so this is probably just a coincidence." Although Maura thought that most of those men had probably said something to a relative or a friend before heading off to who knows what. It would be cruel to let parents — or a wife — think that you had abandoned them deliberately, or to let them believe that you were dead. What a sad choice. Times then must have been hard indeed.

Mrs. Nolan spoke softly, "No, you're right to ask it. Someone might be glad to know the truth of it, even so long after."

"I was wondering if I should tell the police. That's what we'd do back home, if we think we have some evidence they might need."

"I suppose you might, although I'd be surprised if there was to be any record of a man gone missing like that. Will you be going over to Skibbereen?"

"I thought so. I haven't even seen it yet."

"If you should find yourself talking to Patrick Hurley at the garda station, give him my best regards. He's the man in charge there. I haven't seen him for a while, but he's a busy man, no doubt."

"I'll do that." Maura stood up. "I should

148

go now, so I can get back to the pub later. It's Friday — will things be busier there?"

Mrs. Nolan laughed lightly. "Ah, it's been quite a time since I've visited a pub on the Friday. You'll have to tell me."

Maura smiled at her. "I will. And I'll tell you tomorrow what the police say. See you in the morning."

Once outside again, Maura realized that she really could use a map. She had the feeling that there must be a shorter way to Skibbereen than retracing her steps back to Leap, but she was afraid of getting lost in the winding lanes. Back to Leap it was, then, and onto the main highway to Skibbereen and the police. Gardaí. She could only hope they wouldn't laugh in her face.

CHAPTER 12

Maura drove cautiously into Skibbereen, uncertain of what to expect. This early in the day there was little traffic. The place would be bigger than Leap, no doubt, but certainly smaller than Boston. When she heard the word "town," she immediately had a mental picture of the towns outside of Boston, at least the few she had seen. As she approached Skibbereen, the transition from open country to town came quickly. Maybe it was smaller than she had thought?

She navigated the small roundabout Ellen had described, then followed the main road past a school and some sort of official buildings and a church on one side with varied small shops on the other. She came to an intersection of several roads, but there was only one direction she could go, to the left, and she followed obediently in second gear, passing a post office with a brick facade. Once past that she saw the police station, set back from the road. She turned right into the surprisingly large parking lot behind the supermarket, parked well away from any other cars, then locked the car, straightened her jacket, and made her way across the street to the police station.

She walked inside and was surprised to find the station seemed busy, although she had no way to judge whether the current level of activity was normal or extraordinary. It was smaller than the neighborhood station back home, which she'd been to a couple of times with her gran, usually to report a theft or minor vandalism. She'd never been there as a suspect, though she could name several of her high school classmates who had. She approached the main desk, manned by a young officer in uniform. As she drew near, she decided that he couldn't be more than twelve. His uniform, while crisp and clean, hung off his slender frame as though he had borrowed it from his father. What was the legal age for police service around here?

"Uh, excuse me?" Good grief, the kid still had acne.

"Can I help you, ma'am?" he asked politely.

Maura had to resist the urge to look behind her to find anyone who looked like a "ma'am." "Can you tell me who is handling the investigation of the body that was found near Leap a couple of days ago?"

The officer sat up more stiffly in his seat. "And why would you be asking, ma'am?"

"I have some information that might help," Maura answered. "Can I talk to someone on the case?"

She seemed to have stumped the young man. He looked around the room before settling on another officer sitting at a desk at the far side of the room. "Riordan!" he called out. "Can you help this lady, please?"

Officer Riordan rose and came over to the desk. He might have been five years older than the boy on the desk, so Maura hoped that she was moving up the ranks. "What can I help you with, miss?"

"I'm Maura Donovan. It's about that body in the bog in Leap — I have an idea who it might be. Well, sort of an idea. Can I give you the information?"

Riordan looked around the room; everyone seemed busy, either on the phone or on a computer. "I'm sorry, Miss Donovan, but it's Detective Inspector Hurley you'd need to speak with, and he's been called away."

"I just wanted to pass on some information," Maura protested. How difficult could that be?

"Sure, and that's kind of you, but it's not a good time. Could you leave a note, or come back another day?"

So much for her effort to do the right thing. Maura debated for a moment and decided that her evidence would look foolish if she put it on paper — she'd rather try to explain it face-to-face. She could come back later, when there was someone around who might be interested in what she had to say.

"I'll come back, I guess. I'll be staying in the area for a few more days."

As she turned to leave, the atmosphere in the big room changed: everybody suddenly sat up straighter and looked even busier, if that was possible. A man had just come in the front door. Somewhere north of fifty, Maura guessed, and clearly the senior bull in this herd. He was wearing civilian clothes, but he had an undeniable aura of authority. He spoke to two other men in street clothes, and he said something to them that sent them off in different directions. This must be the chief — of something, anyway; or maybe the detective that Officer Riordan had mentioned?

The man surveyed the room briefly, and his eyes came to rest on Maura, who suddenly felt out of place. *I'm glad I haven't done anything wrong!* was the irreverent thought that popped into her mind. *I wouldn't want this man angry at me.*

He nodded politely at her. "Miss." Then he turned to his officer. "What luck with the phone inquiries, Riordan?"

The young man stiffened and said briskly, "Nothing yet, sir."

"Well, keep at it. Anything else come in?"

"No, sir."

The man gave Maura another brief look, then turned and strode toward a corner office.

Another young officer had followed the detective in, but he stopped to talk to Maura. "Did you have a problem, miss?"

"I'm Maura Donovan. I might have some information about that body that was found in the bog on Wednesday." She looked more closely at the young man. "Didn't I see you there? Officer Murphy, is it?"

"Oh, right — you were driving Bridget Nolan's car." He extended a hand, and Maura shook it. "And you think you might know something about that poor man?"

"Uh, maybe. But if you all are busy, I can come back some other time. That guy's been dead for a while, so I'm sure this will keep."

Officer Murphy scanned the room, then

154

looked back at her. "I can spare a few minutes, since you've made the trip to town and all. You're staying around here?"

"Yes, in Leap. I'm, uh, kind of working for a bit, at Sullivan's." Suddenly she wondered if she was breaking any laws — at least she hadn't been paid anything yet. "And everybody at the pub has been talking about the body."

"No doubt they are. Was it something you heard there you wanted to tell us?"

"Uh, not exactly. It's something I found at Sullivan's, but I don't know if it's important," Maura said dubiously.

The door to the corner office opened, and the detective gestured toward Officer Murphy, who nodded, and turned quickly back to Maura. "Sorry, turns out I can't talk to you now. Will you come another day?"

"I guess."

Sean Murphy grinned at her and said quickly, "Grand. I have to go now." And like that, he turned on his heel and headed for the corner office. Maura wondered what on earth could be going on. Her small piece of information would have to wait.

She retraced her steps out to the front of the building and stood indecisively at the entrance. What now? She didn't have to be back at the pub for a few hours. Maybe this would be a good time to explore Skibbereen — on foot. The town didn't look that large. Her car was safely stowed in a lot, and she could see it from where she stood. She also noticed someone leaning against the fence, not far from the car, and he looked familiar. It took her a moment to place him — one of the young men who'd nursed a pint at the pub yesterday. She gave him a tentative smile, but she wasn't sure he'd seen it, as he had turned away and was walking briskly toward the opposite end of the car park. Not exactly a friendly guy.

Anyway, now she could walk around a bit and see whatever there was to see. First, though, she had to find a road map. Would there be a tourist office somewhere nearby? Surely she wasn't the only clueless tourist to find herself in Skibbereen. She walked back toward the intersection she had navigated, which was labeled "The Square," though it was anything but square, with a small traffic island in the middle and roads sprouting off in all directions. Standing in front of the post office, she surveyed the scene: a rather ornate town hall occupied one corner to her right, and she saw a bright blue sign just beyond it: OIFIG FÁILTE/ TOURIST OFFICE. *Perfect!* She crossed the street cautiously, looking both ways more than once, and headed for the office.

The building was painted a cheerful blue, and the windows were plastered with brightly colored posters advertising upcoming events. Inside she found carousels of brochures and pamphlets, and a girl about her own age beaming at her from behind a wide counter. "Is there something I can help you with?"

Maura came up to the counter. "Uh, I need a map."

"Would you be driving or walking?"

"Driving mostly, I guess. Unless the walking map shows what's in town here?"

"I'll give you the both of them, shall I? Are you looking for something in particular?"

"Nope, just trying to figure out where I am."

"American, are you? Where do you come from?" the cheerful young woman asked as she shuffled through a stack of brochures.

"Boston, in Massachusetts," Maura said.

"Ah, grand. Well, *fáilte romhat.* That means 'welcome.' I'm sure you've seen signs that say *cead mille fáilte* — that means a 'hundred thousand welcomes.' "

Only in every cheesy Irish pub she'd ever worked at in Boston. "Yes, I have. Maps?"

"Here you go." The woman spread out

one brochure. "This is for County Cork, as far as Cork City, and over to the Beara Peninsula. This other one" — she fanned out the second map — "this one gives you some more detail about our local roads." She pulled out yet another one. "And this one's for the town here, if you're walking. You came in from the highway?" When Maura nodded, she continued, "Here's the square, where we're standing, and that's the main street there." She traced it with her finger. "The river makes a loop on the one side. The heritage center is down at the other end, if you're looking for your family's history. And between there are shops and some lovely restaurants."

Maura was overwhelmed. "What I really need right now is a place to buy some basic clothes — jeans, maybe a sweater."

"Then I'd go down the main street — there are some small shops that would do. It's not tourist stuff you're after?"

"No, just ordinary clothes."

"Well, then, I'm sure you'll find what you need. Can I help you with anything else? Are you fixed for a place to stay? Petrol? There's a couple of stations out on the highway, back the way you came. Would you be looking for some live music? There's some pubs that have it, although not so much this time of year."

"Sorry, I'm busy nights." Maura hesitated before adding, "I'm working at Sullivan's, in Leap."

"Oh, are you now? Is it still in business? I suppose it must be, if you're working there."

"True." Although Maura wasn't going to place any bets on how much longer that would be true, given its current state of confusion. "Thanks for the information."

As she turned to leave, the woman said, "Come back if you need anything else. It was grand to meet you!"

Out on the pavement, Maura breathed a sigh of relief. How did the girl do it, stay so relentlessly cheerful, cooped up in a tiny office, apparently alone, day after day? But at least Maura had her maps, and now she needed a place to sit down and study them so she could figure out where she was and where she was going. It was lunchtime, and she was beginning to get hungry, despite the tea at Mrs. Nolan's, so maybe she should find some place to eat and then look for something to supplement the meager wardrobe she had brought with her.

Traffic had picked up a bit now, so Maura carefully crossed the road and strolled down the main street, which curved gently to the right. Most buildings were two or three stories tall, and painted in a range of bright colors, with no two quite alike. She passed a bank with an ATM — good to know, even though there was not much money in her account. Further along there was a bridge, and through the gap in the buildings there she could see a fair-sized river, with open ground — marshes? — nestled in its broad loop. At that point the street name changed to Bridge Street, and she continued to follow it, ignoring the rumblings of her stomach, until she came to the heritage center the woman at the tourist office had mentioned. Certainly at this end of town the buildings were drabber, and more clearly residential. She crossed and retraced her steps on the opposite side of the street, noting a bookstore and many more small shops. Finally she stopped at a pub that had tables in the window and a menu posted. It looked affordable, so she pulled open the door and hesitated in the doorway a moment, until the lone waiter noticed her and waved at the array of empty tables. She picked one nearest the window on the street, so she could watch people go by. Once again she had to wonder, how did places like this stay in business? Could they all survive on the proceeds of the tourist season alone?

"You'll be wanting lunch?" the waiter said,

handing her a short menu.

"Sure. What's good?"

He clearly was not very interested. "The stew's the special today."

Maura scanned the menu quickly. "I'll have the stew, then, and a coffee." She hoped the Irish stew didn't come from a can, since this would be her first meal in a restaurant since she'd arrived in Ireland.

The waiter quickly returned and deposited coffee in a thick mug, along with a plate of sliced brown bread and wrapped butter packets. At least the bread looked fresh and locally made, and Maura finished one piece before the bowl of stew appeared. When she tasted it, she was happily surprised: wherever it came from, it was delicious, and the cook hadn't skimped on the chunks of lamb. She finished it quickly, as well as a second slice of bread, and accepted a refill of her coffee before pushing the now-bare plate away and spreading out her maps on the tabletop.

She started with the larger regional map, tracing the road from Leap to Skibbereen. She was surprised at how far inland she was. Leap was also well inland, but opened on the broad harbor she had seen from the Keohanes' house. She tried sounding out in her mind some of the names of what must

161

be townlands marked on the map, and gave up quickly — they all had so many letters, and none of them sounded like anything she'd heard anyone say. Not that she really needed to give voice to them. She knew the way to Knockskagh and back, and people could tell her how to get from one place to another.

She turned to the tourist map for Skibbereen, whose pamphlet included a few facts about the town. The population was only slightly over two thousand, but the labels on the map showed a surprising number of public amenities — a sports center, something labeled "Winter Wonderland," a couple of "Industrial Estates," which she interpreted to mean factory sites. Whatever the town's size, it seemed to be thriving, at least on paper.

She sat back, feeling unexpectedly content. Her stomach was full, and she had some spare time to . . . be a tourist. Something she'd never really had a chance to do. She didn't even know downtown Boston well, beyond the occasional school field trip and a couple of jobs in the swankier areas. Here she had the chance to get to know an unfamiliar place, and it was small enough that she could actually accomplish that. It was a nice feeling.

The waiter ambled by and deposited her check on the table. Maura fished in her bag, pulled out some bills, and looked up at him. "Hey, can you tell me where I can buy some clothes?"

"There's a couple of shops down the street that might do, if you're not looking for high fashion," he said, pocketing the bills. "If it's fancy tourist stuff you're wanting . . ."

Maura held up a hand. "Just stuff I can wear around here."

"Then try Donovan's. Ta." He wandered off again, leaving Maura to gather up her bag and maps and venture forth in search of blue jeans.

CHAPTER 13

After a modestly successful shopping foray that left her bank account less depleted than she had feared, Maura arrived at Sullivan's to find both Rose and Jimmy at work. Rose looked up when Maura walked in. "Ah, there you are. I came in to finish up what we started yesterday — easier to do when it's bright."

"You're right. I see your father's here."

"He's brought in supplies, and I think he's swapping the barrels below."

"There's a basement here? I haven't seen it."

Rose shivered. "Dark and damp it is, so close to the water and all. But it keeps the beer cool, for free."

"I hadn't thought of that." Maura hesitated a moment. "I reread that letter last night."

"Oh?" Rose answered, but with little interest.

"When I read it again I realized that Denis Flaherty had mentioned an uncle who disappeared in the 1930s, and I found myself wondering if the dead man in the bog could be connected."

At least she'd captured Rose's attention. "How strange would that be? Him gone so long, and he pops up just as this letter appears?"

"I agree," Maura said. "It would be a heck of a coincidence. But I decided that the police should know what was in it, just in case it turned out to be true."

"Did you now? Did you take it to the gardaí?"

"Well, I tried, after I talked to Mrs. Nolan."

"And what did they say?"

"They were very busy and told me to come back another day. I got the feeling there was something going on, but of course they didn't tell me what it was. I saw the head guy walk in, and everybody jumped."

"Will you be going back?"

"I guess, if I can find the time. Anything else going on here?"

Rose opened her mouth to speak but was interrupted by the sound of cracking wood, several loud thumps, and a howl, all issuing from — the basement?

Rose ran toward the basement door, and Maura followed. "Da?" Rose called down into the dark. "Are you all right?"

"The fecking stair gave way. I've broken me arm, I think."

Rose looked stricken. "Oh no!" She looked stunned, and helpless. Maura was reminded again of how young she was.

"Is there another way in and out of the basement?" Maura demanded.

"No. Well, yes, but it's locked and nobody's had the key in a donkey's age."

"So we'll have to get him out this way." Maura pushed past Rose and peered down at what remained of the rickety stairs, and Jimmy Sweeney sprawled at the bottom, lit by a single feeble bulb hanging from a cord. She could tell that his arm was bent in a direction that nature had not intended. She could also tell that a couple of the treads of the stairs were splintered — but luckily not all of them. "Jimmy, don't move. I'm coming down."

Maura stepped on to the top tread gingerly, but it held her weight. So did the second and third. By the fourth tread, the stairs were protesting, weakened by the missing treads, but Maura carefully felt her way down, one step at a time, placing her feet at the edges and managing to bypass the broken ones. Once at the bottom, she knelt by Jimmy, who was pale and sweating, even in the cool basement. "Where's the nearest doctor, Jimmy?" she asked.

He looked up at her blankly. "What? We don't have one here."

"Where, then? Skibbereen?"

He shook his head. "Only a clinic there, and they'd only send me to hospital."

Maura was getting frustrated. "Okay, Jimmy, where is the nearest hospital?"

"There's one in Bandon, but it's small. The big one's in Cork."

"The city?" When Jimmy nodded, she asked, "Is there an ambulance service?"

He nodded, then added, "But there's no guarantee they'd be here any time soon, and this hurts like the very devil. You could drive me to Cork?" He looked plaintively up at her.

Maura quailed inwardly. Drive to Cork? She could barely manage country lanes, and he wanted her to drive in a city? But clearly Jimmy was in pain, and it didn't seem right not to do something. "What about Rose? Can she drive?"

"We've no car, and she's never learned."

No help there. "Can you direct me to the hospital?"

He nodded. Maura stood up, then called

up the stairs to Rose. "Rose, your father wants me to take him to the hospital in Cork."

Luckily Rose had recovered from her first panic. "Right. What can I do to help?"

"Stay there — I don't think the stairs will take the weight of all of us at once. I'll try to get him upstairs, and then we'll go in my car."

She turned back to the man on the floor, trying to remember her rudimentary first aid classes. "Anything else hurting you, Jimmy? Did you hit your head?" When he shook his head, Maura said, "You've got to stand up now, so you can get up the stairs. Here, let me help." She went around to his good side and grabbed him under the arm, and somehow managed to get him to his feet, although he complained steadily. "Can you handle the stairs?"

"I think so."

"I'll stay behind you, and Rose will be waiting at the top. Ready?"

Slowly but surely he succeeded in climbing up what was left of the stairs, with Rose pulling him up the last two steps. At the top he leaned against the wall, panting, but at least his color was better.

Maura followed quickly. "My car's out front — just a few steps, Jimmy, and then you can lay down again."

"I'm good," he said, pushing off from the wall, wincing, then clutching his injured arm to his chest. Maura led him out the front door, with Rose trailing anxiously behind.

"I'm coming with you, Da," she said.

"Who'll look after the pub?" Jimmy protested.

Maura looked at him. "Call Mick Nolan, if you're that worried. Rose, you're coming with us."

"Don't worry, Da, I've got me mobile. I'll text Mick. And I'll put up a sign sayin' we're closed for an emergency, shall I?" Jimmy waved a hand at her feebly, and Maura nodded her approval.

While Maura settled Jimmy in the backseat, Rose walked a few feet away to send the text. She'd returned by the time Maura climbed into the driver's seat. "It's done, Da. Mick answered that he'd be round in an hour or two."

"Then let's go," Maura said grimly. The sooner she got on the road, the sooner she'd get off of it. At least it was daylight. "Which way?"

"Take the main road, and I'll talk you through the roundabouts," Jimmy said. He lay back and shut his eyes, cradling his injured arm.

The drive proved easier than she had expected. Most of the route was the main highway, although it did weave through a few small towns along the way, but Rose helped her navigate the turns, and traffic was light. It turned out that she didn't need to go into the center of Cork, because the hospital lay on the south side of the city. At least Jimmy had managed to fall at midday; if he had done it during rush hour, she might have been a second casualty. Maura fumbled her way through a couple of roundabouts and sets of stoplights until the large brick bulk of the hospital loomed on her left.

"Do we go to the emergency room?" she asked Rose as she waited for the light at the entrance to change.

"The what?" Rose said. "Oh, right, A and E. That's Accidents and Emergencies. Turn in here, then go right quickly, and then left. I'll see to getting him inside."

Maura followed Rose's instructions, surprised at how many people seemed to be suffering from accidents and emergencies: there was no place to park. "I'll drop you off, then see if I can find parking somewhere. Here, let me help you out, Jimmy."

She pulled on the parking brake, and

between them, Rose and Maura hauled Jimmy out of the backseat. On the pavement he took a moment to steady himself, then with Rose hovering anxiously, he shuffled toward the entrance. Several impatient honks reminded Maura that she was blocking the drive, and she climbed back into the car and pulled away from the curb. Now where? She tried to recall whether she had any money on her, if she had to pay for parking. If she could *find* parking. There was a lot across the drive from the A and E, but it looked full. Surely a hospital this size must have more parking somewhere? She got herself turned back the way she came, and began a slow circuit of the hospital building. She stopped suddenly when a uniformed police officer appeared — and then she realized she recognized him: Sean Murphy. What on earth was he doing here? She pulled up alongside the curb quickly. He looked at the car once, then looked again and recognized her, and came closer. Maura rolled down the window.

"Fancy seeing you again. Everything all right?" he asked.

"Jimmy Sweeney fell, and it looks like he broke his arm."

Officer Murphy nodded. "Ah, that one. Wouldn't be the first time. So you delivered

171

him here?"

"There didn't seem to be anyone else to drive him. What are *you* doing here?"

He looked around him before answering, but the pavement was empty. "There's been another death."

"What?" Had she heard right?

Officer Murphy rested his elbow on the roof of the car and leaned closer. "A man was found dead in Skibbereen this morning, apparently the victim of a robbery. That's why I'm here — this is where they do the autopsies for the county. I was picking up the report for the poor Bog Man and delivering the next case."

"That's awful. So that's why no one had the time to talk to me this morning. Was he a local man?"

"He was. Just come from the cash point, but no money was found on him. Someone dragged the body out of sight, so he wasn't discovered until this morning."

Maura wondered if he was talking about the same ATM she had noted earlier — in plain sight, on a busy street. Hardly the place she would have expected a mugging. Impatient car horns behind her reminded Maura that she was still in the driveway. "Look, I'm not sure where to park. Will it take long for someone to see Jimmy?"

"If he's not at death's door, it could be a while — hours, at least. Were you planning to wait?"

"I . . . don't know. I'm making this up as I go. Can you point me toward a cheap parking lot?"

"Of course. Go halfway round the building again, and you'll see it on your left." He stepped away from the car.

"Thanks for the help," Maura said as she pulled out and followed his directions, and was rewarded with a parking space. She sat for a moment, turning over what Sean Murphy had just told her: two men dead, in the course of two days. Well, the first one didn't count, because he'd probably been dead for a while. Still, she felt a chill go through her, then shook it off. One problem at a time: right now she had to deal with Jimmy's. She headed for the nearest entrance, followed the signs to the A and E, and found Jimmy and Rose seated on hard plastic chairs in a crowded waiting area.

"What's the word?" she asked.

"Do yeh see that board, over the glass there?" Jimmy said.

Maura looked up to see a digital board with scrolling letters in bright red. "And?"

"I'm number 257. They've reached number 193. I may be called by Christmas." He winced as he shifted in the hard plastic chair.

Rose piped up, "You should go back to the pub, Maura. No point in waiting — it'll be hours yet."

"How will you get home?"

"They'll call a cab for us. Don't worry, we'll be fine. Go on back, help Mick out," Jimmy said.

Briefly Maura wondered why he'd be worried about that, until with a start she realized that this second death that Sean Murphy had told her about would probably boost attendance tonight; Jimmy was more right than he knew. "I guess I'll leave, then, if you're sure."

"Go on, then. Don't worry," Jimmy said. Rose smiled weakly and made shooing motions.

"Then I'll see you later, or maybe tomorrow. Take care, Jimmy — I hope it's not too bad."

Back on the road again, Maura concentrated on remembering the route, only in reverse. Once she'd reached relatively open road past all the roundabouts, she relaxed a bit. She didn't know a whole lot about the Irish health care system — nothing, in fact, except that it covered a lot of people for not much money. Did people here have insurance? Or were services, or at least emergency treatment, free to everyone? Her grandmother's last illness had drained her meager savings, even though she had had basic insurance coverage. Could Jimmy afford to pay for whatever he needed? He and Rose didn't seem to have much. Did the pub face any liability for his accident, or was that just American thinking, planning a lawsuit before the ambulance had even arrived? Only there weren't a lot of ambulances, apparently. She might even suspect Jimmy of having manufactured his accident to get out of doing the heavy work, but she'd seen his arm, and there was no way to fake that.

Maura arrived back at the pub just as darkness was falling. The lights inside Sullivan's glowed warmly. There were already several cars parked in front, and she could see people inside. Smoke eddied from the chimney, so someone had lit the fire. She decided to park back at the bed and breakfast, to leave room for customers' cars in front of the pub. When she walked back and pushed her way into Sullivan's, she was greeted with smoky warmth and the sound of many voices. Mick Nolan looked up, then beckoned her over.

"What's the word?" he asked in a low voice.

"I'm not sure — I left Jimmy and Rose in the emergency room, or whatever you call it around here. They said they would be there for a while, and that I'd be more useful here. Looks like I was right."

"It'll be a busy night. There's been a killing in Skibbereen."

"Oh," she said. News sure traveled fast around here, so clearly she didn't need to worry about keeping it a secret for Sean Murphy's sake. "Then it's a good thing I'm here."

"It is that."

The night faded into a blur as more and more people poured into Sullivan's. There were many new faces, although to Maura most faces in town would be new: the youngest seemed to be in their twenties, the oldest anywhere from seventy to ninety. The latter group included Billy Sheahan, reigning from his customary chair by the fire. He raised a hand to her but didn't seem to expect any conversation, since it was clear she didn't have the time.

She caught snippets as she moved through the crowd, delivering pints and picking up empty glasses. It didn't take her long to hear the name of the dead man: Bart Hayes. She froze in place, shocked.

Mick noticed quickly. He came over, grabbed her arm, and guided her back to the bar. "What's wrong?"

She swallowed. "The dead man, Bart Hayes — he was just here yesterday, late afternoon." He'd been so happy. It was hard to take in that he'd been killed only a few hours later.

Mick nodded. "He's a regular. He drives by here most days, stops in now and then. He was a good man. Are you all right?"

Maura nodded. "I will be, I guess. Such a shame." She picked up the next round of drinks. After a couple of hours she had pieced together most of the story. Bart Hayes had been on his way home, had stopped to celebrate at another pub or two. It must have been later when he stopped at a bank ATM to take out some cash, well after dark. Someone had hit him on the head and dragged him out of sight near the river, then emptied his pockets. Maura could guess how few people there would be out on the streets late in the evening. The blow had proven fatal. There was no useful evidence (at least, none that anyone in the pub knew of), and robbery seemed to be the only motive. The man was local and generally well liked. And now he was dead.

So far there were no suspects, and the gardaí were interviewing anyone who admitted to having been in town anytime after six p.m. The opinion among the crowd at Sullivan's was evenly divided between those who thought an arrest would come quickly and those who believed they'd never find the attacker. In the latter camp, there was agreement that the attacker was not a local man and was probably long gone. Wishful thinking? Maura wondered.

Mick finally shut down the lights shortly past midnight and hustled out the last patrons, locking the door behind them. "Long day," Maura said, sitting gratefully on a stool at the bar. "Any word from Jimmy?"

"Rose left me a message that they were on their way home. He's meant to take it easy for a day or two — it was a clean break — but Rose said she'd cover. Can I get you something?"

"You mean, a drink? Are you having one?"

"I'll join you. A half-pint?"

"Okay." Maura watched as he poured two smaller glasses from the Guinness tap. When he finally slid it across the bar, he raised his own and said, *"Sláinte."*

"And to you," Maura said, raising her glass. Then she reminded herself to go slow:

178

she'd missed dinner again. Had Jimmy managed to bring in any food before his accident? "Mick, what's going to happen with this place? Or maybe I should ask, what do you *want* to happen with it?"

"It's been here for a long time. There used to be music, in the back room. Old Mick ruled the place like his own little kingdom, and he had plenty of loyal subjects."

"Will they keep coming?"

"Hard to say. Many of the old regulars are gone now, except Old Billy."

"How do you attract new people to replace them?"

"I don't know. But that wasn't your question, was it?"

"Not really. What I'm asking is, do you expect to stay on, whatever happens?"

"Maybe. It depends. I'm hoping . . ."

"What?" Maura asked.

Mick looked down at the bar and moved his glass around in small circles. "Old Mick never married, although there are plenty of relatives around. I'm pretty sure Jimmy's hoping that he'll get at least a piece of the place, if there's a will to be found."

"And you? You want a share?"

"It's a good business. Could be better if it's handled right."

He kept ducking the question, Maura

179

noticed. No simple "yes" or "no" answer. "Do you stay around Leap because of your grandmother?"

He looked at her then. "You'd know something about that, wouldn't you?"

"You're right — I do. But Gran was the only family I ever had, or ever knew, and I couldn't leave her alone. Not that I had any big ideas about what I wanted to do. But I bet you have other options."

"We all have choices. I've made mine, for now. My gran's well into her eighties. There's time to decide later. For now, this is a decent place to be."

He didn't seem the least bitter about it, Maura reflected. She couldn't really say whether she was bitter either about giving so much of her life to helping Gran. She'd loved her and believed she owed her something. It had been *her* choice. In any case, she was not one to throw stones at Mick Nolan.

"Sorry, I mean, it's your life. And I do understand your wanting to be around for your gran. When did she move to Knock-skagh?"

"When she married, at seventeen."

"Wow, that was young. Were there a lot of kids?"

"I had my own share of aunts and uncles.

Most are gone now."

"Gone as in somewhere else, or have they passed on?"

"A bit of each. Before you ask, my father Denis died of pancreatic cancer a few years ago, and my mother lives with my sister Bridget in Clonakilty. Any more questions?"

"I didn't mean to pry," Maura replied, bristling. "It just seems like everyone around here knows a whole lot about me, but I don't know them at all. How else am I supposed to find out anything?"

"Sorry, I didn't mean to be short with you. It's been a difficult day, and I'm tired. You must be too, and I'd guess that Jimmy won't be of much use for a bit, so it's up to us to handle the place. Are you good with that?"

"I'm used to working hard, if that's what you're asking. There's nowhere else I have to be, right now. Good enough?"

"It'll do. Drink up now, and go home."

Maura emptied her glass, wondering just where "home" was.

CHAPTER 14

Maura was surprised to find herself awake early, after her late night. She had to stop and count how long she'd been in Ireland: this was only her fifth day here, if she counted the day she'd arrived. It seemed like longer. She had to admit, she felt like she'd been thrown into the deep end of the pool, with no warning. As she'd told Mick, everybody around here seemed to know who she was; most of them knew more about her family history than she did. How many years would it take to fill in that kind of information for all these new people she was meeting?

She jumped out of bed and showered quickly, then went upstairs to find that Ellen's children were still in the kitchen. Oh, right — it was Saturday, which meant no school. She hovered in the doorway, feeling like an intruder. When the children noticed her, they suddenly turned shy.

"You lot, in the parlor," Ellen barked, and the older children took themselves off, leaving Gráinne, who was seated on the kitchen floor playing with several wooden spoons and looking quite content. Maura wondered briefly what it would be like to be one of many kids, much less the last of many. Or maybe not even the last? Ellen couldn't be forty yet, so she could have more if she chose.

My own mother hadn't even wanted to raise one.

"You're up early today. You've heard?" Ellen said. "Oh, would you rather have cereal, or bread and butter? There's jam."

"If it's the brown bread, I'll have that. I'm developing a taste for it. You mean about the murder in Skibbereen? I did; everybody was talking about it at Sullivan's last night. Sad thing. Do you know, I talked to him, the afternoon before he died? He stopped in at Sullivan's on the way home. You don't get a lot of murders around here, do you?"

"It's a rare thing, God be praised. And finding two bodies within the week — even if the man in the bog died long ago — I can't recall it ever happening before. Did you talk to the gardaí?"

"I went over there, but they were kind of busy with this new death, even though I didn't know it at the time. I hate to bother them now, with such a long shot. They'll be busy with this new one, won't they?"

"No doubt they will. I'm sure the man from the bog will keep, until they get this sorted out," Ellen said, before turning to her child. "Ah, Gráinne, you've made a mess of yourself — I'd better be cleaning you up. Could you hold her a moment, Maura?" Without waiting for an answer, Ellen deposited Gráinne, still clutching a spoon, on Maura's lap. Maura and Gráinne stared at each other seriously, then Gráinne offered the spoon to Maura.

"Oh, so you want me to play? All right." Maura took the spoon and looked around for something to bang it on, that wouldn't break — and wouldn't give little Gráinne some evil ideas. She couldn't find anything within reach, and in the end she simply handed it back to the toddler. Gráinne grasped it as if she'd never seen anything so delightful and waved it at Maura. They repeated the process several times, before Ellen approached with a wet cloth to wipe down her daughter — a process that Gráinne didn't enjoy at all. Apparently she had already learned the word "no."

"She's a handful," Maura said once Gráinne had slid back down to the floor.

"They all are, but I love them to pieces," Ellen said, giving Gráinne's face a final swipe with the cloth. "It's easier now that the older ones can help out. So, what're your plans for the day?"

"More of the same, I guess. I'll go see Bridget Nolan, then spend the rest of the day working at the pub. Did you hear about Jimmy's fall?"

When Ellen shook her head, Maura recounted the adventures she'd had taking him and Rose to the hospital in Cork the day before. When she was done, Ellen said, "Jimmy's been known to take a drop, even in the mornings. Could be he was a bit unsteady on his feet."

"Possibly, but those stairs looked ready to fall apart. There's lots that needs to be done to the building, and I'm starting to think Old Mick was beyond seeing or caring."

"True enough. But he kept his spirit to the end, bless him."

After a pause, Maura said, "Ellen, how is it everyone seems to know about anything that happens around here? Like that death in Skibbereen? I mean, back home everyone would be on their smart phone texting the minute they knew anything, but I don't see so much of that around here. It wouldn't have made the television news that fast.

How does the word spread?"

Ellen laughed. "And how do you think people learned such things in the old days? They talked to each other. Take Mrs. Nolan, for instance. You've been visiting her. Michael calls in on her every other day or so. There are near neighbors who stop by to see if she needs anything, or just to chat. Sure, there's more that go off to work now, but they're the ones who'll have the phones, see. And big events — who's had a baby, whose uncle has died, who's had a piece of good luck — they're most often personal around here, and you'd rather tell them to their face than on a phone. You're either related to the person, or you know someone who is. It's a small place. Let me ask you this: if you live in a town that has ten or a hundred or a thousand times more people than Leap, why is it you Americans talk less to each other than we do?"

"I . . . don't know. I never thought about it, really. It might be because most of those people are strangers, not relatives, and we aren't sure we can trust them. It's too bad." Back in Boston, Gran had been on nodding terms with most of the neighbors — at least the ones who stayed around more than a couple of months — but she'd never had much time to "just stop by," much less time to share gossip over a cup of tea. In fact, most of the women Maura had known, growing up, had been working, so none of them had that kind of time either. Most of the people she'd spent any time with had been the newly arrived Irishmen, with no family and no local ties in Boston. They would come by after their own workday, looking for a cup of tea and a friendly face, and Gran had never turned them away. Maura couldn't criticize, because she had ended up with few friends herself. She'd worked as much as she could, including evenings, and what friends she'd had in high school had drifted away, either into marriage or to search for something better, or at least something different, outside of Boston.

"Look, you take in guests, like me," Maura began slowly. "Do you advertise online?"

Ellen laughed. "You mean, do I have a website? Hardly that. I've only the two rooms, and they bring in a bit extra, but it's not a business, exactly. Most of my guests, it's the guys at the hotel that send them over. There's a computer for the kids in the parlor, but I watch how much they use it. I know, they're young yet, and it'll only get worse. I pay for the satellite service, since guests seem to want it more often than not.

But I have to say that it seems wrong to me that visitors should come from thousands of miles away and then sit in front of their laptop as if they were at home. Why bother to make the trip? I see you don't have a computer."

"I don't own one. I know, that makes me really out of things. But back home, I could never afford one, and if I needed one for homework or something, I'd go to the library or the computer lab at school. I notice that Rose is on her phone a lot, even with her father and Mick, not just friends."

"It's the thing, at her age. Oh, wait — I have something for you." Ellen left the room briefly, returning with a cell phone in her hand. "You should have this mobile. And here's the charger to go with it." She held them out to Maura.

"A phone? Doesn't it belong to someone?"

"A visitor a while back left it, saying it would do her no good back home. It's one of those prepaid things, so you can use whatever minutes are on it, maybe even add more if you want."

"Uh, thank you. Not that I know anyone to call."

"Don't be daft. There's me and the pub, for starters. Plus, a woman traveling alone, as you are, with a rackety old car — you might need to call someone to haul you out of a ditch. Which reminds me, if you do have any trouble, call 999 — that'll get you the gardaí. But only if it's an emergency. I hope you won't be needing it, but I'd rather you had it, just in case."

"Thanks, Ellen." Maura felt touched by Ellen's unexpected thoughtfulness. She'd never had more than a cheap prepaid phone back home, which she kept only for emergencies and if she needed to reach wherever she was working at the time, or Gran. "Oh, and I got a few maps in Skibbereen, but it turns out they're too big to show all the lanes around here. Do you have a local map? So far I keep taking the same roads, and I'm sure there are better ways of getting around."

"Goodness, I should have thought of that. Where's my head been?" Ellen rummaged in a drawer and came up with a folded map. "It's turned to the parts you'll be needing. But I should warn you, just because there's a road on the map, doesn't mean it's a road fit to drive. And there's been little money put toward fixing the roads these past few years, so watch for potholes and the like."

"I will. Thanks again."

"You're more than welcome. Oh, look at the time! Gráinne *mo ghrá,* we've got to get

189

ready to go. Have a good day, Maura." And Ellen bustled out, her daughter balanced on one hip. Maura could hear her calling to her sons. Where would they go on a Saturday? Was it like back home, when mothers seemed to be dragging their kids, willing or unwilling, to games and classes and training for something or other? Gran had made her take violin lessons for about six minutes, because the school had offered them for free, but she had quickly demonstrated that she had no musical talent at all, and they'd never mentioned it again.

Maura drank the rest of her coffee and laid the map out on the tabletop, finding the smaller road to the north that took her from where she sat toward Knockskagh. If she stayed on that, past the turn up the hill that she already knew, she'd come to a T-intersection with a bigger road leading left to the highway or right toward Drinagh. That was one option. And the road she'd been using to get to Bridget Nolan's appeared to continue over the top of the hill and down again, to intersect with another larger road. Wasn't that the way Mrs. Nolan had said the children of Knockskagh went to school? The bog where the dead man had lain — or been placed — was almost due east of Knockskagh. So many lanes! Apart from the so-called roads, there were little lines darting off of them, sometimes going to only one or two houses, and in addition there were dotted lines that often led to nowhere. Dirt roads? Footpaths? She had no idea.

All right. Today she would go the usual way, but maybe on the way back she'd return to Leap by a different path. And she should get back to Sullivan's by mid-afternoon, because it would be Saturday night, and besides, she wanted to see what news had surfaced overnight. She had to remind herself that it wasn't exactly gossip; it was a fair exchange of information, with everyone adding something and taking something away. And now there were two deaths to chew upon.

The sky was overcast, but it didn't look like rain. Maura set off for Mrs. Nolan's house with renewed confidence. After all, she'd braved the city — well, at least the fringes of the city — and emerged intact. She'd made it back to Leap without getting lost. She was getting the hang of driving on the left, and she even recognized some of the local landmarks.

However, when she arrived at the Nolan house, her confidence wavered, and she parked in the lane across the road rather than risking the narrow entrance to the house. When she crossed the lane, she could see that the door was open, letting in some light and the spring breeze. Maura heard cows lowing in distant fields, although the field in front of Mrs. Nolan's house remained empty. Would there be cattle grazing there later in the spring? Maura realized that apart from a long-ago field trip to a farm her elementary school had arranged, she had no idea what went into raising cattle. Grass in one end, milk out the middle, and the rest out the back end. Simple, right? Well, probably not, but cow management was not something she had ever thought she needed to know. She rapped on the open door.

"Come in, come in," came Mrs. Nolan's voice from the kitchen.

"How do you know it's me?" Maura asked as she walked into the main room.

"I heard the car coming up the hill, didn't I? And I was expecting you. Awful news about that young man in Skibbereen, isn't it?" Mrs. Nolan emerged from the kitchen with the tea tray; a plate of sliced bread studded with raisins was already set out on the small table next to the chairs.

"It is. How did you hear?"

"Ah, Mrs. Driscoll, up top the hill,

192

stopped in to bring me some milk. She'd heard it on the telly this morning. What is the world coming to, that people should be attacked on the street?"

"I wish I knew." They chatted amiably as Maura enjoyed the bread, along with fresh butter, even though it had been only an hour since her breakfast. After yet another hour had passed, Maura thought she should be going, but she couldn't resist adding, "You've heard about Jimmy Sweeney's fall?"

"Poor man, he has no luck at all. He's been a changed man since he lost his wife. Rose is a sweet girl, but it shouldn't fall to her to look after him," Mrs. Nolan said. "Mick brings Rose up here now and then, to help me clean the place, and I sent her over to Old Mick's now and then, since he had no woman to look after him. Jimmy has no car, you see, so she needs the ride. Just as well, Jimmy not having the car. He doesn't handle his drink well." That was the harshest criticism Maura had heard Mrs. Nolan make of anyone.

"I wish Rose could find something that she wants to do," Maura said. "Tending bar in a village isn't much of a life for her, is it? I haven't seen many kids her age around. Doesn't she get lonely?"

Mrs. Nolan shook her head. "Most of her

friends have gone away now, looking for work, and the ones still here — well, they're not the kind a nice young girl should associate with. But things are hard these days."

"They are," Maura said, "and not just here, but back in the States too." After a moment of shared silence, Maura said, "Well, I should be getting back. It may be another busy day at Sullivan's. At least, I hope so, since it's Saturday."

"You go on your way, darlin'. You don't have to keep coming to entertain an old lady like me."

"It's no trouble. And I still want to hear more about Gran, and you promised to tell me how to find the cemetery where my grandfather is buried."

"That I did. Thank you for reminding me. Tomorrow I can give you the directions — it's a little hard to find, once you pass through Drinagh."

"I'll look forward to it. Bye now." Maura pulled the door closed behind her as she left — the wind had shifted, and had a sharp edge to it now. Back at the car, she started the engine and checked the road: empty in all directions. She consulted the map, looking for a new way back to town; it said she should go right out of the lane she was parked in and over the top of the hill, and

on the way down she'd pass something
called "Lough Gorm" on the right, and if
she turned left at the bottom of the hill and
then right, the road would take her back to
Leap. It should be easy.

CHAPTER 15

Maura came to the crest of the hill, driving at a cautious twenty miles per hour, and stopped to admire the view of the two small ponds — identified as "loughs" on the map — below. The lane she was on looped around to the left, following the contour of the hill. There was room for only one car at a time, but luckily there was no one else in sight at the moment. She began inching forward, her foot hovering near the clutch, and it didn't take her long to realize that this had to be one of the roads that had suffered from a lack of maintenance, as Ellen had warned her. It might be easier to walk it, but Maura had a borrowed car to worry about, and she didn't want to destroy an axle by slamming into one of the many potholes that punctuated what was left of the road surface. Not to mention the ditches a foot or more deep that heavy rains had cut along one side or the other. Getting to the bottom was not going to be easy, but at least she was in no hurry and could take it an inch at a time if necessary.

Which would have been fine if it hadn't been for the car that appeared behind her. Where had that come from? She hadn't seen anyone else on the road when she started. She vaguely recalled that there were rules for who should pull over to allow someone to pass, but they were pointless now because there was nowhere to pull over. Generally she had found that Irish drivers were polite, if impatient, but then, they knew where they were going. The driver behind would just have to wait — she wasn't going far anyway, and she refused to be rushed.

Then the car hit her. At first it was a nudge, and Maura's anger flared — no driver had the right to be *that* impatient. She slowed even further, now alternately straining to see who was behind the wheel of the other car and watching out for the pits ahead of her. All she could make out was a man wearing a baseball cap and dark glasses. Then he sped up and hit her again, harder this time. Maura grabbed the wheel tightly, her knuckles white, and wondered what the hell was going on. Not that there was much she could do. There was only one way out: forward, downhill.

The man had fallen back slightly, but as Maura watched in her rearview mirror, he accelerated and came at her again, aiming for her left rear bumper. This time the hit caused her steering wheel to be jerked from her grip, and she felt a front tire spinning in air as the front end skewed toward the right — the downhill side. Another thud, and the car slowly tilted downward like a seesaw. One more solid thunk, and the back wheels slipped over the edge, and the car began sliding downhill, despite her foot jammed firmly on the brake. As a last resort, she hauled hard on the parking brake — anything to stop her forward motion. And somehow the car skidded to a stop twenty feet down the hill, with the front bumper against a small tree.

She sat for several seconds, waiting to make sure she had really stopped, not just paused in her tumble toward the lake below. She could hear the ticking of the car's engine, now stalled, and the crackling of the brush she had smashed in her passage. Finally she dared to turn her head back toward the road, to see if the other driver had stopped to check on her.

There was no one there. The bastard! He'd just left? Well, of course he had — he'd made every effort to push her off the road.

Intentionally. No wonder he had left in a hurry.

With infinite caution Maura opened her door, inch by inch, afraid of jarring the car loose from its precarious perch. The car didn't shift. Once the door was open, she swung her legs out. Still no movement. And then in one last burst, she thrust herself out, away from the car.

She took one look at the car, tilted at what looked like a forty-five-degree angle, and sat down hard, mainly because her legs wouldn't support her. She looked down at her hands to see them shaking. What had happened here? This made no sense. She looked back at the car, just sitting there, totally out of place in the landscape. Nothing else had changed: somewhere in a meadow below she could hear a cow lowing, but there were no human sounds.

When her hands steadied, Maura remembered the cell phone that Ellen had given her. But the cell phone was in her purse — which was in the car. She'd have to go back to the car or hike to the nearest house with a phone. Which was easier? If she went back to Bridget's house, she'd have to tell her what had happened, but Maura was afraid that the news might be too much of a shock for her. Besides, there were other houses nearer, and downhill. Car, she decided: she'd need her purse anyway, since it held all her identification. She stood up shakily, using a spindly tree for support, and approached the car as if it were a wounded animal and she was afraid a sudden movement would spook it. She had left her bag on the floor on the passenger side, so she cautiously opened the front left door. She held her breath as she reached into the car and extricated the bag. Then she backed away and sat down on the grass again. In her purse she located the cell phone. She flipped it open and punched in 999.

A disembodied voice answered quickly, and she described as best she could where she was. The voice at the other end seemed to know where she meant. Yes, the car was off the road. No, she wasn't injured — no medical assistance required. Yes, she would stay with the car until someone came. No, there was no one to call. The voice promised to have someone there shortly. Irreverently Maura wondered just what the Irish idea of "shortly" would be: Minutes? Days? As she waited, she tried to sort through her jumbled impressions and put together her story. She'd been driving normally, which in her case meant slowly and carefully. She hadn't had anything to drink, or any medication. A person had come up behind her and used his car to run her off the road.

She shut her eyes, to better remember what the other car had looked like. She had never paid much attention to cars in general and couldn't tell one make or model from the next. She knew that the car had been small and brownish. Dirty? She hadn't seen it from the side and had glimpsed the front only through the rearview mirror. She had a vague impression that it was battered — a crumpled fender maybe, or a cracked headlight? She couldn't remember — she'd been a little distracted. Of course, she hadn't gotten a license plate number — he'd been too close for that by the time she had noticed him. At least she could definitely say that the driver had been a "he" . . . unless it was a woman who had made an effort to disguise herself. But somehow she couldn't imagine a woman driving the way this person had.

And that was the end of her observations. Was her car all right? From where she sat, she couldn't see more than a few dents in the front bumper from the trees she'd hit, and a surprisingly small number of dings on the rear bumper where the other car had hit hers, but that didn't mean it hadn't somehow disemboweled itself on the bumpy ride down. What had that other driver been thinking, and where had he gone so fast? Was he some lone crackpot who just wanted to get past her on the road? Back home she had seen plenty of macho men who thought they owned the road, but here?

Maura was getting madder by the minute and couldn't sit still, so she started pacing back and forth, looking alternately at the poor car and down at the road below where the expected police arrived a few minutes later. For a moment she was startled: with its blue light bar and bright yellow stripe; she had forgotten that Irish police cars didn't look anything like the ones back home. She watched it come partly up the road, then stop, and a uniformed policeman climbed out and walked up the lane to where she stood by the car.

For goodness' sake, Maura thought, *it's Sean Murphy again. Is he the only cop in town?*

When he reached her, he said incredulously, "Maura Donovan? Again?"

"Yes, it's me, Officer Murphy. How's your day been so far? Because mine is going downhill fast." *Stop with the bad puns, Maura — this is serious.* "Can I call you Sean? You're no older than I am, and it seems stupid to keep calling you 'officer.' Besides, we really ought to be friends now, since we see each other so often."

"Sean'll do, then." He seemed to be suppressing a smile. "Are you all right?"

"I'm fine. And I think the car is too, but I don't know how to get it back to the road."

"Don't you worry yourself about that. It happens to a lot of visiting Americans. Sure, and it's not easy to learn to do everything on the other side — the wrong side, you'd say."

No way was she going to take the blame for this. "This was *not* an accident," she said through clenched teeth.

Sean nodded in what he probably thought was an encouraging way. "Something wrong with the car, then? The brakes went out, or the steering?"

Maura shook her head. "No, nothing like that. Will you please listen . . ."

The young officer went on, making an attempt to be soothing that only annoyed Maura more. "Sure, this must be distressing for you, on holiday and all. You just stay where you are, and I'll call for assistance."

Maura's anger boiled over. "SEAN MURPHY, WILL YOU PLEASE LISTEN TO ME?" He looked at her, startled, but at least she'd gotten his attention and jarred him from his script. "This was not an accident. Somebody ran me off the road. Deliberately.

Which has got to be a crime around here, and you'd better start looking for the jerk who did it."

Sean gazed mutely at her. Clearly he hadn't been prepared to deal with an angry woman. Then he seemed to gather himself together. "I'm sorry. My chief always says I'm too quick to jump to conclusions. Let's make a new start. What did you want to tell me?"

Maura took a deep breath, then suddenly paused. "You know this is Bridget Nolan's car, which she loaned me to use while I was here — you don't have to tell her about this right away, do you? Because she's old, and I don't know how she'd take it."

Sean Murphy waved that comment away. "Let's see what shape your car's in before we worry about saying anything to Mrs. Nolan. You were saying?" he asked, pulling out a pad.

Maura quickly outlined the appearance of the driver and his determined efforts to force her off the road, and Sean carefully recorded what she said, looking equal parts concerned and puzzled.

"Did you recognize the driver?" he asked.

Maura shook her head. "I haven't been here long enough to know many people. Besides, the guy had on a cap and sunglasses. I didn't get a license plate. I was trying to keep my car on the road. And once he was sure he'd shoved me off it, he disappeared. I couldn't tell you which way he went."

"I see. And I apologize for my earlier questions. We do get a fair number of confused tourists on the roads."

"I bet you do, but I'm not one of them. So, what now? Is the car okay? Do you have to get a tow truck up here?"

Sean Murphy eyed the car critically. "You didn't hear any loud noises — you know, crack, crunch, and so on?"

Maura had to smile at his description. "Only the bushes."

He bent down to peer under the car. "I don't see anything leaking, which is good. It's an old car, and built like a tank, thank goodness." He straightened up. "Let's get it towed back to Skibbereen and have it checked out. I wouldn't want you to come to harm driving it around now, not knowing if it's safe."

"Sounds good to me, but I'll need a ride back to Leap."

"Sullivan's?"

"Yes."

"And you're sure you don't need medical

assistance? Don't blame me — I'm required to ask."

"No, I'm fine, really. I wasn't going fast, and I didn't hit anything — except the brakes, and a few bushes on the way down. Mostly I was scared. And then mad."

Sean Murphy smiled. "Let me make a call, then," he said. He walked away, a cell phone at his ear. Figuring it might take a while, Maura sat down again.

Sean finished his call and sat down beside her. "All set — the truck'll be here in a few minutes. Do you mind if we go over this again, while we wait?"

"No problem," Maura said.

"I don't suppose you noticed any possible witnesses?"

Maura looked around her. Nothing had changed. "Does a cow count?"

"They're not very reliable."

In spite of herself, Maura laughed. "Yeah, I'm not surprised. Anyway, no, I even stopped at the top of the hill to check out where I was going. This guy showed up out of nowhere and started pushing me around."

"You described him as youngish, and wearing a baseball cap and sunglasses." When Maura nodded, he asked, "And the car?"

"What I know about cars would fill a postage stamp. It looked ordinary and dirty. As far as I could tell, it had four wheels and a roof."

The officer smiled. "Well, that certainly narrows down our search. A male in a nondescript car, which might or might not have some front-end damage, maybe before and most likely after he'd pushed you off the road."

Maura leaned back and regarded him. "Do you believe me? You don't think I'm just making this up, to cover up a stupid accident?"

"I believe you," he said solemnly. "I can't think why you'd make up such a story. But I also can't see why anyone would want to do you harm."

"That makes two of us."

CHAPTER 16

To her surprise, the tow truck arrived in less than fifteen minutes. The driver and Sean Murphy spoke briefly, and then the driver maneuvered his truck so that the winch at the back was turned toward Maura's car. After another conference, the winch hook was attached to something or other, and as Maura watched, the car inched slowly up the hill. She winced when some part of the undercarriage scraped on the edge of the lane, but once it was back on the lane itself, Maura released a breath she hadn't known she was holding.

"What now?" Maura demanded. "I don't know squat about insurance here, or if the car is covered."

"Don't worry yourself. We can sort that out later," Sean Murphy said.

"It looks all right, doesn't it?" Maura said dubiously. "But if there's anything really wrong with the car, I don't have any way to pay for repairs."

"Let's take one worry at a time," Sean said in the same patient tone.

"But isn't there going to be paperwork to fill out?"

"Not at the moment. I'm guessing that there's nothing really wrong with the car, so all you'd have to pay for is the tow and having it looked at to be sure it's safe to drive. Is it Bridget Nolan who'd be the owner of record?"

"Uh, I don't really know. It may be Mrs. Nolan, or her late husband. Her grandson Mick would know, because he's been the one taking care of it."

"I'll ask him later, then. Tell me, are you sure there's no one who'd want to do this to you?"

Maura turned to glare at him. "I've been in this country all of five days. I've had conversations with maybe ten people, not including Mick and Jimmy at the pub and Rose and Ellen Keohane."

Officer Murphy was smiling at her. "I had to ask the question, but I agree that it seems unlikely that any one of them would do this."

"So . . . what? There's no one with a grudge against me, so is it juvenile delinquents? Do you get kids joyriding around here? Just letting off steam? Are you going to interview people nearby to see if they noticed anything?"

"I see no point to that. I know the road, and there's no one near enough to have seen anything, even if they were at home. Did anyone know you'd be on this road?"

"No, I've never even taken this road before. I was trying to find a new way back to town, and I'd only just made up my mind to try it. But that's it. Does that mean the guy was following me? Or waiting for me to leave Mrs. Nolan's house?" Even as she said it, she realized how ridiculous it sounded. Suddenly she felt drained. "That's all I know. Listen, can you take me back to Sullivan's now? Or should I go and wait at the garage where they took the car?"

"Of course I'll take you. And I'll see that the car's returned to you as well." Sean led the way to his car, and they headed back along the road toward Leap. Maura found herself counting the houses that they passed. There was an old abandoned building at the bottom of the road — no witnesses there. Around another bend there were a couple of newish houses, but they were out of the direct line of sight for the hill.

They arrived in Leap in a couple of minutes. Sean pulled over and parked his police sedan in front of Sullivan's. Maura gathered up her bag and opened the car door quickly, worried briefly whether the sight of the police car would have an impact on business.

"Thanks for the lift," she said, and shut the door before he could answer. She entered the pub to find Mick behind the bar, polishing a glass.

"What's that about?" he asked, nodding toward the police car parked outside.

"Car trouble," Maura said curtly. "Jimmy's not coming in today?"

"We're on our own. Everything all right?" Mick asked.

"Depends on how you look at it," she said. "Someone ran me off the road near your grandmother's, but the good news is, I'm fine and we're pretty sure the car is too — Officer Murphy there sent it to a garage to have it checked out."

Mick's expression changed quickly to one of concern. "You sure you're not injured?"

She shook her head. "Don't worry, I'm not very fragile. Nothing damaged. Thanks for asking, though."

He gave her a long look but wisely didn't comment. "Jimmy's staying at home today — says he's in a lot of pain from the arm and all. He said Rose'd be in later, and I'll

211

be in tonight. You won't need to stay, if you're not up to it."

"Why wouldn't I be? Besides, I really need the cash now — I've got to pay for the tow and any repairs the car needs."

"Don't worry yourself — it won't be much. The car's been through worse."

Pride and relief fought in Maura's head. If she owed money, she wanted to pay it, but she wasn't sure how much she had, or how much would be coming in from her time at Sullivan's. "Should be a busy day, what with that murder, eh?" She heard the door behind her open and turned to see Sean Murphy coming in. Mick straightened up and set down the glass that he'd polished several times.

"Nolan," Sean said.

Mick nodded. "Murphy."

The officer turned to Maura. "I just got a call — the car's fine. I've asked the man at the garage to bring it over to you. I'll stay here to ferry him back to Skibbereen."

"Jeez, that was fast!" Maura said. "Did your mechanic friend really have time to look at it?"

"He did that. He's just down the road, before you get to the Skibbereen round-about. He knows his business, if you're worried about him getting it right."

"Well, great, thank you. Can I get you anything?" Maura asked, wondering if he was on duty or not and whether that mattered in Ireland.

"Tea would be grand," he said, settling himself on a stool at the bar.

Mick silently filled a mug with hot water, dropped a tea bag into it, and set it in front of him. "Maura was just telling me there'd been some trouble with the car."

Sean looked at Maura, as if asking permission. She nodded. "She was pushed off the road, near your gran's. Is it her car?"

"My grandfather's name is still on the papers." Mick glanced at Maura, his expression unreadable. "Ran her off deliberately, you mean? Why do you think anyone would do that?"

"That's what I've been asking myself," Maura said sharply. "I haven't done anything! I'm not hiding out in Ireland to escape the Mob or the police back home. I'm just a tourist. Why on earth would anyone be interested in me, much less want to hurt me?"

"Well, that's the question, isn't it?" Sean said mildly. He turned to watch a new arrival on the road: Maura's car, with the tow truck driver at the wheel. The driver climbed out and came into the pub. "Car checks out fine, miss. The mechanic says they don't build them like this anymore — real solid." He laid the keys to the car on the bar in front of Maura.

"I'll take you back directly." Sean turned back to Maura and Mick. "Have you seen anyone paying particular attention to this lady here lately?"

Mick laughed. "Over the past few days we've had more people in here than in the full year before. Most people have said hello to her, at least — she's a new face, and American at that."

"True, but it seems everyone's been much more interested in the body you found in the bog, and then last night they were all talking about the new death," Maura protested.

"Well, keep an eye out, both of you," Sean said.

"Of course," Mick answered, and Maura nodded.

"Then I'll be on my way. Let me know if anything else unlikely happens."

He and the driver went out to the garda car. Maura turned to Mick. "I'm sorry — you can take the car back if you want. Looks like I'm not taking very good care of it."

"He said it's not your fault," Mick said, nodding at the garda car as it pulled away.

"If you tell me it's no accident, I believe you."

"Are the . . . gardaí, is it? — going to find out anything?"

"They're bright enough lads," Mick said, "but it sounds to me like they've little to go on, and they've got other things, like this murder, to worry about."

"Which sounds like a no to me. Should we tell your grandmother? About the car, I mean?'

He shook his head. "It'd only upset her. The car's fine, and you should keep it for now. Just be careful, will you?"

"I thought I *was* being careful."

"Listen, if you want to go have a rest or something, I can cover here," he said again. "You seem upset."

"No, really, I'm fine," Maura insisted. "I'd rather keep busy than have to think about what happened up on that hill."

"At least go have yourself some lunch — there's time enough for that," Mick said.

"Thanks, I guess I will." Maura went out the door and stopped in front of the car. The garage had actually shined it up a bit, and the only signs of her encounter on the back road were a few scratches in the paint. Even she could tell that it was a relic from an earlier age, when car bodies were actually made of metal rather than plastic. But she wasn't ready to get behind the wheel again — not just yet. She decided to walk up to the small market and pick up some food, and then find somewhere to sit and eat it — and think about why anyone would try to do this to her.

With sandwich and drink in a bag, Maura came back along the road to the Keohanes' house, but rather than going to her room there, she followed the lane that ran alongside the harbor. Actually, she realized, what she had thought was the Keohanes' driveway merged into a graveled lane that led to a couple of other houses, past a field with a grazing horse, and ended near a large, empty stone building three stories high. Since the land sloped steeply upward to the road above, she was sheltered from the wind down below, although she could see riffles in the water far from shore. She found herself a spot overlooking the water and sat. There was no noise, no crowds; no sirens blaring in the distance, no airplanes passing overhead. How often in the past had she found herself surrounded by such quiet? It was unsettling. She didn't open her lunch immediately, but looked out over the water, waiting for her pulse to stop racing and her mind to stop spinning.

The peace and quiet were soothing, and did their job: after a few minutes she felt calmer. Even she had to admit there was a kind of magic here. If she who had always been a skeptic could sense it, it must be real. Had Gran seen this view of the harbor, countless times? Had she missed it when she got to Massachusetts? How had she gone from this kind of silence to the endless bustle of a city? What would have happened if Gran had stayed here to raise her son? She must have hoped for a better life in America, and maybe that would have worked out if her son, Tom Donovan, hadn't died. Maybe they would all have moved to a nice house in the suburbs and lived happily ever after. *Ha!* Maura thought to herself. Gran couldn't have known what was in store — she had just tried to do the best she could. Throughout her life she'd worked hard and tried to help other people.

Kind of like the way people here have been helping you out, Maura?

That thought stopped her cold. She'd always secretly thought that Gran was a softy, a pushover, and that people took advantage of her kindness. Maybe she should be looking at it in a different light. Gran had just been doing what the people she had grown up around had done: she of-

217

fered help and support to those who needed it. Payback, or paying it forward? Gran's generosity hadn't been a weakness — it had been her strength, and Maura had refused to see that.

How many other ideas was she going to have to toss out? About her Gran, about her own life?

Maura shook her head to rid it of such troubling thoughts. She picked up the sandwich she'd all but forgotten and wolfed it down, then trekked back to Sullivan's. It was going to be a busy day.

CHAPTER 17

When Maura walked back into Sullivan's Mick looked up and nodded but didn't say anything, which was fine with her. After some food and the walk, she felt calmer and didn't want to risk breaking that spell. She took a quick look around the pub; she and Rose had missed a few spots in their cleaning, but overall it looked pretty good, or at least better than it had when she'd first seen it. Not that the previous evening's customers had seemed to notice, but Maura was pleased with it. Gran would have approved, Maura was sure — she was a stickler for keeping things clean, even when she was working two jobs, and she'd trained Maura well.

Billy Sheahan was already dozing in his seat by the fireplace, where a small fire was lit. Maura leaned over the bar toward Mick. "Is he always here?" she said in a low voice.

Mick smiled briefly. "Mostly. He's been

coming in for years — he and Old Mick were quite the pair, when they'd get going. I haven't the heart to move him — he's too old to change his stripes now. And he does no harm."

It figured. Maura had already noticed that the Irish didn't go in much for change, at least if something was still working. The very essence of the "if it ain't broke, don't fix it" philosophy. "You know, Mick, I get the feeling this place is caught in a time warp. I mean, everybody else in the world is putting in fancy digital CD players and big-screen TVs and Wi-Fi, but here, it's like nothing's changed in the last fifty years. How does this place stay in business at all?"

He shrugged. "It was Old Mick's place, and he ran it to suit himself. He saw no need to change."

Maura waited a few moments, but Mick didn't elaborate. It made a kind of sense — as long as Old Mick hadn't needed the money. "I've been meaning to ask — you guys more or less set your own hours here, right?"

"That's true. You're thinking that's no way to run a business? You'd be right, but Old Mick was here most of the time, so it didn't matter much. And we haven't had the time or the heart to reorganize yet. Are you worried about the local laws? Age limits? You have to be eighteen to drink."

"And drunk driving? Don't I have to look out for that?" At least she'd finally gotten some answers. It was only then that Maura noticed a new addition. "Where on earth did the espresso machine come from?" Maura nodded toward a machine against the wall. It looked brand-new.

"Ah, that was one of Jimmy's grand schemes — he thought it would bring in a better crowd. He got it on the cheap somewhere. But he lost interest fast, after he'd burned his fingers a time or two. It was down in the cellar collecting dust. I'd forgotten about it until I went down to fix the stairs."

"I'd forgotten about the stairs. I'm glad you remembered. Why'd you bring the machine upstairs now?" Maura asked.

"I figured we should either use it, sell it, or dump it. Have you ever used one?"

"Now and then, but not this model — seems like each one's different. This looks like a good one, though."

"Will it be worth it, do you think?"

"Not for the customers I've seen so far. But who knows? It might attract more women. What did Old Mick think about having an espresso machine in here?" Maura walked behind the bar to where the machine sat in all its stainless steel glory, and poked around a bit.

"I never said he used it, did I? He had a soft spot for Jimmy — I think they were related somehow, maybe through his father's people. Jimmy's always been a sharp one, looking for a quick deal."

Maura smiled in spite of herself. "Seems everybody around here is related to everybody else."

"It's true, most of the time. You've heard of the Potato Famine?"

"Of course, but what does that have to do with anything?"

"This area was hard hit — there's a mass grave at Abbeystrowry, the other side of Skibbereen, where there were thousands of dead dumped in a pit. Of course, a lot of people left the country — it was better than starving to death. I'd guess it made the ones who survived, and who stayed behind, all the more close. For a while there, it looked as though we might have a chance — that Celtic Tiger business — but we should have known better. We muddle on, in our own way. I think the Irish expect to be knocked down. We're used to it. But that's why we stick together."

Maura thought about how different the

attitude was back home, where it seemed that some people expected the government to create jobs where there were none and hand out money the government didn't have, just because they felt entitled. She had no patience for that, nor had the people she'd grown up with. They worked, sometimes at more than one job. Like Gran. Maybe the Irish had it right: expect the worst, and be happy about anything better.

"Mick, do you think you could make a go of this place? Once the legal part is settled?"

He shrugged. "We don't know what will happen. We don't make much off-season, but it's enough to keep us going until summer each year. And whoever ends up with it will get a place that's ready to step into, if that's what they want."

"What if that person wants to turn it into a tacky souvenir store selling plastic leprechauns? And why keep it a pub at all, if it makes so little money?"

"The place has a history — remind me to tell you about the days when there was music each week, and people would come for miles to hear the *seisuns.* That was Mick's doing. It's fallen off the past few years, but it could happen again."

"Are you saying you don't want to see the place just fade away?"

"We'll see." He turned away then, and Maura wondered if he felt he'd said too much.

"You know, maybe you could just ship it to Boston — pubs go over real well there. All these wannabe Irish types, pining for a place they never knew, that probably never existed anyway except in their heads. Green beer and sappy songs after you've drunk enough of it."

"Aren't you the bitter one? And what's so wrong about selling this nostalgic Ireland, if it makes people happy?"

"Because it's a lie, a myth, a fake. Gran left here with nothing, worked hard all her life, and died with nothing plus not much. She didn't spend time glorifying her days here in Ireland."

"She had you, did she not? You're thinking her life would have been better if she'd been born somewhere else, or if she'd stayed on here, after her husband died?"

Maura struggled to put her feelings into words. "No, not that. I just wish that she'd put herself first, fought for something better. She gave so much away that there was nothing left for her or for me. I wish we could have enjoyed the last few years of her life." She turned away from Mick so he wouldn't see the tears starting. She must be more upset than she had realized.

Mick's voice was surprisingly gentle when he answered. "Did you never stop to think that it made her happy to help people? And I wouldn't say she looked back on her time here as unhappy. Why else did she keep in touch with my grannie?"

"I don't know!" Maura burst out as she turned back to face him. "She never talked to me about it! Why did she think it had to be a secret? Why didn't she ever tell me about all this? Why couldn't she have shared some of the good parts? Told me about family or friends, like your grannie? Or did she hate this place? Was she glad to get away from this place, where with no husband there was no way to support herself or her child?" If Mick kept on being nice to her, she really was going to lose it.

"Maybe the only way she could handle the regret at leaving was to try to forget," Mick said, then added gently, "Maura, are you all right? You've had a bad few weeks since she died, and a worse day today."

Maura shut her eyes for a moment. *Damn all these kind people!* She took a deep breath, then looked at him again. "Sorry, you're right, and I shouldn't unload it all on you. As for now, like I said before, I'd rather be around people than sit in my room and stew. But thank you for asking." She changed the subject. "Listen, if you want, I can have a go at that espresso machine, since it's here."

"Surely you don't mean we'll need to get some of those sissy little cups with handles too small for a man's fingers?" He smiled.

"Of course not. But if you're going to offer coffee, it should taste like something other than the roofing tar you've got coming out of those pots there."

"Point taken. It's all yours." He paused for a moment. "Maura, there's something I think you'd like to see. Do you have plans for tomorrow morning?"

Why was he being so mysterious? "Other than visiting your grandmother again, no, not really. You're not planning to kidnap me, are you? Because that's the way my luck has been running this week. But then, you know nobody's about to pay you a ransom for me."

"You've nothing to fear. I'll be bringing my grannie to town for church, but this is better done early. You'll understand when you see it. I'll meet you at the Keohanes' at, say, eight? I'll drive."

She studied him a moment. She'd been joking about the kidnapping thing, but maybe there was just a bit of truth in it.

226

Someone had it in for her, if that incident with the car on the hill wasn't just a jerk making trouble, and Mick was one of only a handful of people she'd met in Ireland. Not that she could see any reason why he'd want to do her harm. If anything, he seemed to be trying to cheer her up. Well, she couldn't go around suspecting everyone of a hidden motive, could she? "Fine."

The door opened and Rose came rushing in, apologizing. "I'm sorry, but Da kept wanting something else like a glass of this or that and a bite to eat, and he looked so pathetic I couldn't say no. The doctors said he'd be right in a few weeks, and he could do everything but the heavy lifting, but you'd think he was at death's door to hear him talk."

"Gran always said that most men are lousy patients — they feel a twinge and they're convinced they're dying." Maura laughed. "And worse, they want you to be sympathetic." And then there were the women like her gran, who wouldn't complain about a physical problem until she dropped.

People began trickling into Sullivan's in ones or twos, and greeted Mick, who they all seemed to know, and nodded to Maura. They joked with Rose, who bantered with them and smiled as she poured their drinks.

By six the place was full; there was a constant stream of people, both in and out. There were more women in the crowd now, mostly with husbands or boyfriends. The noise level rose, and so did the temperature in the room, with the smell of damp wool joining the constant background scent of burning peat. Maura circulated around the room and tried to keep what she hoped was a friendly smile on her face as she picked up glasses. All the while she listened, and the words she picked up most often were "murder," "death," "that poor man," and "awful." Maura scanned the faces in the crowd. A few already looked familiar from the last few days, presumably regulars. She seemed to be the only tourist there, this time of year. Most people would be local, stopping in for a bit of news and a quick drink before going home.

She saw a middle-aged woman approaching her. "Can you give me a cider, darlin'?"

"Magners?" Maura asked.

"Grand. So, you're the American?"

"I am, from Boston. But my grandmother was born around here."

"That's right, I heard you were Nora Sullivan's granddaughter?"

"Yes." She really should get over being surprised that everyone knew.

"My mother has Sullivan cousins, though they moved to Clonakilty, I think, or maybe it was Bandon. They knew each other at school. Me ma said . . ."

Maura listened, amazed anew at how everyone she met seemed to have an encyclopedic memory about their families, no matter how distant, extending back at least a century. Of course, she'd met a few people in the Boston area who were happy to tell you how many of their ancestors had come over on a boat in 1623, and how many had fought in the Revolution, and so forth. She wondered if everyone here could trace their family back to the seventeenth century.

"You know how to manage that thing?" the woman asked, pointing behind Maura.

"What, you mean the espresso machine? I think so. You want a cup? I'm not sure what kind of coffee we have."

"Wouldn't mix well with the cider, now, would it? But I might try one tomorrow, if you're up for it."

"I'll make sure I'm ready for you." Maura smiled.

"Grand. By the way, I'm Johanna Burke, and that lout in the corner is my husband, Seamus." She nodded toward a burly man in a dark sweater laughing with several other men. She slipped a few coins across the counter and raised her glass. "I'll see yeh."

CHAPTER 18

The evening had been busy right until closing and then beyond, and Maura had been happy to fall into bed. She'd chatted with more people than on earlier nights — maybe they'd finally accepted her as one of them. Ellen was still feeding her family, including her husband, who was wearing a sports jacket, when Maura came into the kitchen upstairs the next morning. "You're up early, Maura. No, Sean, that's Patrick's toy — yours is over there. Kevin, finish up or we'll be late for church. Tom, can you start herding them toward the door?"

Oh, right, it was Sunday. The tolling of the bells up the road should have clued her in. "This early?"

A harried Ellen replied, "I like the early Mass. If we wait for the later Mass, the day is lost. Will you be coming?"

"I, uh, don't think so." Gran had dragged her to Mass as a child, but by the time

Maura had reached high school Gran had given up. Maura couldn't remember the last time she'd been to church on a Sunday; the last time she'd been in a church at all had been for Gran's funeral.

"Sorry, I didn't mean to make you uncomfortable. We get all kinds here, those that are wanting to go daily, and others who think Sunday is for sightseeing. Have you other plans?"

"I'm meeting Mick Nolan at eight — he said there was something he had to show me. There, now I've told you where I'll be, in case I disappear."

"You're thinking Mick's going to throw you off the bridge?" Ellen smiled, quickly sponging breakfast crumbs off the counters.

"Or kidnap me," Maura said cheerfully. "Is he the type?"

"And what would I know about kidnappers and the like?" Ellen retorted. "Okay, out the door, now! Kevin, you keep an eye on the little ones. Maura, there's a later Mass if you find you've the time."

"Ma, I'm not little!" Patrick complained.

"Then you're big enough to follow instructions, aren't you? Now, come along!"

The three older children followed their father out the front door, and Ellen brought up the rear, carrying Gráinne. At the door she turned and said, "There's coffee, and food's ready on the stove there. Can you see to yourself?"

"Sure," Maura called at her retreating back. She made a quick circuit of the kitchen, grabbing and filling a mug, loading a plate with the contents of a covered pan on the stove — apparently the whole family indulged on a Sunday — then sitting down to eat. As she made her way through eggs, sausage — including the blood sausage that she was growing fond of, much to her surprise — she wondered what Mick thought was important enough to show her, and why so early. She hadn't seen much of the local sites, apart from the middle of Skibbereen. But between talking with Mrs. Nolan mornings and filling in at the pub, she really hadn't had much time to sight-see. What should she see? she wondered. And why should she care? It had always seemed pointless, to pack up and drive across a state or two just to look at something, take a few blurry pictures, then turn around and drive back again. Not that she'd done much of it. Now and then she and Gran had spent a few hours at one beach or another near Boston, but that didn't really count as sightseeing. She knew in theory that Boston was rich in history and art, but she had to admit, deep down, that she really wasn't interested. What did it have to do with her?

She cleaned up her few dishes, then went downstairs to find her bag and, after a glance out the glass doors, put on a rain jacket: it was either raining lightly or misting heavily, and the fields across the harbor had disappeared into the murk. She went back upstairs and let herself out the front door to find that Mick was already waiting for her, his car idling at the top of the drive.

He greeted her with a nod. "Come on," he said, reaching over and opening the passenger-side door.

"Where are we going?"

"You'll see."

"I told Ellen I was going somewhere with you. In case you're kidnapping me."

"What?"

"In case you're an ax murderer. Maybe you belong to some weird cult that demands ritual sacrifice, and I'm the guest of honor."

He seemed amused. "Paranoid, are we? Besides, if I wanted to hide your body, I know where all the good spots are."

"Well, that makes me feel *so* much better," Maura said with a hint of sarcasm. She was enjoying herself, despite yesterday's problems and the wet state of the weather.

"Is this mysterious thing far?"

"You'll see," he repeated.

Maura fell silent and watched the scenery. Mick took a right onto the road that ran along the harbor. It twisted and turned, with a sheer cliff on one side, the water below on the other. Maura saw a long bridge crossing the harbor, and beyond it across the harbor, another town. "What's that?" she asked.

"Union Hall." He didn't volunteer anything further.

After a few more minutes they came to another town. "Okay, what's this one?"

"Glandore." Again he stopped speaking.

"Mick, if this is your idea of acting as a tour guide, you suck at it. Just so you know."

He smiled without looking at her. "We're not there yet."

Past the village, the two-lane road veered away from the water, and Maura was completely lost. She decided to just sit back and enjoy whatever Mick had planned, since she'd come this far.

After another mile or so, Mick turned off the main road, down an unmarked dirt road. A few hundred yards later, the road widened to a small graveled area. There were no cars and no people in sight. He pulled in and stopped the car. Maura looked at him quizzically.

"We walk from here," was all he said.

She sighed: whatever it was, it was going to be wet. She was glad she'd brought her jacket. The heavy mist — or was it light rain? — continued to fall, obscuring any possible views. Mick set off toward a grassy path at one end of the graveled area, and they passed through a revolving gate of some sort, apparently intended to keep out grazing animals rather than humans. The path twisted through tall hedges with dark-green leaves, and changed direction several times. Maura plodded along the slick grass, trying to avoid puddles.

After another turn, Mick waited for her, then stepped aside and motioned her forward. She moved into the open, stopped, and stared in wonder. The land before her fell away down a gentle slope, and she could not see beyond the hedges that bordered the large clearing because of the sweeping grey mist. But in the center of the space, she could make out the ghostly outlines of . . . a circle of grey stones. She shivered: they appeared so at home in this wet, lonely landscape. "What is it?" she breathed. She'd seen pictures of Stonehenge, but that was in a different country, and this had to be a lot smaller — but no less powerful.

Mick said quietly, "The Druid's Altar of

Drombeg. It's prehistoric, probably between two and three thousand years old. There are quite a few of these circles around, although this is one of the most complete — and probably the most dramatic."

Maura took a few more steps into the clearing. "I've heard about these — I saw some National Geographic special a while ago. Aren't they supposed to be aligned with the sun or the moon or something?"

"There are different theories, but a lot of the circles do line up with one or the other, particularly at the solstices." Maura could feel Mick's eyes on her as she began to prowl around the stones, running her hands over them. On the far side, one stone lay horizontally, unlike the others. There was a single shape carved on the flat top. Maura traced it with her fingers, trying to imagine the effort it would have taken someone to chip this simple form into the rock two thousand years ago, and why they had done it. The whole place was eerily silent — no birds, not even any sheep, just the drip of water. She felt as though she had stepped out of time. She had no trouble envisioning this as a religious site.

There were some other heaps of stone not far away, and after another minute Maura walked over to examine them.

"That's a pair of huts," Mick said as he followed at a distance.

"And that square thing in the ground?" Maura pointed.

"It's called a *fulacht fiadh*. It was a cooking pit. There are other examples in the area. You heated up stones in your fire and threw them in the water along with your meat, and after a couple of hours you had boiled meat. Some scientists have tried it, more recently, and it worked. This was before metal cooking pots, you know."

"Yes, I figured that part out," Maura said absently. She sat down on a low stone near the pit and fell silent, lost in thought. She studied the ancient monument, wanting to fix the scene in her mind. It really was eerie, particularly under these conditions. Had Mick checked a weather forecast? In bright sunlight it would be much more ordinary.

She looked up at him from her perch on the stone. "Thank you." She didn't want to have to say any more, but suddenly she felt very happy. She never would have believed that she could sit in a field with a bunch of rocks, in the rain, and be thrilled by it.

But Mick had to feel it too, because he had brought her here, and he was hanging back, letting the place work its magic on her. She could sense it here. She stood up, walked back to the center of the circle, and shut her eyes. She wasn't sure what she was seeking, but apparently it wasn't to be found in the middle of the circle, so it had to be the whole place that was so moving. She walked back to where the path entered, then turned and surveyed the scene once again. Mick followed, and at some unspoken cue, they both headed back up the winding path. In the parking area another car had arrived, and a couple of older women climbed out, clutching guidebooks. Maura nodded politely at them but didn't speak, almost afraid to break the spell. She was glad they had not arrived earlier, and she thanked the unknown local gods for giving her a bit of solitude.

Once back in the car, Mick pulled out and retraced the way toward the main road. After a few miles Maura said, "Maybe I wasn't so wrong about the ritual sacrifice thing. But what an amazing place." She fell quiet again, and they drove back to Leap in silence. Mick stopped at the top of Ellen's drive to let her out of the car. Before she closed the door, she paused, then said, "Thank you, Mick. I mean it. I would never have found the place on my own, and it really is special."

Mick looked at her, a half smile on his

239

face. "I thought you'd like it. I'm off now to pick up my grandmother for church."

"Oh, right." Maura was torn; her recent memories of being in a Catholic church were sad ones, but at the same time, the church in Leap was likely the one where her grandparents had been married and where her father had been christened. She should probably make at least a token effort to see the church; it would have pleased Gran. "Can I come with you?"

Mick gave her a quick, puzzled look. "Sure, if you like."

"Do I need to change clothes?" Maura asked, before remembering she had nothing better to change into.

"Father Driscoll is more than happy to have people in his church these days — he won't mind, nor will the others. Shall I go straight on to Grannie's house, then?"

"Yes." Maura settled back in her seat, wondering what she had just let herself in for.

CHAPTER 19

Maura sat silently for most of the drive to collect Bridget Nolan, trying to fit what she had seen — and felt — at Drombeg into what she knew, or had thought she knew, about Ireland. It wasn't an easy job. When they reached Mrs. Nolan's house, she was already waiting at the door, wearing a hat that was probably older than Maura, and carrying a prim purse, its handle over her arm. Her face was turned to the sun, as if seeking the spring warmth. Maura noted that the mists that had clung to the coast at Drombeg seemed to have melted away.

Mick pulled up in front of the house, and Maura climbed out of the front seat.

"Oh, how lovely," Mrs. Nolan said on seeing her. "Will you be joining us for church?"

"If you don't mind. I thought I should see where Gran was married. Nobody will care, will they?"

"Of course not, love. If you'll just give me

a hand in, we can get on."

Maura guided her to the front seat and then sat behind.

"Will you be joining us for dinner at the hotel, after?" Mrs. Nolan tossed back over the seat.

Dinner? She must mean lunch. Maura mentally reviewed how much cash she had with her and wondered if it would be enough. Which also reminded her to ask Mick when she would likely get paid for the hours she was putting in at Sullivan's. But now was not the time. "I don't want to be a bother," she ventured.

"Don't trouble yourself — the rest of the town'll be glad to get a look at you," Mrs. Nolan said complacently.

Great. Her first public appearance — in church, no less — and she was wearing grubby clothes and would probably have to beg for her lunch. She hoped the local citizens were forgiving.

Maura had been past the Church of St. Mary, first on the bus the day she had arrived, and then when she'd picked up food at the quick mart across the street, but she hadn't yet ventured inside. It was a substantial rectangular stone building, with few decorative frills. To the front lay a large parking lot; behind, the steep cemetery. The lot was no more than half-filled and looked rather forlorn. At least Mick could park fairly close to the entrance. He was already helping his grandmother out of the front seat by the time Maura had her own door open. He took Mrs. Nolan's elbow and guided her slowly to the church door, while she nodded and smiled to several people along the way. Maura trailed behind, feeling alternately painfully exposed and invisible.

The church's interior was large, well lit, and surprisingly bare. Maura wondered just what she had expected, but this wasn't it — not at all like the churches she had seen in Boston. At Mick's gesture Maura slid into a seat, then he settled Mrs. Nolan beside her and took the seat on the aisle. Once Mass began, Maura listened to the liturgy with half her mind; with the other half she watched the people around her and then checked out the windows and plaques on the near walls. Funny how quickly the ritual came back, even though it had been years since she had attended any Mass other than at Christmas; she stumbled on the responsorials but still knew when to kneel. At least she'd outgrown the fidgeting part. What would Gran think if she could see her now? Or maybe she could?

Maura tried to picture her grandmother

and James Donovan, the grandfather she had never known, standing in front of the priest and friends and relatives in this echoing space. Would there have been many watching? The current priest wasn't young, but not old enough to have known them. As she scanned the thin crowd, Maura realized that she and Mick were the youngest people there. Maybe all the people with young children made a point of going early, as Ellen and her family had?

When the service ended, Maura waited for Mick and Mrs. Nolan to make their way back outside. Instead, Mrs. Nolan slipped her hand through Maura's arm and began to introduce her to friends, and to the priest. It took some time before Mrs. Nolan ran out of people to introduce her to. Maura smiled and nodded, knowing she would never remember all the names. She wondered if any would show up at Sullivan's.

"I'll take you down to the hotel, shall I?" Mick said.

"Lovely, dear. Maura, you'll enjoy the meal — Sheahan's lays on a nice spread for a Sunday."

Mick drove them down the street to the rear of the hotel, where the restaurant was located. Mrs. Nolan seemed reenergized — or was looking forward to the meal? — and guided Maura to the entrance, her hand on Maura's arm.

As she opened the door, Maura realized that *everybody* in town must be there. A wave of loud conversation rolled over her, and she could smell cooking lamb and cabbage, and other things she didn't recognize. A tiny bar tucked in one corner was enjoying brisk business, mainly among the men. The food was arrayed cafeteria-style on several long tables against a wall, and Maura realized how hungry she was. There were no prices listed anywhere, but before Maura could say anything, Mrs. Nolan leaned toward her and said, "It's our treat."

When Mick returned from wherever he had parked, Mrs. Nolan said to him, "Find us a place to sit, will you? Maura and I will fill our plates."

Mick grinned at Maura over Mrs. Nolan's head. "Sure, Grannie." Once they'd done so, Mrs. Nolan led the way to the corner table where Mick was leaning protectively. When the ladies were settled, he took his turn in the line for food.

Maura felt something inside her relax. This was a family place, and a family event, as if the whole town gathered once a week to eat together and catch up on each other's news, for there was as much talking going on as eating. She didn't feel out of place, even though she didn't recognize anyone beyond Mrs. Nolan and Mick — although if Mrs. Nolan had anything to say about it, that wouldn't last long. Just as she had at the church, the older woman introduced Maura to whoever came up to the table, and repeated the same mantra — "Boston, grandmother, Donovan" — and people seemed to put the pieces together quickly. Maura found she was smiling a lot, probably more than she'd smiled in the past month. It felt odd.

After an hour or so, the din quieted, and people, especially those with children, started to leave. Mrs. Nolan leaned toward her. "If you don't mind, I'll take my leave of you now. Will I see you tomorrow?"

"Of course." Then a thought occurred to her: maybe Maura could seize the time and go visit her grandfather's grave. It seemed like a fitting ending to the afternoon. "Mick, could you tell me how to reach the cemetery where my grandfather is buried?"

"No problem." He snagged a paper napkin and began sketching out a simple map; Bridget leaned over to correct him at the last bit leading to the cemetery itself. She also kept up a running commentary. "It's not hard to find — just go down the bog

246

road till it ends, then turn right, up the hill to Drinagh," she said. "But you won't be wanting to stop in Drinagh, though the new church is there, for the family's in the old cemetery up the hill. You'll turn right at the main road through Drinagh — if you pass the creamery you've gone the wrong way. Then there's a small road on the left that goes up the hill, until you see a tall stone tower on the left — that's all that's left of the old church. The cemetery's just below it. They couldn't move the dead, now, could they?"

Mick added quietly, "Can you manage that?"

"I think so. There aren't enough roads to get lost, are there?"

"Most likely not. I'll see you later down the pub — no need to hurry."

When Mick left to get the car, Maura turned to Mrs. Nolan. "Who else is there in that cemetery, do you know?" Maura hadn't thought beyond her grandfather, about whom she knew very little. She felt a pang: the last time she'd visited a cemetery, it had been to bury Gran. She'd known that cremation would be cheaper, but Gran had been careful to hold aside enough money to pay for a real burial, and a few Masses said for her as well, and Maura had honored her

grandmother's wishes. She had been pleased
when the priest said some very nice things
about Nora Donovan, and it was clear that
he'd known her grandmother and hadn't
just been reading off a standard text. Gran
would have been happy.

"No other Donovans, I'm afraid," Mrs.
Nolan said, "but quite a number of Sullivans, and a Herlihy or two. When your
grandfather died, we all thought your grandmother would be laid to rest alongside —
that's why he's there, rather than with his
own people."

"Were they from far away?"

"Only the next townland over, but in a
different parish, so they went to another
church."

Maura looked around before saying, "Can
I ask you something?"

"Of course, love. What is it?"

Maura tried to choose her words carefully.
She had a strong suspicion that Mick had
stayed around mainly to take care of his
grandmother, but she didn't want to make
Mrs. Nolan look too hard at Mick's motives
or think that she was holding her grandson
back. "Ellen's told me a bit about Mick, but
he seems kind of out of place working in a
pub. What's his story? I mean, did he go to
college? Does he have a profession other

248

than barkeep?" Maura wasn't sure she'd managed to hide her real question: why would anyone want to hang around such a dead-end place?

"Ah, and would you be thinking of making a run at him? There's no woman in his life, although I've told him time and again he's not getting any younger." At Maura's horrified expression, Mrs. Nolan laughed. "I'm just having a bit of fun with you. He studied business at uni, but there's not many that's hiring these days. I've told him he should be in Dublin, or at least Cork City, but he claims he's happier here. I know he wants to keep an eye on me, see that I don't get into any trouble."

"What if the pub closes, or the new owners want to bring in other people?"

"Well, we'll just have to wait and see, won't we? He knows which way the wind is blowing, and he'll be all right, whichever way things fall out. If you're going up the hill, you should start now, give yourself a little time to spend there."

Maura stood up. "I'll report back to you tomorrow, then."

"Say hello to your grandda Jimmy for me, will you? He was a grand figure of a man," Mrs. Nolan said.

Jimmy. James. Her grandfather. It took

Maura a moment to put it together. "I'll do that. See you tomorrow."

CHAPTER 20

They said their good-byes to various friends and acquaintances, then Mick escorted his grandmother out of the restaurant, and Maura retrieved her car from behind the Keohanes' house and headed north. It was only when she was halfway there that she realized that she hadn't given a second thought to driving. There were no problems with the car, as far as she could tell, but she didn't know a whole lot about fixing cars. That had always been a guy thing when she was in school, and she'd never had a car anyway. But the fact that the old car had stood up to some pretty serious abuse was strangely reassuring; Maura felt protected, like she was driving a tank. Patting the steering wheel affectionately, she promised the car that she would avoid small roads in the future, at least whenever she could. She'd already learned that most of the roads around the area would be called "small" by any standards, clearly meant for a horse cart. Of course, she wouldn't have any more luck managing a horse — she'd never been near one. She suddenly realized that she was laughing at herself.

Taking her on that little excursion to Drombeg this morning had been a really nice thing for Mick to do. It was almost embarrassing that she had been in the country nearly a week and hadn't done any sightseeing — all she'd seen was Leap and the inside of the pub, and a bit of Skibbereen — including the garda station. She wasn't going to count the hospital in Cork, a place she'd rather not have seen. None of it was the stuff that made it into tourist brochures. Maybe Mick had wanted to show her a different side of the place, a more mystical, primal one. Strip away all the organized religious stuff — easier now that the Catholic Church was losing its grip — there was still this weird underlying sense of unseen forces lurking, particularly out in the country. Maybe leprechauns had been invented to sell beer and greeting cards, but at the same time, maybe they held just a dash of truth. Maura was almost willing to concede that there were spirits here, and if there were, some of them lingered at Drombeg.

As she followed Mick's napkin map, Maura realized that none of the roads except the main highway had road signs, much less directional signs. The road that she turned onto when the bog road ended was the Drinagh road because it led to Drinagh, nowhere else. You had to know where you were going, or know someone who did, or you'd be hopelessly lost.

The Drinagh road took her to another T-intersection, where she stopped. Looking left she could see what Mrs. Nolan had called the creamery, so she must be in the right place. When she'd heard the term "creamery," she'd pictured something small and quaint, but in fact it looked like quite a modern thriving operation, with multiple buildings and a few tanker trucks in sight. At least one business around here seemed to be doing well. Maura turned right, and the road took her by a lovely small lake, below her on the right. But she was looking for a road on the left, leading uphill. She crept along, grateful that there were no other people on the road, or she would have missed it. She turned carefully, passing some ramshackle sheds with a couple of chickens scurrying around, and after a few hundred feet she could see what had to be the tower from the old church, looming through the trees.

Just past the tower there was a wide turn-in on the left, and Maura pulled over, close to the well-kept stone wall. When she got out of the car, she could see an old cemetery spread out below her, its headstones canted in all directions. The tower was near the wall, and the empty space to its left had to be where the old church had stood. It was a good landmark, but why had whoever demolished the building bothered to leave just the tower? Noisy black birds she couldn't identify flew in and out of the open windows in the upper stories. She glanced briefly around her. To her right there was nothing but open fields. Further up the hill, there appeared to be a home and some farm buildings, and the lane petered out in the farmyard. She couldn't see any people around. So much space, so much silence — it all felt so foreign to her.

Before heading for the gate, Maura stopped to read a large and new-looking sign. Apparently the local Cork County authorities had recently decided to allow only approved grave diggers to work in county burial grounds. Maura smiled: what did it take to be approved as a grave digger? Did the sign mean that until now family members could just show up, dig a hole, and deposit their dearly departed? Looking out over the small graveyard, she could easily believe that people might do just that.

She unlatched the gate and let herself in, carefully closing it behind her. There was nothing as orderly as a path, just space between the rows of headstones, which ranged from short stubs to a few that were taller than she was; from old to a few that looked like they'd been put up last week. Were people still using this place, even though there was a newer cemetery down below? Or were they only coming to visit their dead? Someone was taking care of the place, because the grass was short; she spotted a rusty scythe resting against one side of the tower, and tattered bunches of plastic flowers on some of the graves, so at least there were occasional visitors.

Just like her. What was she doing here? Maura didn't like cemeteries — they were depressing. She'd visited her father's grave a few times, but only with her gran. Looking at the headstone of a man she'd barely known didn't do much for her. So she was here now to pay her respects to her unknown grandfather, mainly because she knew her grandmother would have wanted her to. Burying Gran had been hard, but only because it drove home that she would never see Gran again. Whatever had been buried in that cemetery was not the person she had known and loved, the strong, kind woman who had raised her.

Mrs. Nolan had said to send her greetings along to James Donovan — how odd to think that she had known him. Were Mrs. Nolan's people buried here? Maura had forgotten to ask. She wandered along the rows, trying to avoid tree roots, silently apologizing to whoever she was stepping on, even though they were long gone. After she saw two stones with the exact same names on them, she started counting, and ended up with four. They had certainly stuck to naming patterns around here, hadn't they? Was it confusing or comforting if everyone had the same name? It must have been hard on the schoolteachers.

Her grandfather's stone turned out to be a fairly modern one — well, he had died in 1968, which was probably a hundred years later than most of the burials here. Who had erected it? As far as she knew, the family hadn't ever had much money, and not only had Nora had a child to support, but she'd also somehow paid the fare for both of them to come to Boston. But the stone looked professional, and expensive. She'd have to ask Mrs. Nolan, if she could figure out how to do it tactfully. There was plenty of room left on the stone, probably intended for Gran at least, if not her own dad and his family. *Like me,* Maura realized.

The ground in front of the stone seemed dry enough, so Maura sat down cross-legged and tried to figure out what to say. She shut her eyes for a moment, listening to the birds and what sounded like a distant cow, or maybe sheep. And to the silence: no cars, no airplanes, no useless annoying noise. It could be any century. She opened her eyes again and looked at the stone erected for a man she had never known. One whom her grandmother had loved, and had had a child with. If he'd lived, there might have been more children — Gran had always loved taking care of people. Of course, if he'd lived, Gran probably wouldn't have gone to America with Maura's dad, who then might never have met Maura's mother, meaning that then Maura wouldn't have existed, and wouldn't be sitting here now, surrounded by relatives she had never met but who shared her blood. And they had all mattered to some-one, because there were stones to honor them; and they apparently mattered still, if the garish plastic flowers were any indica-tion. It certainly wasn't like any cemetery

Maura had seen before; the ones in Boston were big and impersonal, and suddenly she felt bad for her father and grandmother, parked in the middle of hundreds of strangers, with only her to remember them.

Her increasingly maudlin thoughts were interrupted by the sound of an approaching car. Another person coming to visit a dead relative on a Sunday afternoon? As far as she knew, this road didn't lead anywhere but the farm. She sat still, waiting to see if the car kept going, but instead it stopped next to the cemetery. So much for privacy.

Maura stood up, brushed off the back of her jeans, and turned to check out the newcomer: a young man wearing a baseball cap, leaning against the gate, with a dusty brown car behind him.

CHAPTER 21

Maura's senses went on high alert at the sight of the man and his car, which she recognized as the one that had pushed her off the road the day before. This wasn't a random meeting; this guy, whoever he was, must've followed her here. What did he want?

She checked him out: about her age, dressed like every other twenty-something guy she knew, in jeans, a hoodie, and that stupid cap. He looked slightly grimy, although she couldn't put her finger on why. A sneer was plastered on his face. So much for a warm Irish welcome.

He was watching her too. What was he thinking? She'd faced off against tougher guys than him — her neighborhood, school, and the places she'd worked all had had their share of bullies. If Brown Car was expecting a meek tourist, he was in for a surprise.

Maura looked around her: still no other people in sight, although she thought she could hear a tractor now, several fields away. Yeah, that would be a lot of help to her. Maybe Brown Car Guy wanted to apologize. And maybe pigs could fly.

But she wasn't looking for trouble, and her business here was done. Might as well leave. She could be wrong and he really *was* here to honor his dead mother or something. Maura started walking toward the gate, and he straightened up from his slouch, but he didn't move out of the way. When she was about five feet away, she said, "Mind letting me by?"

"Mebbe I do," he said. To Maura's ears his accent didn't match the others she'd heard around here, but she didn't know enough to place it.

"You want something?" she asked. Not the smartest move in the world to challenge him, but she hadn't survived Southie by being timid.

"Yer not from around here. Go home where yeh belong."

Was this some punk kid who liked to throw his weight around? Someone who hated Americans on sight? What was his problem?

"What if I like it here?"

"That can change fast."

This standoff was getting them nowhere, although Maura's gut was telling her that this guy had more on his mind than picking on a tourist. What should she do? She had the cell phone in her pocket: she could call 999 and say . . . what? That a man was annoying her? Still, maybe the threat of a call would be enough to discourage him. She pulled the phone out of her jacket pocket.

He laughed. "Think the guards'll be any help? It'll take 'em forever to find this place. Besides, I've a message to give yeh: Yer pokin' yer nose where it don't belong. Leave it go."

What on earth was he talking about? "Oh yeah? Says who?" Maura retorted. To her own ears she sounded like a twelve-year-old on a playground.

Maura was relieved when he didn't push back. "I've said my piece. Back off or yeh won't be happy." The punk turned and strolled back toward his car, ignoring her questions. Instead of using the gate, he vaulted over the low wall — showing off? But at least he did nothing more threatening than get into his car and back out of the lane too fast, spraying gravel as he sped down the hill. Maura had time to notice

261

part of a license plate this time. Would that help?

She gawped at the phone in her hand. She didn't need 999 now, but she thought she ought to tell the gardaí that she'd seen the car that had run her off the road again, and now she'd gotten a good look at the driver as well as part of a license plate. She didn't have Sean Murphy's mobile number, but she could go to the station at Skibbereen and tell him face-to-face, so he could add one more piece of information to their skinny file on her. And she even knew how to get back to the main road from here: the Drinagh road led to the main road, which led to Skibbereen.

As Maura drove to Skibbereen, following the Drinagh road to the main highway, she had time to think about what Brown Car Punk had said. Stay out of what? She'd been minding her own business, talking to a few elderly people, and pulling pints at the pub. The guy had apparently wanted to warn her off — but from what? Why was he picking on her when he didn't even know her? She pulled abruptly into the small lot in front of the garda station, nearly empty on a Sunday. She got out and headed for the front door.

The same ridiculously young officer was stationed at a desk in the front, and he

262

looked up and smiled politely at her. "Hello, miss, can I help you?"

"Is Officer Murphy in?"

The young officer stood up. "I'll see if he's free," he said, and darted across the room. He didn't have far to go, and reemerged quickly with Sean Murphy in tow.

"Ah, Maura Donovan. How's the car running?" Sean asked with a smile.

"Fine, thanks. But, uh, look, can I talk to you about that?" Maura said.

He looked around, finally locating an empty desk in the corner and nodding toward it. They walked over, and he gestured Maura toward a chair while he went around and sat on the other side. "What is it you wanted to tell me?" he asked.

"I saw the guy in the brown car again. And this time he got in my face."

Suddenly Sean Murphy was all business. "Just now?"

Maura nodded. "Yes. I came straight here. I was visiting my grandfather's grave — he's buried in the old cemetery at Drinagh. Do you know it?"

"Up the hill, by the old tower?"

Maura nodded. "That's the one. I drove from Leap directly there, and when I got there I was alone. I spent some time in the cemetery, and I found my grandfather's gravestone. But then this other car showed up, and the guy got out and came into the cemetery. He had to have followed me."

"And he threatened you?" Sean asked. "What do you mean by 'got in your face'?"

"Well, not exactly threatened — at least, not physically. He watched me for a while, and when I tried to leave, he told me I wasn't welcome and I should just go home. He didn't say why, except that he didn't want me 'poking my nose' into something. He didn't get close enough to touch me."

"Did you respond to him?"

"I asked him what he wanted, and he just laughed at me. I pulled out my phone to call you guys, and he said you'd never get there in time. But then he left."

"You were lucky. Did you happen to —"

"— get the license plate? Part of one. He took off pretty fast, so by the time I got to the gate he was making the turn. All I got was 99-C-8 something."

"That at least tells us it was a Cork plate, then. Can you describe the man?"

"He looked . . . ordinary. About my age, no taller than I am. He had on jeans, a hoodie, running shoes — none of it was new. A baseball cap, no logo on it, so I couldn't see the color of his hair. I didn't get close enough to see his eyes." Sean was writing all this down, and Maura waited until he had finished. "Does that help?"

He sat back in his chair and looked at her. "You're sure now the car was brown, and we have a partial license. That's good. The way you describe him, he could be about anyone. But what matters is that he's come back after you a second time. He seems to want you to go away. Why would that be?"

"I can't tell you. You think he's hanging around, like, stalking me?"

"I can't say. I'm sorry — I don't know what we can do to keep you safe from him. Of course I'll check the car registration, but we're out flat with these murders and all, and we can't put anyone on it right away." At Maura's puzzled look, he added, "We've few violent deaths in Skibbereen. Or in all of Cork, for that matter, even in Cork City. Few of us have ever worked on a homicide at all. And the people in town are on edge, looking over their shoulders all the time, if you know what I mean. So we're doing our best to figure this out, and that leaves little time for complaints like yours. I'm sorry."

"You mean, he'll have to kill me to get your attention?" As soon as the words left her mouth, Maura regretted them. Of course the small police force here was stretched thin. Of course the fresh murder of one of their own people took precedence. She kept having to remind herself that this was small-town Ireland, not Boston. "Look, I'm sorry," she said quickly. "That didn't come out right. I'm glad you're willing to talk to me now, at least. Have you made any progress on Bart Hayes's death? Were there cameras on the cash machine, or anything like that?"

"The machine has cameras, but the attacker knew enough to wait until Bart Hayes had moved away before he struck. It may be that he's done this before, or he'd planned it."

"It was just supposed to be a robbery, wasn't it? I mean, it wasn't like somebody wanted the guy dead." She flashed on a memory of Hayes at the pub; he'd seemed so happy.

"We've no reason to think anyone held anything against Bart Hayes. The shopkeepers are hoping it was someone passing through who saw his chance and took it. Which would make it nearly hopeless for us to solve, of course." He shook his head. "The blow probably wasn't meant to kill, but nobody saw the body until the next morning, and by then it was too late." Sean sighed. "Nobody saw the attack. Shopkeepers hadn't seen anyone suspicious loitering about. Wasn't even very much money."

"Happens all the time back home," Maura said. "And it seems like everybody has guns these days. Kids, even. They get into some argument with another kid and blam, they shoot him. It's stupid."

Sean smiled at her. "You won't be finding that kind of violence around here. Maybe in Dublin, or Cork City. I won't say we're all angels, but we do draw the line at gun violence."

"Still, what a waste that Bart Hayes is dead." Maura shook her head and stood up. "I'll let you get back to work. I'm due at Sullivan's anyway."

To her surprise, Sean stood as well and said, "I'll see you to your car."

"What, you think Brown Car Guy is waiting for me outside a garda station?"

He smiled. "Criminals aren't known to be smart." He walked her to the front door, but he seemed to be in no hurry. "You've been having quite the time of it since you arrived."

Maura nodded. "I guess. I never had this kind of trouble back home, and nobody ever claimed that our neighborhood was a good one, at least when I was growing up, although it's cleaned up its act in the past few years. Is this normal, or is there something weird going on?"

"How do you mean?"

"Well, the first day I'm here you drag a body out of the bog, and I happen to be driving by. Then Jimmy at the pub falls down the stairs and breaks his arm, and when I take him to the hospital you're there and tell me there's been a murder in Skibbereen. Then there's this jerk who tries to run me off the road, and follows me to a cemetery. Am I attracting this crazy stuff?"

Sean shook his head. "That I can't say, but I will tell you it's not the usual order of things."

"Do you know yet who the guy in the bog was?"

"That we do not. We've had the people from the National Museum down, and they said he was modern, been dead no more than a century, which is much too young for them. No documents on him, no wallet, no keys, but that's not necessarily unusual. We'd guess he died sometime after 1925, based on the few coins in his pocket. We've yet to find any record of the man's disappearance. We may never put a name to him."

"Poor guy — you want to think that somebody missed him. What do you do now?"

"We've been handling it like any other

crime scene — the detective inspector thought it would be a good idea for us to get some training in how to handle one. Good thing too, what with the second murder hard on the heels of the first. Anyways, we performed a thorough search of the crime scene, collected the poor man's few possessions and inventoried them, had the official autopsy done. But clearly we've no witnesses to his death and no likely suspects in our sights."

"But he was murdered, right? No way that was an accident?" Maura asked.

"That's what the autopsy tells us," he said.

"Maybe he just fell and hit his head on a rock or something?" She found she wanted it to be an accident, not a murder.

"I'm afraid not. The marks on his head were unmistakable — a strong blow to the back of the head with a long, narrow object, a cane or a stick. That much we know. And then this other killing comes along, so who knows when we'll get back to our man in the bog."

"Will he be buried? Or I guess, reburied?"

"Most likely, although it's still an open investigation right now. It would be good to have a name for the stone, though." He leaned up against her car. "So, will you be staying around much longer?" he asked.

Maura wondered briefly why he wanted to know. "It looks like it — I'll be helping out at Sullivan's until they figure out what's going to happen with it." She could have sworn he looked pleased. "Well, it was nice talking to you, Officer Sean Murphy, but I need to get back to Leap." Maura fished in the depths of her bag for her car key and felt the crackle of paper — the letter addressed to Old Mick, that she'd picked up in the pub. She'd forgotten she was still carrying it. "Oh, shoot."

"You've lost your key?"

"No, I've found that letter. So much has been going on that I forgot all about it." She pulled the letter out of her bag and looked at Murphy. "I think we'd better talk to that detective of yours. I may have something about your Bog Man that he should hear."

CHAPTER 22

Maura had to give Officer Sean Murphy credit: after a first startled glance, he said simply, "Follow me," no questions asked. Good for him — at least by now he seemed to trust her judgment. Although Maura worried that when she presented his boss with her small bit of information, they'd both look foolish.

Inside, Sean said, "Wait here, will you?" and headed for the corner office. The door was open, and after a brief rap on the door frame, he went in. The man seated behind the desk looked up, then listened. Sean nodded toward Maura out in the common area, and after another word with the higher-up, he beckoned her forward.

The man behind the desk stood up courteously when she entered. "I'm Detective Chief Superintendent Patrick Hurley. Please, have a seat."

He was the man she'd seen before — the

one who was in charge. *Now* he wanted to talk to her? He waited until Maura had settled in a chair before sitting again. Sean remained standing, behind Maura's chair.

"My officer here says you have information regarding the dead man from the bog?" Detective Hurley began. Deep voice, cultured accent, Maura noted. She squared her chin and quickly assessed the man's appearance: his dark hair was tinged with silver, and his eyes were a color that she would have said was impossibly blue. He was solidly built — and he exuded authority. She could see why he was the man in charge here.

Maura found her voice. "I'm Maura Donovan, from Boston. I'm just visiting, staying in Leap. And I wouldn't say I have information — only a guess, but I thought someone here should know, just in case, you know." She stopped: to her ears she sounded like she was babbling.

The detective nodded, once. "I'm in charge of investigations of all murders in this district. How did you come to know about that body?" He gave the impression that he was paying close attention, without any sense of hurry.

Maura took a breath to calm herself. Why should she be nervous? "I happened to be

272

driving by when your people were pulling the body out of the bog a few days ago. And of course everybody was talking about it at the pub in Leap after that. Sullivan's."

"Ah. Mick Sullivan's place. He was a good man, and he'll be missed." Detective Hurley paused for a moment. "What was it you wanted to tell me?"

"Well, it kind of relates to Mick Sullivan. I've been helping out at the pub, and I was cleaning up behind the bar and found this letter with a bunch of other mail. It's addressed to Mick, and it was already open so I figured he'd read it. I read it too, to figure out whether it was important and who should get it. I suppose I just could have taken it to the post office and told them to send it back, but it was from a guy in Australia, and I guess I thought it was kind of a cold way to find out that Mick Sullivan was dead." She pushed it across the desk. Detective Hurley looked briefly at it but didn't touch it. "I didn't know what to do with it, so I asked Mick Nolan's grandmother if Old Mick had any family living around there, or who was handling his estate or whatever you want to call it. She couldn't help much, and no one else seemed to know. I tried to bring it to you the other day, but everyone was busy with Bart

273

Hayes's death, so I put the letter in my bag, and then I kind of forgot about it. The last few days have been, uh, distracting." Maura stopped to take a deep breath. The detective must think she was an idiot, the way she was rambling.

When Detective Hurley raised an eyebrow, Officer Murphy spoke for the first time. "Miss Donovan was run off the road, this side of Knockskagh — no damage, and she couldn't identify the car or the driver at the time. Today she came in to report that she saw the same man today, and he threatened her. Then she recalled that she still had the letter."

The detective turned his attention to Maura. "Is that correct?"

Maura nodded. "More or less. Look, before you ask, I've been here less than a week. I don't know anybody or anything, and I have no idea why somebody would be pissed off at me."

"I understand. Murphy, you're dealing with this harassment issue?" When he nodded, the detective turned back to Maura. "Let's go back to the letter and how it relates to our man in the bog. What's in this letter?"

"Well, it came from a guy named Denis Flaherty in Australia. His family emigrated from Ireland when he was young, and now he's getting old and wants to fill in his family tree while he still can. All he knew was that they were from Cork somewhere, possibly from around Leap. He thinks he and Old Mick might have been related, and he mentions a family story about an uncle of his who kind of disappeared back in the 1930s, and no one ever heard from him again. I know it would be a huge coincidence, but I couldn't help wondering if that missing uncle might be the dead guy you've got." Maura stopped, appalled at how confused her story sounded.

Detective Hurley was looking at her with curiosity. Which at least was better than contempt. "So you've brought the letter to me."

"Well, I figured somebody should have it. I know, it sounds crazy. You must be busy, and I'll just get out of your hair now."

The detective smiled. "Please, don't rush off, Miss Donovan. Your information is no stranger than some we've had. Everyone has an opinion, as no doubt you've already seen at Sullivan's."

At least he hadn't dismissed her as an idiot. "Can you tell me anything more about the body?"

After a few seconds of consideration, he

said, "We have the postmortem from the county pathologist, of course. The body appears to be male, no more than fifty."

So far, so good, Maura thought. "Do you know how long he's been in the bog?"

"That's more difficult. Do you know much about bogs?"

"Nope."

"Well, they're peat, a plant that used to be used as heating fuel — after it's dried. It's still used for power generation these days — there are quite a few bogs around. As bogs are usually very wet and acidic, they can preserve things for a very long time. Sometimes things — and bodies — have been preserved for centuries. This body was found a foot or two below the surface, so we're guessing it had been there a good long time, but not more than a century. We could make a rough estimate based on the rate of growth of the peat, but we also had what's left of the clothes as well — buttons and such."

"No buttons in the Middle Ages?" Maura asked.

"Not like these."

"So it's possible that it could be Denis McCarthy?"

He cocked his head at her. "It is. Did your Denis Flaherty know the townland?"

"He didn't seem to." Maura said. "Me, I'm barely clear on what a townland is. I asked a couple of people at the pub if they knew of any local McCarthys, and they practically laughed at me. Seems there were lots of McCarthy families around."

"There still are. Murphy, you can check the records, see if any McCarthys reported the man missing."

"Already done, sir," Sean Murphy responded quickly. "We've been through what few records we have for people who have gone missing, and found no one who fits the description. Of course, the early records are a bit scant, and not everyone would have made a report, nor are those earlier records in the best of condition."

Hurley turned back to Maura. "We'll hold on to the letter for now, if you've no objection."

"Please! It's not exactly mine — I kept it only because I couldn't figure out what to do with it. And it didn't seem right just to throw it away."

"I'm glad you brought it in." He glanced at it again, and his focused sharpened. "Your letter writer says here that the only thing that went missing with this uncle of his was his favorite pipe, carved by his brother, with a knot pattern on it. Murphy, do you have that list of items found on the body?"

"I do, sir. Give me a moment." Sean Murphy went quickly to his desk in the open area and returned a few moments later with a folder, from which he extricated a sheet of paper and handed it to the detective.

Detective Hurley looked at the page, then looked again at Maura. "It appears we have a match."

Maura went cold. This was ridiculous — she just happened to be around when the body was found, and she just happened to find a letter that could just as easily have been thrown away, or lain in the pub for years, and the two just happened to be connected? What were the odds of that? "So the Bog Man is Denis Flaherty's missing uncle? And he was murdered?"

"It appears likely. Too bad we can't ask Old Mick what the connection was, if Denis had the right family. I understand there's some issue as to who inherits, so I assume someone is looking into the family history. Check on that, will you, Murphy?"

"Right, sir."

Maura wondered briefly why the head police officer of the entire district would know about Old Mick's lack of heirs; obviously she still had a lot to learn about how things worked around here. "What do you do now?" she asked.

"We are still treating it as a murder investigation. You've done us a great favor by providing a possible identity for the body. Can I count on you not to share the information about the murder?"

"Sure, of course," Maura said, "but I'm pretty sure most people know about it already. You know, people talk in pubs."

He nodded. "If they talk, listen carefully, then let me or Murphy know if you hear anything that might be of value." He stood up, signaling the end of the interview. "Thank you for stopping by. Most people might not have done. Officer Murphy has your information, if we should need anything further?"

Maura nodded. "Yup. If you need to find me, try the pub, or maybe Ellen Keohane's place by the harbor — that's where I'm staying. And Officer Murphy has my mobile number."

"He'll see you out, then. Thank you again."

Sean Murphy opened the door and waited while Maura went through. At the front door she found herself standing on the station steps, feeling confused.

"What just happened?" Maura said.

Sean Murphy smiled at her. "You identified a man who died long before you were born."

"But things like this just don't happen!" Maura protested. "I don't understand. Why me?"

"I can't say. Why did you bring the letter in at all? Others wouldn't have."

"It seemed like the right thing to do. I felt bad for the poor old guy in Australia, hoping to find an answer after all this time."

"It was good of you to bring the letter in — you never know what might be important. Will you be all right, getting back?"

"You mean, driving back to Leap? I think I can handle it." Maura smiled at him. "I'll let you know if I see that damn brown car again. Thanks, Officer Murphy. Sean." Maura extended her hand.

"Take care, now." He shook her hand, then let her go.

Maura made the loop around the town and found herself on the main road once again. The drive back was uneventful, although she kept glancing in her rearview mirror, looking for the brown car. There was little traffic, and none of it looked ominous.

Her mind kept jumping around. What could that jerk want? Was he actually following her? Why? As far as she knew, she didn't have any enemies, here or in any country. She had to admit that he hadn't looked very bright; maybe he had her mixed up with someone else? Not that there were too many people of her description around at the moment.

And then that thing with the letter. How weird was that?

She arrived back in Leap and left the car behind the Keohanes' house, walking up the drive to the road above. She looked both ways for cars but could see only one, at least half a mile away, and it was red. *Getting paranoid, are you?* She crossed over to the pub and found Rose behind the bar. Her father, Jimmy, was seated in front of the fire, giving Old Billy Sheahan all the details of his hospital stay. To hear him talk, he'd survived intricate major surgery, not a simple cast for a broken bone in his forearm. Maura dumped her bag and jacket behind the bar and went over to the two men.

"So, Jimmy, are you back to work?"

"There you are, Maura my dear. My doctor says I should take it easy for a few more days — no heavy lifting and all. But I didn't want to leave you two ladies here on your own, not with a killer running around the streets."

Maura tensed, then realized he was talking about the mugging death. She wondered how long he could spin out the "no heavy lifting" excuse. Apparently a full pint of Guinness didn't fall in that category. "Can I get you anything, Billy?"

"I'm grand, thank you very much. If you've the time, why don't you come sit with me awhile? I've heard all this fella's stories more than once." He nodded at Jimmy.

Jimmy struggled to look offended. "You cut me to the quick, sir. But I could use a quick bite, before the evening rush. I'll leave you to your tales." He extricated himself from the sprung seat of the chair, waved at his daughter, and headed out the door, whistling.

Billy was still watching her expectantly. There were a few other customers in the place, but Rose was handling them, so Maura sat in the chair Jimmy had vacated. "You've had a spot of trouble, I hear," Billy began.

As far as Maura knew, the man never moved more than fifty feet from where they sat. Which trouble was he talking about, and who would have told him what? "You mean when I nearly ended up in the lough?"

"It's always been a bad road, but I can remember when there were children aplenty running up and down it, and carts goin' to the creamery at the bottom, by the water. You'll have been by it, although it's been closed for a while now. The old school's just there to the left, where the lane meets the road."

Maura wondered what the definition of "a while" was for Old Billy and whether it was measured in years or decades. Then she realized that the school he spoke of might have been the one her grandfather had attended, maybe even her father. "Tell me more about the school. How many students were there?"

"They kept the boys and the girls apart, back in those days . . ." And Billy was off and running, stopping only now and then to take a swallow of his stout. In truth he needed no push, now that he'd found a new and willing listener for his tales. Probably everyone who passed through Sullivan's had heard them all before. Realizing it could be some time before she got back to work, Maura looked briefly at Rose, who winked at her. Maura winked back and settled into the sagging chair for the long haul.

CHAPTER 23

People began to drift in, in ones and twos, later in the afternoon, and Maura had to tear herself away from Billy's storytelling session, with some regret — she had enjoyed listening to him more than she had expected. His recollection of local events was deep, though their breadth extended no more than ten miles from Leap. Still, Maura was sure he could tell her more about her own family, if she could get a word in and nudge him in the right direction. But she would have time for that, wouldn't she? She wasn't going anywhere soon. She was still getting used to that idea.

Still, it was nice to be in the company of other people — she was beginning to worry about going anywhere alone, with Brown Car Guy following her around. If he stepped up his threats . . . she didn't know what she was going to do.

She was behind the bar taking the espresso

machine apart to clean it when Johanna Burke came in, making a beeline for the bar. Maura recognized her and greeted her. "If you're back for that coffee, you may have to wait a bit, as you can see."

"Haven't yeh got it goin' yet?" Johanna asked, settling herself on a stool.

"Almost. It hasn't been used much, so it's mostly a question of cleaning the dust off. Oh, and we'll have to get some ground coffee."

"I got some," Rose said. "I wasn't sure what sort was needed, though, so I got what they said was the strongest. Will that do?" Rose reached under the counter and pulled out a bag of ground coffee and thrust it at Maura.

Maura read the label. "Should be fine." She turned back to Johanna. "Well, Johanna, are you willing to be our guinea pig? Because I can't make any promises about the results."

Johanna grinned. "If that means I'd be the first to try it, fire away, dear. I'm pulling for you."

Maura squared off against the machine. Had she plugged it in? Yes. Filled the water bin? Yes. Maura packed ground coffee into the thingy with the handle, tamped it down, then clamped it into place, sliding a cup under it. Rose and Johanna looked on intently, clearly enjoying watching Maura take charge of the machine — and anticipating the results? — and she gave them a brief smile. "Here we go." And she pushed the button.

For a moment nothing happened, but then the machine began to make a noise between a hum and a hiss — and coffee began dribbling into the cup. Johanna and Rose clapped and whooped, attracting attention from the men in the bar, who gave them a look of bewildered disgust and then returned to whatever they'd been discussing. Maura focused intently on the stream of coffee, and when it finally slowed, then stopped, she turned and slid the cup across the counter to Johanna. "There you go. Unless you wanted a cappuccino, with steamed milk?"

Johanna waved a hand at her. "This is grand. You can fuss with cappa-whatsis later. Have you any sugar?"

Rose passed a bowl with sugar packets in it over to her. Johanna took three, ripped them open, and dumped the contents into the cup. Silently Maura offered her a spoon. Johanna stirred, then lifted the cup to her mouth and sipped. A smile bloomed on her face. "Perfect. Points to you, Maura. You may be seeing a lot of me, come afternoons. What're you charging?"

Maura and Rose exchanged blank looks. "Since it's the first cup, it's on the house. Rose and I will have to work out what to charge."

"Will I get a discount, if I buy a month's worth, say?" Johanna asked.

"We'll see," Maura replied, feeling ridiculously pleased with herself. It was only a cup of machine-made coffee, and Johanna's enthusiasm seemed greater than the cup deserved, but if having espresso available made people happy — and kept them coming back — Maura wasn't going to argue.

"You want to try it?" Maura challenged Rose.

"Drinking it or making it? 'Cause I'm not much for strong coffee, but I'd like to know how it works." She watched as Maura reversed the process, removing the coffee grounds and cleaning out the holder.

"Always make sure there's water in the container here," Maura told the girl as she worked. "I can show you the milk part after you've figured this out. Your father wouldn't happen to still have the instructions, would he?"

"Nah, he got the machine from somebody he ran into somewhere, not a store. Maybe they were settling a debt or something."

"Then we'll just have to figure it out on our own, right?"

"That we will," Rose replied. "I push this button here?"

Rose completed brewing the coffee, and Maura accepted it and clinked cups with Johanna. The coffee was good, and Maura was filled with a sudden sense of contentment. The pub was as clean as it had been in years, she'd gotten the coffee machine up and running, and she'd made a new customer happy. She'd even done her good deed for the day by passing on Denis Flaherty's letter to the gardaí in Skibbereen.

After darkness had fallen, Jimmy breezed in again, flaunting his cast. "Ah, I see you've got my toy to work. Good on you! I could see the possibilities in it from the start."

"You're going for the female crowd, are you?" Maura asked. "Or do you intend to wean the men from their pint?"

"We're covering all the bases, we are. Besides, it's paid for and all." He turned to check out the crowd, which to Maura's eye looked larger than it had the previous night. "Ah, Seamus, there you are . . ." Jimmy headed toward a man in the corner. Maura and Rose exchanged a glance.

"Is he planning to do anything more than

hang out with his friends?" Maura asked, nodding toward Jimmy.

"I've no clue. He usually comes and goes as he pleases. But with you here now we've got plenty of staffing, right? At least until the summer season."

Maura pulled a couple of pints, wondering just what busy might look like in summer. She knew that the current night-time crowd wasn't exactly the norm, because of the murders, but no one should count on that to continue. She realized how ignorant she was about Irish regulations for pubs. Was it all right if people brought their children in? And she also considered the issue she had run into tending bar in Boston: did they have any liability if they sent someone out of here drunk and he caused an accident? She wondered if Jimmy would have answers to any of these questions; Mick seemed more likely to know.

Whoa, Maura — aren't you getting a little overinvolved here? It wasn't her problem if Rose was underage or if Jimmy was skimming from the register. If she was just helping out for a while, what did it matter to her what the rules were? She was in no hurry to leave, but she hadn't decided how long she wanted to stay. She topped off the waiting pints and pushed them across the bar, collecting the money handed her. Then she turned to Rose.

"Rose, what do you want to do?"

"What do you mean?"

"Do you see yourself here behind the bar, pouring drinks, forever?"

"I told you, I've done with school," Rose protested. "It's a decent enough living here. Da and me, we need the money, not that the pay's good, but it's something coming in."

"Isn't there anything else that interests you? Like living somewhere else, maybe in a bigger town, a city? Or aren't there courses you could take, to learn some kind of skills?"

"What're you getting at, Maura? I don't have a lot of training, and jobs are hard to come by. Besides, who'd look after Da?"

Maura felt frustrated. She wanted more for Rose. She wanted Rose to want more. *But, Maura, be honest with yourself: are you thinking about Rose or about your own life?* Maybe Rose was happy doing what she was doing; and maybe it was Maura who was chafing at the narrowness of her life. Sure, she'd never figured out a so-called career path for herself, and none of her high school counselors had pushed her to try harder. She'd taken some classes on her own, after high school, just to fill in the afternoons during those stretches when she was working nights. But nothing in her had caught fire. And there was no boy or man past or present she'd ever met who she could imagine settling down with. She'd seen enough of her high school classmates make that mistake and end up divorced at twenty-two with a couple of little kids. Not for her.

So how was she so different from Rose? She'd had more options available, but she hadn't done much with them. Instead, she'd usually found herself working in one bar or restaurant or another and coming home to Gran. They'd needed the money, just like Rose and Jimmy did. Funny thing: the bills kept coming, whether you were following your dream or just marking time.

Maura my girl, you'd better clean up your own act before you start telling Rose what to do.

What would happen to Rose and Jimmy, and even Mick, if the pub closed? Where would they go? And when would they know what was going to happen? Old Mick had been dead and buried for, what, two weeks now? She scanned the room again: everyone seemed comfortable and content. There was a low hum of conversation, the sound of the television over the bar blending in. Everything at Sullivan's was probably as it had been for decades, yet it could disappear with a single phone call from a lawyer, once they'd found either a will or a next of kin.

Rose left to see to supper at home. Shortly after that Mick came in the front door, shutting it quickly to keep out the cool night air. Smoke from the peat fire swirled briefly through the room. Mick made his way through the small crowd, stopping to say something to Old Billy, greeting a few other patrons, exchanging words with Jimmy, who looked comfortably settled with some friends in a corner. Then he made his way to the bar and leaned against it, keeping an eye on the room.

"Evenin', Maura. You're looking somber. Was it visiting your grandfather that got you down?"

"No, or at least, not altogether. Why, is my expression scaring away customers?" She debated whether to tell Mick about her encounter with the Brown Car Guy again. One the one hand, it was her business and she should take care of it on her own; on the other hand, the guy might decide to come after her here at the pub, which would make it Mick's business. "Look, Mick, I have to tell you . . ."

He turned his back on the customers to face her and cocked his head at her. "What?

As Grannie would say, trouble shared is trouble halved."

"I don't think you want half of it." She hesitated, then plunged ahead. "I saw the guy in the brown car again, the one who ran me off the road, up at the cemetery."

"Did he try to harm you again?"

"No, but he told me to go home, more or less. Then he left. But I got part of his license plate, and I took it to the gardaí in Skibbereen. Not that I expect much to come of it."

"They've a lot on their plates at the moment, what with that murder and the fellow in the bog. Did they offer you any hope of catching the man who's been bothering you?"

"Not really. The whole thing is so stupid — what could I have done to set him off?"

"Who's to say, but maybe I should be walking you home for a bit."

"Oh, come on — it's just across the street." Maura wasn't sure how she felt about that, but she had to admit that she was trying hard not to think about someone who might want to do her harm.. And she wasn't about to play the helpless female part. She sighed.

"Penny?" Mick asked.

"What?"

"Penny for your thoughts," he said.

"Oh, sorry, it's just so different here from what I grew up with. Do you get the TV show *Cheers* here?"

"We have done, now and then. Why?"

"Well, in the theme song there's a line about going to a place 'where everybody knows your name, and they're always glad you came.' But most of the bars I've worked in around Boston weren't like that."

"And?"

"And this place *is* sort of like that, or at least a whole lot closer to it. Is it typical? Or is this some kind of never-never land?"

"I'd say it's typical of its kind in a small town. Dublin, now, they cater to tourists, at least in the center, so maybe the cheer is false. But here? Going down the pub of an evening is tradition; it's just a place for friends to get together, have a quick pint, and talk for a bit. You might have noticed there's not much else social to do here."

"I guess. Maybe I grew up around a big city, but what I did with my time was kind of like what Rose is doing now, except I didn't know everybody who walked in the door."

"Were you not happy there?"

"I never thought about it, really. I wasn't college material, even if I could have afforded it, and then there was Gran. She was the only family I ever knew, and I didn't want to leave her on her own."

"Then it's not so different, is it?"

"I guess not." Maura wondered why she felt sorry for Rose, thinking she was trapped in a dead-end life. Much as she hated to admit it, she was in the same boat, and while she was maybe ten years older than Rose, she still didn't think she had any answers, and clearly she had no idea what she was going to be doing in another week or month, much less a year. What would make her happy? Right now she didn't know.

CHAPTER 24

Another good night for Sullivan's, Maura thought as she walked out of the pub. Mick watched her leave but made no move to follow her. After almost a week, she didn't feel like the new kid anymore. Actually she was pleased: it meant that she was doing her job well, doling out pints quickly and correctly, with no fuss. Part of the furniture. She was fine with that.

The night was misty, the air a bit raw. She darted across the wide street and crunched her way down the gravel drive to the back entrance to her room. The rear of the house, the side toward the harbor, was unlit, but her eyes had adjusted to the dark by the time she reached it. She had her key in her hand, ready, but when she stuck it into the lock on the glass doors, the door panel slid under her hand. She knew she had locked it when she'd left that morning; it was a habit drummed into her over many years. She slid it open fully and stepped into her room.

And stopped, senses alert. There was someone in the room. She couldn't make out much, other than that he was male, dressed in dark clothing, and huddled in the farthest corner, his back against the door that led to the rest of the house. Her choices: back out and run like hell to . . . where? Scream her head off and hope the Keohanes upstairs woke up before the guy killed her? Neither seemed useful, so she decided to push back.

Odds were it was Brown Car Guy — again. "What do you want?" she demanded. "If it's money, I don't have any, or anything worth taking. And if you're the jerk who's been following me, I've told the police all about it, and they're looking for you."

The man didn't answer, but he finally made his move, lunging straight at her. But she'd anticipated it, and instead of retreating backward as no doubt he had expected, she feinted to the side, ducking under the weapon he was swinging. Stick, pipe? It was too dark to tell, but whatever it was, Maura was sure it could do some damage if it connected.

He turned quickly, but Maura had jumped over the bed and down on the other side, nearer the door. Her defensive options hadn't improved much: she could throw a blanket over him, slam him with a pillow . . . or there was the lamp, an inexpensive china thing. As the attacker came at her again, Maura grabbed up the lamp and walloped him on the side of the head with it. The flimsy lamp base made a satisfying crash, shards of china flying. Her attacker cursed, stumbling backward and fell out the glass door, which Maura had left open.

The noise had finally wakened the household, and Maura heard the thud of heavy feet above her. Outside she saw a bobbing light — a flashlight? The man on the ground clearly saw it too, and he leapt up and disappeared, running away from the house toward the lane that ran along the harbor. Thanks to his dark clothes, he disappeared quickly into the night, as the bearer of the flashlight came around the corner and peered into the room.

"Maura? You all right?"

"Sean?" Maura said incredulously. "What the hell are you doing here? Aren't you going after him?"

Even as she spoke, she could hear the sound of a car starting up on the road above, its engine loud and rough.

"He's gone," Sean said. "Could we get some light here?"

Maura looked at the remains of the lamp in her hand and started to laugh. "I think I just killed the lamp. Come on in — there's a switch by the door, at least." Even as she moved toward the door to the hall, it flew open to show Tom Keohane, a heavy wrench in his hand, followed closely by his wife in a droopy robe. Ellen found the light switch quickly.

"What in the name of all that's holy is going on here?" Even in her chenille bathrobe Ellen bristled as she peered around her husband's broad back. "Sean Murphy, what are you doing here in the middle of the night?"

"I've only just arrived, ma'am. I was doing last rounds after closing time and heard sounds of a scuffle down here. I was just about to ask Maura here what had happened. It seems someone broke in."

"He was waiting for me when I came in," Maura said tersely.

"Did you get a look at him?" Sean asked.

"Not his face. It was dark." Maura looked at the remains of the lamp in her hand, then tossed it onto the bed. "Sorry about the lamp."

A sleepy Kevin appeared behind his parents, rubbing his eyes. Ellen turned and told him, "Back to bed with you — now!" and

Kevin disappeared quickly. Ellen pushed past her husband. "Don't worry yourself about it. Did he harm you?"

"He never touched me. I think he was kind of surprised when I hit him."

"Good on you! Thomas, will you see to the door there? Maura, Sean, come up and I'll fix you both a nice cup of tea."

"Ma'am, I need to ask . . ." Sean began.

"Of course you do, but you can do it just as well upstairs. Come on, then."

Sean and Maura exchanged a look and followed. When they arrived in the kitchen, Ellen had already set the kettle to boil.

"Sit, the two of you," Ellen commanded.

"Won't we wake your children?" Maura asked.

"Ah, they'd sleep through the end of the world. Kevin only noticed because he was next door. The others'll be right mad that they missed all the fun."

Sean pulled a small notebook out of his pocket and sent Ellen a warning glance. She smiled and busied herself with making tea. "Will you tell me now what happened, Maura?"

"I left Sullivan's at closing time. I crossed the road, but I didn't see any cars or anyone moving. I walked down the driveway and came around the back, like I always do.

300

When I went to open the door, I realized it was already unlocked, and when I opened it, I could see someone lurking inside by the other door."

"And you didn't run?" Sean said, incredulous.

"And go where, out there in the dark? I'd probably just trip over something and he'd catch up with me. And there was no time to wake the Keohanes."

"Good point. Description?" Sean said in an official voice. "Or would this be your mate with the brown car again?"

"I couldn't see much, but it's likely, isn't it? Male, maybe an inch or two taller than me, dressed all in black or some other dark color. Come to think of it, I bet he had gloves on, because I didn't notice his hands at all. He had some kind of bat or pipe or something, and he came at me. I ducked and got around back of him, and when he tried again — that's when I used the lamp on his head."

"Hard enough to leave a mark, do you think?" Sean said, making a note.

"At least a good lump. But the lamp shattered, so he might be bleeding. Then he fell out the door."

"Anything missing from your room?"

"I haven't had time to check, but I don't

have anything worth much. I carry my passport and cash in my bag, which I keep with me. Although right now I think it's on the floor downstairs."

"Mrs. Keohane, any trouble in the neighborhood lately?"

"Of course not, Sean. Most of us have little to tempt a thief — there are better pickings elsewhere, maybe over in Glandore. Unless it was just mischief, but why would he be in Maura's room, then?" She filled three mugs with dark tea and handed them around.

After Ellen had sat down, she and Sean turned to look at Maura. "What?" Maura demanded. "I don't know what's going on, Sean, but this makes three times the guy's gone after me, assuming it's the same man." When Ellen looked confused, Maura added, "I'll fill you in later, Ellen, but it makes me think that this has nothing to do with you or with the neighborhood."

Ellen's husband, Tom, stomped up the back stairs and joined them in the kitchen. "Door's fine — I put in a bar to keep it shut. I'll be going back to bed." He lumbered down the hall.

"So, what now?" Maura demanded. "Do you call in crime scene people, take fingerprints and all that?"

302

Sean's mouth twitched in a half smile. "We call them out only for the serious crimes. I don't mean to belittle what happened here, but it doesn't qualify."

Maura stood up abruptly and paced around the kitchen. She felt wired and shaky — too much adrenaline? "So you're not going to do *anything*?"

"I didn't mean that. Of course I'll report this at the station, and we'll look to see if it's happened to anyone else around. But we have little to work with, especially if he was wearing gloves, Maura. I wish I could be of more use to you. It's good you were alert enough to escape any serious harm."

"Yeah, right, thanks a lot. If I hadn't, maybe you'd be investigating another killing. I bet you're all jumping for joy now that you're all learning how to handle murders." Sean looked stricken, and Maura immediately took a deep breath and apologized. "Sorry. I know you're doing what you can. But I'd just like to know why anybody would want to do me harm. I haven't done anything to anybody. I've never even been here before. I show up, and suddenly there's a crime wave?"

Sean was staring at a point somewhere over Maura's head, thinking.

"Hello, Mr. Policeman?"

He brought his attention back to Maura. "Sorry, I was trying to see a pattern here. You're right — this all seems to have started when you arrived, a week ago. The old body in the bog, the mugging in Skibbereen, your car accident, the guy threatening you in the cemetery, and now this."

Ellen looked shocked. "It's never been like this! Sean, what's your lot doing about it?"

"Investigating as best we can. We're a small department, but bringing in people from the outside wouldn't be much use, now, would it, when there's little more than a partial license plate to go on, and we're working on that? Sorry, Maura. Will you be all right here?"

Where else would she go at three o'clock in the morning? Maura wondered. "I'll get by. I don't think he'd dare come back tonight."

"You're welcome to the divan in the parlor, Maura," Ellen said anxiously.

"Maybe I'll take you up on that, Ellen," Maura said.

Sean looked relieved. "I'll report all this to Detective Hurley in the morning. I'll let you know what he has to say."

"Thank you, I guess. I sure don't have any better ideas," Maura said.

Ellen stood up. "I'll see you out, Sean,

and lock up behind you." They left together.

Maura sat without moving, cradling the cooling cup of tea. She could see no logic in what had happened to her over the past week.

She wanted to go to sleep but wondered if she'd be able to face spending the night in her room. Still, surely the Keohane kids would be up and about early on a Monday, and she doubted she could sleep through that from the couch. Downstairs it was, then — but maybe she should find a sturdy club to keep under her pillow. She stood up slowly and met Ellen coming back down the hall.

"I'm running on empty, Ellen. I'm going to go to bed."

"You're sure, then?" Ellen asked, searching her face. "You don't want the divan?"

"I am. Don't worry — I'll be fine. Maybe by tomorrow the gardaí will have caught whoever is behind this." Maura wasn't sure she believed that, since the sole evidence seemed to be a partial license plate, but she could hope, couldn't she?

"God bless you, aren't you the brave one! But I'm sure my Tom will sleep with one ear out, in case there's any more trouble. Good night, then."

"Good night, Ellen." Maura went back

downstairs, guided by the overhead light that had been left on. In her room she surveyed the damage: minimal. Thomas had removed all the shards of the lamp. Otherwise, everything looked the same as always. Maura lay down on the bed, and then she was out.

CHAPTER 25

It seemed only minutes later than Maura
was awakened by an insistent rapping at her
door. "Maura, are you in there? Maura?"
Ellen's voice. Maura looked at her watch
and was amazed to see that it was after nine.

Since she'd fallen asleep fully dressed, she
rolled to the edge of the bed, stood up, and
went to open the door. "Ellen? What's up?"

"You've visitors to see you, that's what,"
Ellen said in a near whisper.

"Who?"

"Sean Murphy from last night, and he's
brought along his boss, Detective Hurley.
They're waiting in the lounge. Will you be
wanting breakfast?"

Good grief — Sean had said he'd talk to
her in the morning, but why so early? "Sure,
fine. Do I have time to wash up?"

"I'll keep them entertained. You take your
time." Ellen closed the door quietly, and
Maura grabbed some clean clothes and

dashed for the bathroom.

She emerged in record time and roughly toweled her hair dry, then dressed and headed up the stairs. The two men stood politely when she came in. "Sit down, please," Maura said.

Ellen appeared with a tray bearing empty cups and plates. "Let the poor girl have her breakfast, will you? There's nothing that won't keep that long." She left again, and Maura could hear Gráinne whining from the kitchen.

"Have you found the guy with the car?" Maura asked.

It was Detective Hurley who answered. "No, but we've traced that partial plate you gave us, and there's only one local vehicle that fits the description. It belongs to a Denis McCarthy, over in Clogagh."

Despite a lack of caffeine, Maura came to attention. "McCarthy? Related to Australian Denis Flaherty?"

Patrick Hurley smiled. "I wouldn't jump so fast to that conclusion — there are plenty of McCarthys in this county. But it could be more than a coincidence. Families tend to stick to the old naming patterns around here."

"I've noticed," Maura said. Every other man in the pub seemed to be called Patrick

308

or Michael or Sean. "Where the heck is this Clogagh?"

"Not far."

Ellen reappeared, this time bearing a carafe, a teapot, and plates of scones and toast. "Here we go. There's butter and jam in those pots there. I'll go see to Gráinne, if you don't mind." She vanished again, leaving Maura and the two men staring at the trays of food and drink.

Maura broke the silence first. "I need coffee. How about you two?" The men nodded, so Maura filled three cups, then helped herself to a scone and jam. "So," she said through the crumbs, "why'd it take two of you to come and tell me about this?"

"I'd like you to accompany us to see if you recognize anyone," Detective Hurley said.

"Where? This Clogagh place?"

He nodded. "Yes. This particular Denis McCarthy is an older man, which doesn't fit your description of your attacker, but I understand from the local guards that his grandson has been living with him, helping him look after the dairy farm. His name's Jerry. He's twenty-five — close to your age — and until recently he's been living in Dublin with his father. I guess he got into a bit of trouble up there, so his father sent him down here to do some honest work on his grandfather's farm. He might be a more likely lad for this harassment."

"Why would these McCarthys be bothering me?" Maura asked. "They're not even from around here, are they?"

"It's no more than twenty miles, and that's a question we'd be better able to answer there. If you don't mind the ride?"

"Of course I don't, if you think it'll help. But will this be risky? I mean, would they know that you're interested in them? Considering them suspects?"

"It seems unlikely."

"Huh," Maura said, reflecting. "So we're supposed to just walk in and have a chat with whoever's home, right? No flashing lights, no police, er, gardaí wearing bulletproof vests with guns drawn?"

"It hasn't come to that yet in Ireland." Detective Hurley smiled. Maura could have sworn that he was trying hard not to laugh. He nodded at Sean Murphy, who said crisply, "Uniformed officers in the Garda Síochána do not carry firearms, although plain clothed detectives may. Furthermore, we may search an individual whom we have arrested without a warrant and seize goods so obtained as necessary or to support the charge. Although in most cases a warrant

310

should be obtained for any search of a person, a vehicle, or a premises. Right, sir?" He glanced eagerly at Detective Hurley.

"Just fine, Murphy. But in any case, Maura, this is not an official search. We only want to ask some questions with regard to the harassment you've been subjected to. If it's any comfort to you, we may make an arrest without a warrant if we suspect that an arrestable offense has been committed and have reason to believe the person is guilty of that offense. And we may search without an arrest warrant any residence where we believe a suspect to be. Of course, the easiest course is if the owner gives permission."

Maura reached for another scone. "Okay, I get it. We're just going to talk to one of the many, many McCarthys around here, who may or may not have anything to do with what's been happening to me this week, or even with the dead guy in the bog. And you're hoping that whoever answers the door will be happy to let you in and chat?"

"Precisely. Are you willing?"

"Why not? Let me tell Ellen we're going." She grabbed up her cup and plate and went to the kitchen in search of Ellen. She left the kitchen and found the two men stand-

311

ing in the front hall waiting for her. "Do I need to drive?"

"No. We brought the two cars, in the event of an arrest," Detective Hurley answered. "You can ride with me."

That statement sobered Maura quickly. It seemed to her that they had hardly enough information to even think about an arrest, but she guessed she would find out soon enough. She followed the men up the driveway, where the detective guided her to his unmarked car, then held the door for her.

Once they were on the main road, Maura asked, "How far is the place?"

"Clogagh? As I said, twenty miles, more or less, mostly by the main road. It should take less than an hour. Have you seen much of the country around here?"

Maura laughed shortly. "Only what I could see from the bus between Dublin and Leap, and the local roads around here to Skibbereen, Cork, and Drinagh, and a couple of townlands. That's about it."

"Pity. There's much that's lovely. Though this must seem dull to you — we're mainly farms and open land."

"We do have scenery back home too, you know, and it's pretty. But I grew up in the city."

"Of course." Several miles passed in silence. She checked to see the other car, driven by Sean Murphy, trailing behind them.

Then she said, "I don't know much about Irish law. If this grandson Whatever-His-Name-Is turns out to be the guy who's been following me around, what's he looking at? I mean, what can you charge him with, and what would be the penalties?"

"Do you want the long speech or the short one?"

"Whatever there's time for."

"Our crime rate here is very low, certainly compared to your country, and that's something we're proud of. So when something like this string of incidents happens, particularly to a visitor, we're not going to send the fellow on his way with a slap on the hand. Assuming this is the same man, he's committed quite the list of crimes. There's assault with intent to do harm — that's the event with your car. Endangerment. Dangerous driving. Harassment. Forcible entry, although we don't know that he had any intention of stealing anything. Those are what we call headline offenses here."

"And would that mean he'd go to jail?"

"Most likely. I don't know much about your justice system in America, but if this is our lad, he's committed more than one crime, and he has to face the consequences."

"Amen," Maura said. But still, she felt torn. On the one hand, Jerry McCarthy, if he was the right guy, had threatened her more than once, and she wanted him to pay for that. On the other hand, she was the outsider here, and she didn't want to seem vindictive. What she wanted most was to understand why he was trying so hard to drive her away. If there was so little crime around here, then he must have had an important reason to come after her.

They said little more for the rest of the trip. Maura read road signs, trying to figure out what was where. Past Clonakilty the main road veered north, inland. After another five miles or so, Detective Hurley turned onto a smaller road that led east, running straight for two miles or so. Maura watched the scenery unroll, wondering what they were going to find ahead.

They turned, crossed a small bridge, then turned again, the lanes growing ever narrower. Then Hurley pulled into a muddy, rutted drive and stopped. He turned to her. "This is it."

Maura looked around her. They had parked in the open area that lay between a house and a cattle barn — or what she assumed was a cattle barn, based on the wisps of hay and clumps of manure she could see. This was not a picturesque slice of scenic Ireland: it was a relatively modern dairy farm. The house, like so many she'd seen, could be fifty or a hundred years old, and the barn was corrugated aluminum. Sean Murphy's car pulled in behind theirs.

Maura had to ask, "How the heck do you guys ever find any place around here? There are no road signs, no house numbers. Does GPS even work, in a place where the roads don't have names?"

"This is the right place," Detective Hurley said.

"What happens now?" she said.

"I'll need a word with Murphy."

Maura waited while he conferred with Sean and then sent him around to the other side of the property. Hurley and Maura waited together until Sean returned.

"Brown car behind the barn, sir. Plate matches."

"Come on, both of you." Hurley gestured toward the barn. Maura followed reluctantly, wrinkling her nose at the pungent smell of manure. When they reached the corner, she peered around and saw a dirty brown car.

"Is that the car?"

"Yeah, that's it. There's the cracked head-light, and a fresh-looking dent on the front fender."

"Then we'll go have a word with Denis and Jerry McCarthy. You come along and tell me if you recognize young Jerry. If he's not here, we'll talk to his grandfather, see what he can tell us. I'll go first — there's always the chance he might be unwilling to let us in."

"Fine." Maura realized her heart was pounding. She hung back behind Detective Hurley as he rapped on the door, then rapped again. He listened for a moment and then relaxed. It took another half a minute for Maura to hear the sound of shuffling footsteps approaching. Finally the door opened.

The man who faced them was old, very old. He had probably been tall once but had shrunken into himself and was now thin and wiry, like his skin had shrunken to his bones. His face was beyond wrinkled: it was folded into lines worn deep by decades of use. His white hair wisped around his half-bald head. But, Maura noted, his eyes were sharp and knowing. He looked up at the detective and nodded to himself, then looked beyond him, taking in the uniformed garda behind. And then his gaze shifted to

316

Maura, and she would have sworn she saw a flicker of surprise.

Finally his eyes swung back to Hurley. "Gardaí, eh? I've been expecting you."

Hurley spoke. "Denis McCarthy?" The old man nodded again. "We'd like to have a word with you, if you don't mind." His tone was polite, even respectful. Denis McCarthy said nothing more but stepped back into his hallway to let Hurley pass, followed by Maura and then Sean. They found themselves in a long, narrow hall, with doors on either side.

"Straight on to the back," Denis said. Like dutiful children they filed down the hall, Denis making his slow way after them. Despite the tension, or maybe because of it, Maura found herself noting odd details. They passed a kitchen on the right, littered with dirty dishes, pots, and cans; it stank of long neglect. On the left, a dining room with a large table, strewn with papers, clothes, and odd pieces of greasy machinery. At the end of the hall they came to the formal sitting room. Maura wondered idly where the bedrooms were — behind, above? The room was filled with unmatched overstuffed furniture, faded and worn, and several generations of gewgaws — all in serious need of dusting. Clearly the McCarthys had

317

not enjoyed the benefit of a woman's presence for a long time.

"Sit, will yeh?" McCarthy Senior had finally entered the room, and gestured vaguely around. One of the chairs clearly belonged to Denis, and he crossed the room and sank into it with a small sigh of relief, settling into the contours worn by years of use. Hurley waited for Maura to perch gingerly on a dusty straight-backed chair, then took the mate of the upholstered chair close to Denis. Sean remained standing at the door to the hallway.

When they were settled, Hurley began, "Mr. McCarthy, I'm Detective Chief Superintendent Hurley, of the Skibbereen Gardaí. This is my colleague, Officer Murphy. We'd like to have a word with your grandson, Jerry. Is he here?"

Maura could have sworn that the question surprised Denis McCarthy. Was he expecting something else?

"He's out seein' to the cows. In the barn."

Hurley looked at Sean. "Murphy, would you go round him up?" Sean disappeared back down the hall.

"You and your grandson live here alone?" Hurley continued.

"Yes."

"And you have a car?"

"I do — it's out back, behind the barn."

"Does Jerry use the car?"

"He does. What're you after?"

"Mr. McCarthy, I have reason to believe that your grandson has been harassing this woman." He gestured toward Maura. "Her name is Maura Donovan, and she's an American visitor. Do you have any idea why your grandson might threaten her?"

"And why would he be doin' that?"

"That's what we'd like to ask him."

Maura heard the front door open again, followed by the sound of heavy boots approaching. She looked at the doorway to see a young man, none too clean, his arm in the firm grip of Officer Murphy. Around Jerry's neck dangled an incongruously modern iPod, which explained why he hadn't heard them arrive. The odor of manure wafted into the stuffy room.

Hurley stood. "Jerry McCarthy?"

The young man gave him a sullen glare, then nodded. "Yeah."

Hurley looked to Maura. "Maura?" he prompted.

Maura wrestled between confusion and disappointment: the young man looked vaguely familiar, but he was not the one she'd come face-to-face with in Drinagh, and she was pretty sure that if he'd been on the receiving end of her lamp the night before, it would show. "Detective, this is not the man I saw in the cemetery."

"You're sure?" Hurley held her glance a moment, his eyes questioning, then turned back to Murphy and his charge. "Jerry, sit down. We have some questions for you, about the car."

Jerry's eyes darted to his grandfather, then he pulled a chair from against the wall, dragged it next to his grandfather's chair, and sat. The two exchanged a wary glance, and Maura wondered what they were worried about. "So?"

Hurley resumed his former seat. "Where were you last night?"

"Out. Round at the pub."

"Which one?"

"Stopped in at a couple of places."

"And would one of those have been in Leap?"

"No."

"What time did you return home, Jerry?"

Again, the furtive exchange of glances with the old man. "Late, after the pubs closed."

Hurley turned to the older man. "Mr. McCarthy, do you know when your grandson returned?"

He shook his head. "Nah. Me hearin's not

320

what it once was, and I sleep sound."

Detective Hurley lapsed into silence, and Maura wondered just what else he could ask. She had recognized the car but not Jerry McCarthy. Who else might have used the car? It couldn't have been Denis McCarthy — no way the person she had seen was this old man.

The elder McCarthy finally said slowly, "I hear there's been a bit of a ruckus over to Leap — they've found a body? One that had been there fer a while?"

The detective said, "Yes, sir, in a bog near Knockskagh. Why do you ask?"

The old man sighed and seemed to deflate, settling deeper into his chair like a turtle into its shell. "I might know something about that. I've been expectin' you at my door before, as I always knew it would come out. The body — I'm thinkin' that would be me uncle Denis, my mother's brother."

CHAPTER 26

A thick silence fell. *I was right,* Maura cheered silently. The Bog Man *was* a Mc-Carthy, and the odds were looking good that he was the missing uncle. She looked triumphantly at Patrick Hurley, who responded with a smile and a small nod.

Detective Hurley turned again to Denis McCarthy. "Do you know how he came to die?"

He nodded. "I do. My father killed him."

Maura was startled when young Jerry jumped up from his chair. "Grandda! Don't tell 'em nothin'."

His grandfather regarded him gravely, and for a moment Maura saw a flash of his authority. "Jer, give over. It's goin' ta come out anywise. And it's right that it should." He squared his shoulders and faced Hurley.

Hurley nodded once. "Can you tell us about it, sir?"

"I will. But it may take a bit. Can I give

you some tea, or something stronger?"

"Thank you, but there's no need."

"I think I need something. Jerry?"

An exchange of glances ensued: Denis looked at Hurley with a hint of challenge in his watery eyes, Jerry still glared at his grandfather, Sean appealed mutely to Hurley for guidance, and Hurley glanced at Maura and considered. Finally he said, "Murphy, why don't you take Jerry to the kitchen to make the tea? He won't be going anywhere. I'm sure it's in his best interest to have us hear what his grandfather has to say."

"Right, sir," Murphy responded promptly, and he and Jerry clomped down the uncarpeted hall toward the kitchen.

Hurley and Denis eyed each other appraisingly, as if sharing some unspoken dialogue. Denis spoke first. "The girl here — you say she's from America?"

Maura answered him. "Yes. I'm Maura Donovan, from Boston," she said clearly.

"Mmh." He lapsed into silence, and Hurley did not press him. *Maybe the rules of interrogation are different in Ireland,* Maura thought. *Or maybe everything is just slower here.* After a few minutes, she could hear the other men coming down the hall, the clink of china. Jerry emerged from the hallway carrying a battered metal tray laden with mismatched mugs, a teapot, glasses — and a half-full bottle of whiskey. At the sight of the bottle, Maura almost giggled: this was definitely not the way things were done back home. Jerry thumped the tray down on a wobbly table, china rattling.

"Here's your tea, then." He sat again and retreated to his sulk, under the watchful eye of Sean Murphy. All other eyes turned to the old man.

Until another man appeared in the doorway, a twenty-something man who looked the worse for wear. Apparently he hadn't expected to find a roomful of people: he was wearing only a grimy singlet and briefs, and he sported a clumsy bloodstained bandage taped to his forehead. Mid-twenties, small and weaselly — and given that he was in his underwear, couldn't be hiding a weapon. "Wha . . . ?"

Maura stood without thinking, staring at the newcomer. "Detective, *that's* the man from the cemetery!"

If it had not been for the guy's threatening glance and the startled reaction from the others in the room, Maura might have enjoyed the scene. Jerry had jumped out of his chair as well and backed away; he looked scared. Officer Murphy had come to attention and slid over to block the door to the front, so no one could leave that way. Patrick Hurley was out of his chair fast, turning to face the latecomer. Maura began to retreat, not that anyone noticed. The latecomer scanned the group in front of him and took their measure quickly — he was no stranger to the gardaí, Maura guessed. How would he play it? Bluff? Cut and run? Or attack?

For a long moment everyone stood frozen, but then, having figured out his odds weren't good, the young man turned to flee the way he had come, and Hurley moved quickly to intercept him. Unfortunately the younger man knew how to fight, and he reacted equally quickly. If the detective had hoped for an easy grab, he was disappointed, and found himself wrestling the man around the room, at the expense of the knickknacks. Old Denis McCarthy had shrunk back into his chair. Maura pressed herself against a wall, trying to keep out of the way; poor Sean Murphy was torn between keeping track of Jerry and joining the fray. But before Sean could make up his mind, Detective Hurley subdued the man, twisting his arm behind him.

"Murphy! You have handcuffs?" Hurley barked.

"Yes, sir!" Sean disentangled them from his belt and clapped them on the man, then stood eagerly awaiting his next instructions.

"Sit him down there, and keep an eye on him," Hurley ordered. Sean complied, pushing the man down into the chair Maura had vacated and keeping one broad hand on his shoulder.

"Jerry, stay where you are." Hurley remained standing. "All right, you. What's your name?"

The newcomer glared at him and said nothing. Hurley turned to Denis McCarthy. "You know this man?"

Denis looked briefly at his cowering grandson. "He's a mate of Jerry's — he's been stayin' here. Name's Danny Mullan, from Dublin."

"Shut up, old man," Danny spit out.

Denis seemed to swell. "This is my home you've dirtied, and I'll say what I want!"

Danny's bandage had slipped off, revealing a bruised lump around a scabbed gash. "Nasty bump on your head there," Detective Hurley said. "Mind telling me where you got it?"

"You chargin' me with something? I ain't sayin' nothing."

The detective glanced at Maura. "Your work?"

Maura nodded from the safety of her corner. "Probably. I know I hit him on the head, on that side."

He turned back to Danny. "All right, then. Let's begin with assault with intent to do bodily harm. Mr. Mullan, you are not obliged to say anything unless you wish to do so, but whatever you say will be taken down in writing and may be given in evidence."

Maura wondered irreverently who in the room would have a free hand to write down anything.

Danny's only response was a dour glare. Hurley looked at Sean, who was almost panting with eagerness. "Murphy, think you can get him back to Skibbereen?"

"Yes, sir! What about the other one?" He nodded toward Jerry, cowering behind his grandfather's chair.

"No, just that one — Mullan. I want to talk to Jerry here. You start the paperwork on Mullan, and I'll be along directly, after I've sorted this."

Sean hauled Danny out of the chair, with somewhat more force than necessary.

"He might need some trousers," Detective Hurley noted with a hint of amusement. He turned back to Denis. "Mr. McCarthy, as it's your house, will you give me permission

327

to search the room this man's been using?"

Denis McCarthy nodded. "Gladly. It's up the stair, first on the right."

"Murphy, wait here." Hurley went back to the hall, and soon Maura could hear footsteps overhead. He returned a minute or two later with a pair of grimy jeans over his arm and a pair of shoes in one hand — and a battered leather wallet in the other.

Hurley tossed the jeans toward Danny. "Here."

He waited until Danny had struggled into the jeans, hampered by the handcuffs, then asked neutrally, "Is this yours, Mr. Mullan?" He held up the wallet, protected by a handkerchief. Danny Mullan didn't answer. "I'd guess not, since the cards inside carry the name of Bartholomew Hayes, who was found dead in Skibbereen a few days ago, following a mugging. Have you anything to say about that?"

Sean Murphy's hand tightened on Danny Mullan's shoulder. Jerry was watching Danny with a mixture of fear and hostility. Jerry didn't look like he could hurt a rabbit, but he had to know by now — if he hadn't already known — what his mate Danny had done.

Maura saw the flicker of alarm in Danny's eyes before the shutter dropped again.

"Who?"

"You're not that stupid. The dead man in Skibbereen."

Danny avoided the detective's eyes. "Found the wallet in the street."

"Did you now? Where were you last Thursday night?"

"With my mate Jerry. We might have gone for a pint or two."

Suddenly Maura realized why Jerry had looked familiar to her. "Wait!" Maura interrupted. "You were in Sullivan's in Leap, when Bart Hayes came in. You and Jerry both, sitting in the corner. Sorry, Detective, but I didn't think of it before — that was only my second night at the pub, and there were a lot of people coming and going. But now that I see him up close, I recognize both of them."

Danny glared at her, and Jerry somehow managed to look even more scared, with a dash of guilty thrown in. Maura could envision Danny going after Bart Hayes, and she could even see him bullying Jerry into keeping quiet, but she had trouble seeing Jerry as anything but a follower. Danny had to have been behind whatever had happened, to Bart Hayes and to her.

Hurley nodded at Sean. "You take Mullan along now, and we'll sort it out at the station. I want to talk to the McCarthys here, but I won't be long."

"Right so. You, let's go." Sean Murphy all but dragged Danny Mullan out the door.

Detective Hurley sat down in the chair next to Denis's. "Not a welcome guest, I take it?"

"Pah!" the old man spat out. "If I was twenty years younger, I would have pushed him out the door when he first showed his face."

"And that was . . . ?"

"Two week gone?" He turned to his cowering grandson. "Eh, Jerry, he's *your* mate. Sit you down and tell the garda what you know."

Reluctantly Jerry sidled into the circle and sat. "He's no friend of mine, Grandda."

Denis gave him a long look, then turned to Hurley. "The boy's an eejit, but he's not all bad. That Danny, he's led him astray."

"Let's start with that young man," Hurley said. "He's not from Cork?"

"Nah," the old man said contemptuously. "Jerry here — he's me son John's boy. John didn't want to have nothin' to do with the farm, took himself off to Dublin when he left school and stayed on, even after he married. But Jerry fell in with the wrong crowd there, so John sent him back here to help

330

me out with the cows and all, now that I'm gettin' on. He's done a good job, considerin' he couldn't tell one end of the cow from the other when he first came — it's been a year or more now. But then, oh, two, three weeks ago, this Danny fella shows up and makes himself at home."

Hurley turned to Jerry. "You knew him in Dublin?"

Jerry nodded, staring at his knees. "Yah. We used to hang out together."

"What was he doing here? Don't tell me he wanted a nice vacation in the country."

Jerry shook his head, his unwashed hair tumbling over his eyes. "Things got a bit warm for him in Dublin, so he thought it might be good to be somewhere else fer a while, and he remembered that I was out here with me grandda."

"So let me help you out here. Danny arrived and made himself at home. And I'm willing to bet that after the first few days he found the place a bit dull and went looking for some excitement in your grandfather's car. Am I right so far?"

Jerry nodded.

Hurley went on. "Did you always go along with him?"

Jerry shook his head. "Not always."

"What about that night in Skibbereen,

when Bart Hayes died? Were you there?"

Jerry shook his head vehemently. "No ways! He went off on his own that night."

"The two of you were together at Sullivan's," Maura interrupted, "the same time Bart Hayes was there. I saw you. You had only the one car. Did you follow Bart Hayes to Skibbereen?"

The whites of young Jerry's eyes flashed, although he kept his mouth shut.

"Hang on," Maura said more slowly, as bits and pieces came back to her. "The next day — the day they found the body — I went to the garda station, because I wanted to give somebody the letter I found at the pub." Detective Hurley was watching her curiously, and Maura turned to him. "I didn't get to give it to you then because you were all so busy with the murder, but when I was leaving I saw Jerry here lurking in the parking lot near my car. Did you follow me there, Jerry? Were you wondering what I was going to tell the gardaí? That I knew you'd seen Bart Hayes, and I knew you'd left not long after he did?"

Hurley gave her an approving nod, then turned back to Jerry. "So you and Danny ended up in Skibbereen, and you saw a chance to help yourselves to some quick cash?"

"No, it weren't me — Danny did it!" Jerry now looked terrified.

The detective pushed on. "Did he know he'd killed the man?"

"Honest to God, no, sir! I didn't know what he was planning, neither. We split up for a bit in Skibbereen — he said he had something to do, and I didn't ask what. But then he shows up with a pocket full of money, and when we're back here he brags that he'd seen this guy — Hayes, you said? — and he's not too steady on his pins, flashing some bills. So Danny said he followed him and kind of hustled him into the alley and down he went. And that's all I knew, until I heard people talkin'."

Maura wondered just how much of Jerry's story was true. She had no doubt that Danny had done the deed, but would Jerry really have gone off on his own? Would Danny have let him? There was probably no way to prove it.

"Did you see it happen?" Hurley asked.

"I did not," Jerry protested quickly, "and that's God's truth."

Hurley glanced at Maura. "Can you tell me why Danny was threatening this woman, then?"

"He figgered she was the only one could tie us to the dead man. He thought she'd

333

be easy to scare off, so he started giving her a hard time. He took the car." Jerry appealed to Maura, "You saw him, in the car, right? I wasn't there, was I?"

"No," Maura said slowly. "I saw only one man in the car. And only one man at the cemetery."

Jerry turned triumphantly back to Hurley. "There, you see? It was all Danny, like. Not me."

For the first time Maura realized that Denis McCarthy was staring at her. "There's more to the story," he said, "though young Jerry here doesn't know all of it." He looked squarely at Detective Hurley. "But it's a long tale." With a gleam in his eye, he said, "Will you drink with me?" When he hesitated, Denis added, "It's a rare story I have for you, but a dry one."

Hurley cast a quick glance toward Maura, then spoke, "My pleasure, sir." He picked up the whiskey bottle, which had miraculously remained upright through the scuffle, and filled two of the glasses with an inch of the whiskey each, then handed one glass to Denis. He didn't offer any to Jerry or Maura, but she figured there was some obscure ritual going on in front of her.

When they were supplied with drink, Denis took a substantial swallow from his glass before launching into his story. "It's an old story, not a new one. And I'm thinking you'd be a part of it."

He was looking at Maura.

CHAPTER 27

Old Denis returned his gaze to the detective.

"You, sir, have you not put a name to the body that came out of the bog at Killinga?"

"We have, sir. But I'm guessing you know who he was?"

"I do. My father Jeremiah was one of the Carrigeeny McCarthys, and his father was Denis. There were four children in the family: Denis, Jeremiah, and the girls Bridget and Ellen. The farm wasn't much, maybe forty acres, all bits and pieces scattered about, but it had been the home of the McCarthys for as long as anyone could remember, since the days of the old landlords."

Maura sat silently, her eyes intent on Denis's face. She had a feeling that she knew what was coming.

Denis's eyes kept drifting toward Maura, although he spoke to Hurley.

"And then came the Republic, and new laws and new ideas. My family was scraping by, but there was no way that two sons and their families could live off that land, and there were no jobs to be had. And then a bit later the government came round, saying they'd buy them out, get us a better place, keep the payments low and all. But it wouldn't be in Carrigeeny."

He stopped to take another drink from his glass.

"Problem was, Denis — he was the oldest — didn't like the idea. He thought he could make a go of it in Carrigeeny, and he didn't want to leave the old place. Jeremiah — me da— thought different. He wanted to sell. He wanted to improve things, put up a better house. And they fought about it, time and again. Bitter fights, I remember, even though I was only a young lad. Near tore the family apart."

The thin voice drifted to a stop as the old man lost himself in his memories. Hurley caught Maura's eye and signaled patience. Not that she would have dared to break the fragile spell in the room. Finally Denis's eyes focused again, and he surveyed his audience before resuming.

"And then one fine spring night, back in the early thirties, if memory serves, me

337

uncle Denis went for a pint of an evening, like he always did, but never came home. Days passed, no word. And then months, and years. Gone, just like that."

"What did the family do, sir?" Hurley's voice was gentle. "Did anyone ever report him missing?"

The old man shrugged. "What was there to do? The family asked around amongst the relatives and neighbors and at the pub. No one had seen him. You have to remember the days — hard times they were. Sometimes people got fed up and went away. Maybe to America if they could scrape up the passage money. We just figured that was the story." His eyes shifted to Maura once again.

"And what happened with the farm?"

"Ah. There's the tale. Me uncle Denis was gone, no sign of coming back. And then one day not long after, Da ups and says, 'Denis signed the farm over to me, and it's mine to do what I want with.' And he's got the paper in his hand."

"What did Denis's wife have to say about that?"

"Hanora? Ah, she was weak. And she wouldn't say it, but she couldn't read — never learned. No way she could tell what was on that paper or what her husband

338

might have signed. In the end she took her daughters and went back to her family, up past Dunmanway, and Jeremiah took over the farm. And me aunt Bridget, seein' which way the wind was blowing, married and lit out for Australia. After things had settled for a bit, Da swapped the farm like he wanted, and came to this place — 1933 it was. And here we've been ever since."

Maura felt like she had wandered into a stage play, one set in some other time. Nothing seemed real — certainly not the wizened old man in front of her, telling tales of days gone by. But given the detective's patience with Denis, apparently he thought it was important to hear him out, or maybe he was just being respectful to his elder. "There's more to the story, isn't there?" Hurley said now, not unkindly.

Denis met the detective's look squarely, and there was another silent exchange.

"There is, sir. My father wasn't a bad man. He made a success of the farm here, and he raised us children right. But at the end of his life, his conscience came to bother him, and he wanted to die in the good grace of the church, which he couldn't do with this weighing on his mind and heart. And one night after he'd lifted a few pints, he told me the rest of the tale. He'd gone to the pub with his brother that night, and they'd started to walk back together after closing. He'd asked his brother again to consider selling, and his brother had said no, like always. And Da lost his temper and rose up and hit him with his stick, and Denis fell down dead in the road. Da swore he hadn't meant to kill him, but once done, he couldn't undo it. So he looked around, and there they were in the dark alongside the bog, with no one about. He dragged Uncle Denis over and sank him. Put some rocks on him, so he wouldn't come back up." The old man was lost in his memories again. "I've been waiting all these years for me uncle Denis to turn up from the bog, wondering if he ever would. And in the end he did, didn't he?"

Hurley nodded. "Yes, he did. How did you come to learn of the body?"

"I watch the telly now and then. When I heard the place he was found, I knew."

All right, this is getting weird, Maura thought. The body that was found in the bog and the body of the poor guy in Skibbereen — they were connected, to this house, this family, even though they were eighty years apart? Those two deaths had somehow led the police — and her — to this seedy farmhouse?

"The letter," Maura said suddenly. "Jerry, you were at Sullivan's when I was talking about the letter from Australia. And you told your grandfather about it, right?"

Jerry's eyes darted to Denis's, and it was Denis who answered. "He didn't know the story then, but when he came home talking about it, I knew that if you went to the gardaí with it, they'd figure it out soon enough." Denis's eyes flooded with a new kind of sadness. He spoke directly to his grandson. "Tell them, Jerry."

Jerry avoided his grandfather's eyes. "Grandda, won't help nothin'."

"Tell them!" The old man's voice still held a hint of steel.

Grudgingly Jerry said, "Me da didn't want to have nothin' to do wit' farmin'. He took himself off to Dublin, and he's there yet. But like Grandda said, *he's* still here, and the land, so Da sent me back to help out. But when we heard the news about the body in the bog, and Grandda told me about what the old man had done, I come to think maybe we didn't exactly have the right to the place, since we don't know if Jeremiah McCarthy got it honest, like, and we might lose it if the body came back to us. I told Danny I seen you going into the garda station, and he thought you'd be telling about

341

seeing us at Sullivan's, close to the time that man was killed, and I let him go on thinking that. That's when Danny decided to try to scare you off, and I didn't try and stop him, because I wanted you gone too, for the other thing. You" — he turned to Maura and spoke with surprising vehemence — "you coulda let us be, just gone home and left us alone."

Maura glared at a belligerent Jerry. Then she found her voice. "You idiot! This is *my* fault? I came here minding my own business, not bothering anybody, and that pal of yours tried to kill me! He seriously thought I'd just pack up and take myself back to wherever? It was a coincidence that I knew about the man from the bog — your relative — because I was driving by when the gardaí pulled him out of the bog. But if you two hadn't come after me, I might have just gone home like you wanted, and that would have been the end of it. But it was because you two who were so thickheaded that I ended up leading the gardaí right to your door."

Maura fell silent, realizing only slowly that everyone was staring at her. Well, let them; she knew she was right. "So, Mr. Detective, what're you going to do now?"

"Yes, Detective, are you going to charge

the boy?" Denis's voice was surprisingly strong.

Hurley looked at Denis for several seconds without speaking. "I haven't decided. At the least, he's been conspiring with his Dublin friend, and we've plenty to charge him with."

"Jerry here's not a bad 'un, just . . . he doesn't use his head. That's no crime, is it?"

If it was, a whole lot of people would be in jail, Maura thought. She couldn't sit still any longer. Abruptly she stood up and stalked to the edge of the room. Without thinking, she started picking up pieces of the bric-a-brac that had been tossed around and broken in the brief struggle. Someone had collected these things, years ago, and placed them around the room, and there they had sat for decades, until a policeman and a Dublin thug had smashed them to bits. She sneaked a glance at Denis McCarthy. He looked older than he had when they arrived. Jerry had settled into an expression that was one part surly and two parts scared. She almost felt sorry for him.

Among the debris was an old carved pipe, its stem snapped off — and she recognized the carved pattern on it. Mutely she handed it to Hurley, who looked at Denis. "I'm

343

guessing this was your father's?" he asked.

"It was, and me uncle had one like it — I remember my father carving them by the fire at night."

Hurley nodded once and slipped the broken pipe into an inner pocket of his jacket. Maura might have smiled: not exactly a standard way to collect evidence. She'd put money on that pipe matching the one taken from the Bog Man's pocket.

Hurley finally said, "This isn't the first time you've been in trouble, is it, Jerry?"

The old man sighed, then answered for him. "Nah. His da thought maybe things would be different for him here. But he's no farmer, and he still finds trouble, or it finds him. I don't know what to do with him. He never finished his schooling, and he has no trade. There's no other work for him here, nothing apart from the farm."

True, Maura thought, stacking shards of china in her hand. Jerry's future looked dim, with or without the farm. And yet . . . he'd been willing to fight to let his grandfather keep the farm. Maybe there was some good in him? Over the mantel hung a standard religious print, framed in chipped gilt, festooned with desiccated palm fronds. The mantle had been crowded with framed photographs, until they had been swept to the floor, where they now lay amidst slivers of broken glass. Maura gingerly extricated the pictures, shaking off the glass. The photos covered several generations. So many ancestors, and yet this branch of the family had dwindled down to this poor mismatched pair, grandfather and grandson.

The largest picture was a handsomely matted ensemble, the work of a professional studio: a cluster of oval shots, with one larger central picture. From the faded sepia tone of the photos, and the hairstyles and dress, she figured it had to be from about 1900. It must have been expensive for a farming family. A stiff portrait of a middle-aged man and woman occupied the central place of pride: the parents? There were younger people in orbit around them, two boys and two girls, all in their finest clothes. The family resemblance was undeniable.

And then her eyes widened. She had seen one of those photographs before. She set the picture down carefully and retrieved her bag from where she'd left it under a chair. Fishing in its depths, she pulled out the envelope that held everything she'd brought to show anyone who had known her grandmother. The sad fact was, that single slender envelope held almost every personal document and picture that her grandmother had kept over the years. She leafed through it and found what she was looking for: a picture that was a match for the one she'd picked up from Denis McCarthy's floor. The mother and father in the picture were her own great-great-grandparents, and one or the other of the girls had been Gran's mother. Which meant . . .

"Maura?" Hurley's voice broke into her thoughts. "Are you all right? You've gone pale."

Maura turned to him. "I'm fine, but . . . Wait a moment."

She retrieved the group photograph and perched on the chair next to Denis McCarthy, whose eyes — old but still sharp — were on her face. She leaned forward.

"Mr. McCarthy, when I first came in, you were staring at me. Why?"

For a long moment the old man's eyes looked inward, searching his memories, and then he spoke. "You reminded me of my aunt Ellen. I knew her only a short while, until I was maybe six or seven. That was at the old place. You have the look of her."

"I think she was my great-grandmother," Maura said. "My gran didn't have many pictures, especially from Ireland, but she had this one, and she told me about it when I first found it in a drawer. My grandmother

346

married Ellen McCarthy's son James Donovan." Maura showed the old man her copy, and gestured at the group shot. "Which one was Ellen?"

"Bridget — she's the one on the left — went to Australia, and Ellen's on the right." He held on to the picture, lost in thought.

Maura turned to Patrick Hurley. "So that makes Denis Flaherty, who wrote the letter, Bridget McCarthy's son, not to mention some kind of cousin of mine. And I'm related to poor Denis from the bog, and to Denis here, and to Jerry. Detective, everybody in this mess is related!" She didn't know whether to laugh or cry. "Except maybe Old Mick, and who knows how Denis Flaherty found his name." She turned to Denis McCarthy. "I'm sorry if I stirred up . . . things that might have been better left alone. I didn't mean to." What would Gran have made of this mess?

The old man shook his head. "No fault on you — it's not your doing. My father did wrong, and you shouldn't have to pay the price. And now we can give my uncle a proper burial."

Maura was relieved when Patrick Hurley stood and said, "Mr. McCarthy, I need to get back to Skibbereen and see to Danny Mullan. Jerry?" He turned to Jerry, who looked at him with feeble defiance. "Your grandfather needs your help here. If I don't charge you, can you keep yourself out of trouble? And I'll need you to testify about what Danny did."

"Yes . . . sir. And, uh . . ." He seemed confused about what to say to Maura. "I'm sorry about Danny — I shoulda stopped him, only I didn't know how."

"Thank you." She looked to Hurley for guidance. "And thank you, Detective Hurley. Jerry deserves a chance. Mr. McCarthy? Maybe I can come back and talk to you again, when things aren't so crazy."

Hurley said gently, "Maura, we need to be going now. I'll drop you back at Leap."

"Sure. Fine." Maura followed him wordlessly out the door and sat in the car while the detective went around to the other side and started the engine, then pulled out of the farmyard. Then she asked, "How much do you know about fraud and inheritance and property rights and all that stuff?"

"Why do you ask?"

"Because to me it sounds like Denis's father killed his brother so he could get control of the farm and sell it, or at least swap it. That document he came up with was probably a fake, which means he stiffed the poor widow and her children — isn't that fraud or something? So who does the farm really belong to? Jeremiah sold the old place in Carrigeeny based on a murder and a forgery, but is there a statute of limitations for this sort of stuff?"

"Maura, I can't answer most of that." He glanced at her briefly. "I'm good on criminal law, but for the rest, you need to speak to a solicitor." After a pause he went on. "You'll press charges against Danny?"

"Damn straight I will — he deserves it. But I don't want that poor old man to lose his home because of me. Is that all right? Legally, I mean?"

"I think it can be done. I'll talk to the Clogagh gardaí, make sure they keep an eye on Jerry. But from what I've seen, he's not bad — he's just too easily led by someone like Danny. But as for Danny, I have no problem sending him to prison." He drove for a few miles before speaking again. "Are you all right, Maura?"

Maura turned over that question. "I . . . don't know. I'm not sure why I came here at all, except that Gran wanted me to, and she'd never asked for much, so I promised her." She took a deep breath. "I've been here a week, and in that time I somehow seem to have ended up discovering relatives I didn't even know I had, and that includes one who was murdered by another one. And now I'm supposed to decide if my whatever-cousin should go to jail for being dumb and picking the wrong friends, which might mean that his grandfather will end up out on the street. Detective, what the heck am I supposed to think?"

"Maura, I can't even begin to tell you."

CHAPTER 28

Maura fell silent, trying to wrestle her feelings under control, and Patrick Hurley didn't interrupt her, no doubt preoccupied by his own responsibilities in the case. But after a while the silence began to weigh on Maura. "What was that land business Denis McCarthy mentioned all about?"

"You mean the exchange? How much do you know about land ownership in Ireland?"

"Not a heck of a lot. Didn't the English control everything, so the Irish couldn't actually own land?"

Hurley nodded, watching the road. "That was true for a time. The tenants were Irish Catholics, and the landlords were English Protestants, who most often lived somewhere else. And the English didn't want to put much into improving the land — they just wanted to collect their rents. The Irish population kept growing, and that meant that the Irish landholdings kept getting smaller as they were split up within families."

"So the Irish really did have something to complain about?" Maura said, almost to herself.

"They did. Did you think they complained for no reason?"

"I don't know," Maura said. "All I know is that a lot of the Irish guys I met around Boston thought that somebody owed them something. I guess I never believed that there were any facts behind it."

"We Irish have been oppressed for centuries, and it colors our view of things. I can see that it would grate on you, taken out of this setting here. But things began to change in the nineteenth century, when the landlords first made it possible for the Irish tenants to buy the lands they'd rented and lived on for generations. That was the start."

"You mean the guys I met in Boston were whining about something that had stopped over a hundred years ago?" Maura demanded.

Hurley glanced at her. "Do you want to learn something or not?"

"Sorry. I guess that sounded rude. It's just that I can't believe that Irish people hang on to a grudge for so long. But I guess it shouldn't surprise me, considering Northern Ireland is still separate, right?"

"It's changing — slowly. But let's not get into politics, right? The attachment to the land runs deep in Ireland, so we're still living with the results. As you yourself have seen. In the case of the McCarthys, it led to a murder, whether intended or not. It began in the late 1800s, when the English government started letting the Irish buy certain areas of land, though the English were still in control up through the 1920s. After independence, the 1923 Land Act bought out the remaining landlords and sold the land to the tenants. It sounds like that was when the McCarthy brothers started arguing. The Land Commission financed the farmers, made it possible for them to buy land at favorable rates. And over time, that became a financial, political, and social issue. Some in government wanted to keep the farmers on the land, to maintain the traditional rural culture of the small family farm, but at the same time, to guarantee some economic stability for those farmers and their families. Others thought that was a bad thing for the agricultural economy — that system was inefficient and discouraged modern improvements."

Maura held up one hand. "Enough! The landlords caved, then the government came along and made it easier for the farmers — which was about everybody — to buy land. Some people liked the idea, but others wanted to stay where they were. Does that cover it?"

"Near enough. It made sense in practical terms, since in the old days the land was broken up into many tiny lots, so the farmers spent a lot of time just going from one to another. We tend to see the old system as just another way the English tried to keep the poor Irish peasants down. It made it difficult for them to do more than hang on, so Jeremiah McCarthy had the right idea, only he ran head on into his brother's emotional connection to the land. Once his brother was dead, he did take the deal and made a go of it."

Maura mulled over what Hurley had said. Apparently she hadn't inherited the Irish need to have a piece of earth to cling to. But then, it had never been an option — for Gran or for her.

Detective Hurley dropped her in front of Ellen's. Before shutting the car door, Maura leaned in and asked, "Do you think you'll need me for anything else?"

"Most likely. I'll give you a call once I've got Danny squared away. But you can stop looking over your shoulder now. You'll be around for a bit longer?"

"Yeah, I'll be here." Maura watched as he pulled away, headed back toward Skibbereen. She checked her watch and was surprised to see that it was barely one. So much had happened, in so little time!

Maura realized that the first thing she needed to do was apologize to Ellen for bringing so much trouble to her household, even if it wasn't her fault. At least she could tell her that both murders had been solved and that nobody was likely to come after her again. Instead of using her key, she knocked at the front door.

Ellen answered promptly. "There you are, Maura! Oh, come in, come in. How'd you fare?"

"Very well, actually. We figured out who the man from the bog was *and* who the guy who broke in was, all at once."

"You're having me on! The two of them together? Come sit and tell me all about it."

Repeating the story to Ellen over another cup of tea in the kitchen made it clearer in Maura's mind. Danny the Dublin thug had wanted to keep his thug skills polished by using them on unsuspecting locals and clueless tourists, and he'd decided that Maura posed a threat to his cushy little hideaway in Clogagh. Jerry was a jellyfish who couldn't stand up to Danny. Old Denis was . . . old and couldn't control his grandson, much less a Dublin delinquent. But his memory was intact, and he had given them the whole story behind the old murder. *Does every family around here have this kind of story lurking in their past?* Maura wondered.

Ellen was satisfyingly sympathetic. "Oh, you poor girl. So they arrested the Dubliner? I'm not surprised someone from away was behind it all. Poor Denis McCarthy — the Clogagh one, not the one from the bog, although he's had no luck either."

"I'm going to go see Bridget Nolan next — I'm sure she'd want to hear how this all came out." And about Maura's own connection, going back to the dead man in the bog.

"Ah, she's a grand lady, isn't she? And Mick's so good to her," Ellen said. When Maura didn't respond, she added, "Maura? Are you listening?"

Maura shook her head to clear it. "Sorry, Ellen. I was just trying to figure out all the connections. On the one hand, it's not a big country, right? But on the other hand, a move from one place to another twenty miles away made a big difference for the McCarthys. It's all new to me, although I

356

suppose everybody around here knows who's related to who. It makes me sad now to realize how much Gran never told me, that I'm just finding out. I don't know why she never talked about any of this, and now I can't even ask her anything." She paused before adding, "Though I know I shouldn't be mad that Gran didn't tell me, when I guess I never asked either and didn't want to know a lot about it. I wish I could talk to her now, but it's too late."

"Ah, love, I'm sure she knows. Maybe she's even watching out for you." Ellen glanced at her watch. "Heavens, is that the time! I've got to retrieve Gráinne from the creche. You'll be back later?"

"Much later — I'll be at Sullivan's tonight, after I've seen Mrs. Nolan. Let's hope we can all sleep better tonight."

"God willing," Ellen said, bustling out the door.

CHAPTER 29

One week. She'd been in Ireland all of one
week, Maura realized as she drove toward
Bridget Nolan's house in Knockskagh. She
couldn't remember ever having spent a
more bizarre week in her whole life. It
wasn't all bad, and it could have been so
much worse, but she really didn't know
what to think. People had all been kind to
her — well, with the exception of Dublin
Danny — but she felt like such an outsider.
She didn't know even the most basic things
about her own family that other people
expected her to know. And that was her own
fault. Worse, it was not something that could
be made up in a week, or even in a year.

She pulled into her usual space across
from Mrs. Nolan's enclosed yard and
parked. What looked like Mick's car was
already parked in front of the house. Thick
clouds were moving quickly through the sky,
and Maura wondered if it was going to rain

again. With a sigh she climbed out of the car, but before she could reach the door, Mick opened it, then closed it quietly behind him.

"She's napping," he said.

"Oh," Maura replied. "Should I wait?"

He didn't meet her eyes, looking down at his feet rather than at her. "There's something we need to talk about. Will you walk with me?"

"Sure, okay," Maura said. "Where did you want to go?"

"No matter. Down the lane will do." He turned abruptly and started walking up to the lane that bordered Mrs. Nolan's land, and Maura followed, bewildered.

She caught up with him at the turn. "You're being kind of weird. Have I done something?"

"I'm guessing you found out who the man in the bog was, you and the detective," he said flatly, stopping to lean against the stone wall at the side of the road, staring out at the landscape. "I'd hoped that it wouldn't come out, when they found him," he said, more to himself than her.

Maura came up and stood beside him, trying to see his face. "Help me out here. You knew who it was, and you didn't tell anyone? Why not?"

"I didn't know for sure, but I had my suspicions. Denis McCarthy was my great-grandfather. Bridget's father."

Oh. Maura was stunned into silence. She leaned against the wall and tried to work out what that meant. The most important question was, did Bridget know? But if she had, wouldn't she have said something days ago? Either she was a darned good actress, or she really was in the dark about this. And why had Mick known?

She took a deep breath. "Okay, you're going to have to explain. First, does she know?"

Mick shook his head, without looking at her. "She does not. I'd hoped she would never know, because it will cause her pain — she doesn't deserve that."

"She doesn't know that her father disappeared?"

Now he turned to look at her. "You find that hard to understand, no doubt. Bridget was a very young child when her da went missing — you do the math. Her sisters were a bit older, but young still. Her mother wasn't a strong woman, and then Jeremiah McCarthy more or less stole the land from under her, and she had no choice but to take the girls and go back to her own family. She broke off all ties down here. Worse,

360

she took back her family name and never told the girls they were McCarthys. She forbade her family from mentioning Denis McCarthy, thinking he'd run off and abandoned them all. Bridget was too young to know what was going on, and if her sisters did, they were frightened into silence."

"But why do you know this?" Maura pressed.

"Would you be content if I said no more than 'curiosity'?"

Maura regarded him steadily. "No, not really. What made you look?"

He returned his gaze to the timeless landscape. "I was checking some property titles and the like — I wanted to be sure that Grannie was taken care of. After a bit I realized that no one in my family had looked for some of the basic documents like birth certificates and marriage licenses, which seemed odd to me."

Maura digested that. "But . . . didn't her mother have to sign them up for school? Or tell your grandmother her real name when she married?"

"Things were simpler then. I have no idea what the priest knew, but he made no trouble for her. Grannie only came back here as a married woman, and nobody remembered the old story, or if they did, they didn't mention it, out of kindness. When her husband — my grandfather — died, she inherited the land, and she has enough to live on, so there's no government meddling. She could easily never know."

"Except for me sticking my nose into it? I was just trying to help."

"I know. It's no fault of yours." Mick fell silent.

After a moment, Maura said, "Shoot — that means we're related too, you and I."

"I make it third cousins," Mick said with an amused smile.

Maura turned to face him. "Do you know how many people I've added to my family tree in just one day? This is ridiculous! I'm going to have to start assuming I'm related to everyone I meet around here."

"It happens," Mick said. "You won't tell Grannie any of this?"

"She already knows about finding the Bog Man, obviously. Will it be possible to hide his identity from her?" Maura felt a stab of guilt: she didn't want to hurt Bridget Nolan, but she was the one who had figured out the connection.

"I hope so."

"Did Bridget's mother ever remarry?" Maura asked softly.

Mick shook his head. "How could she?

There was no proof that her husband, Denis, was dead — until now."

"So Bridget never had a father," Maura said.

"Her mother's people lived in a townland much like this one — all the families clustered together. It was a happy place, to hear her tell it."

And Maura didn't want to spoil those memories for Mrs. Nolan. "Mick, I won't say anything if you don't want me to, but don't you think it's bound to come out, one way or the other? And if there's a funeral for Denis, won't that stir up more memories around here?"

"I'm trying to keep it quiet. For her sake."

Maura wondered if that was Mick's real reason, but she couldn't find another one that made sense. But if it had been her . . . she would have wanted to know the truth, even if it was unpleasant.

Just like you've gone looking for the truth about your mother?

That thought stopped Maura in her tracks. All right, Bridget had led a long and happy life, and Mick wanted her to end it happy, not mourning a father she had never known. Was there anything wrong in that? And it certainly wasn't her place to question his decision — it was his call. But that still left one question.

"Fine. I'll keep my mouth shut — about everything. She doesn't know about the guy trying to run me off the road?"

Mick shook his head.

Maura sighed. Neither Mick nor his grandmother knew about what had happened at the Keohanes' house the night before, and she wasn't going to tell them. Although it was hard to keep such stories quiet around here, she was finding. "Are we going to go see Mrs. Nolan now? And who'd you leave in charge of Sullivan's?"

"Jimmy's there, and Rose. It's a quiet day, so they'll manage." He straightened up, pushing away from the stone wall. "You can go now — I'll explain to Grannie why you didn't stop by."

"Can I visit her tomorrow? After I've had time to think about all this?"

"Of course."

CHAPTER 30

The rain had finally made up its mind and was falling heavily. If Maura hadn't had to drive in it, she might have enjoyed watching it: clouds scudded across the sky in the distance, dragging curtains of rain. The gullies alongside the road filled rapidly, creating their own little streams. Maura was thankful that she could follow fairly well-paved roads back to Leap.

Mick had stayed on to talk with his grandmother, saying he'd be in later. Maura parked the car in front of Sullivan's and dashed for the door. When she opened it, the place smelled damp and smoky; the small peat fire in the fireplace was not enough to disperse the clammy air, and there was nowhere for it to go anyway. Old Billy was dozing in his usual chair. Rose was behind the bar, Jimmy was nowhere in sight, and there were a few customers, mostly minding their own business. It was not a day for cheerful chat.

"Hi, Rose." Maura greeted her, and stashed her bag behind the bar. "Anything going on?"

"I'm guessing you've seen more excitement than we have. I hear you laid out a burglar with a lamp last night."

"I hit him, but it was Sean Murphy who scared him off. Anyway, we found him again, over in Clogagh, and he's been arrested. Do you know, that all started right here in Sullivan's?" When Rose raised her eyebrows, Maura explained, "The guy and his friend were in here the day I opened that letter from Denis Flaherty — remember, we were talking about it? What I hadn't figured out was that Bart Hayes, the man who died in Skibbereen, was here when they were, and when he left, the other guys followed him, thinking he'd be an easy target. One of the guys saw me later going to the garda station and thought I could put them all together. They were worried that I'd make trouble for them."

"So instead they made trouble for you," Rose said.

"Exactly. If I'd been a regular tourist, I probably would have packed up and left, which is what they wanted. They were kind of surprised when I didn't." Rose had to hear the whole story, and then Maura had to repeat it to Old Billy. Finally Rose said, "Good for you! No doubt we'll have a busy night, if the story gets 'round. You're a local heroine."

"Shoot, I didn't think of that. I really didn't do all that much. You know, it seems that every time I open my mouth I end up saying something I shouldn't, or spilling somebody else's secrets. I hope there aren't any left." Except for Mrs. Nolan's.

Jimmy emerged from the back of the building, carrying some tools, awkwardly bundled in his good arm. Before speaking, he gave her a long look, one that Maura couldn't interpret. "There's someone wants to talk with you," he said, nodding toward a woman seated at a table in the far corner.

"Oh, right, I was to tell you that, but your news drove it clear out of my mind," Rose said, contrite. "Sorry, Da, I forgot."

"Uh, okay. You mean she asked for me?" Maura said. "Do you know why?"

"You'd best ask her," Jimmy said.

Maura went over to the table. When the woman looked up, she said, "I'm Maura Donovan. You were looking for me?"

"Maura Donovan, from Boston?" When Maura nodded, the woman gestured toward the chair across from her. "Please, sit down."

Maura sat and studied the woman, who was in her thirties, and better dressed and groomed than most of the people who came through Sullivan's. She had to be some kind of professional. What could this woman want from her?

"Your grandmother was Nora Donovan, nee Sullivan, correct?"

"Yes. You know she died recently?"

"I do now. But in fact it was you I was looking for. I sent a letter to the last address I had for you, but it was returned, stamped 'not at that address.' "

"That's right. I just moved out, and I didn't leave a forwarding address because I didn't know where I'd be, and I wasn't expecting any mail anyway — I'd settled all the bills before I left. Why were you looking for me?"

"Ah, forgive me, I'm doing this backward. My name is Elizabeth Flynn. I'm a solicitor in Skibbereen. It's a happy chance I found you here! Did you know Michael Sullivan?"

"You mean, the former owner here? No. I gather he died not long before I showed up, so I never met him. Why?" Did this woman enjoy spinning out a story? Maura had to keep reminding herself that things moved more slowly in Ireland than she was used to, but she wished this Elizabeth would just get to the point.

"Not long ago Mr. Sullivan came to me and asked me to draw up a will for him. As you might know, he was not a young man. He never married, nor had children, and his brothers and sisters had passed on. He didn't know most of their children or grand-children, who are scattered all over. He came to me to ask what restrictions there might be as to leaving his property to someone not of his immediate family. I told him that would not be a problem, so long as he was still fit and able, and I was sure that he was. Together we drew up a simple will for him. He named you his heir." The woman sat back in her chair and beamed, having delivered what she must have consid-ered good news.

"What?" Maura wasn't sure she'd heard the woman right. "He never even met me! How did he even know I existed?"

"Ah, well. It seems that Michael Sullivan and your grandmother kept up a correspon-dence over the years. He was her uncle, on her father's side. Did you not know that?"

Maura shook her head vigorously. "No, I did not know that. My gran never talked about anyone in Ireland."

"He knew all about you, and he knew she'd had a hard life and had little to leave

369

you. Hence, the will."

Maura was almost afraid to ask the next question. "What did he leave me?"

"All he possessed — his house and land, and this pub, both the building and the business. And what money he'd put away, enough to cover the costs of burial and taxes."

Maura couldn't breathe. How could some old man she'd never met just hand her everything he owned? Had Gran known about this?

"But, how . . . I can't." Maura stopped herself and took a deep breath. "I don't even know if it's legal for me to own something in Ireland, much less run a business here."

"I understand that you have Irish citizenship already?" Maura nodded, and the solicitor went on. "There'll be some formalities, but I'll be glad to help you sort that out." The woman looked ready and eager to take on any such pesky problems that might arise.

Maura was not ready to begin to think about it. What about Mick? She thought he'd had some expectations of inheriting the pub. And Jimmy Sweeney? No doubt he'd pinned his hopes on the pub as well. Had he already guessed why the lawyer —

solicitor — was asking for her? She stood up abruptly, just catching her chair before it fell over. "I have to think about this. I can't . . . I can't do it right now. Sorry."

She fled, leaving everyone in the pub gaping after her. Out into the rain, into the late afternoon gloom. She passed Mick climbing out of his car, but if he called out she didn't hear him. She didn't know where she wanted to go, but she knew she couldn't stay in the pub, not with people watching — people whose livelihood could depend on her, people who were likely to be disappointed or, worse, angry that she had somehow snatched an opportunity away from them. She couldn't take it all in, not on top of all that had already happened this day. It was too much.

She darted across the street, blessedly empty. She couldn't face going back to the Keohanes'. Who else knew about this inheritance? Oblivious to the rain, she stalked past the house, down the hill, and kept going along the path that followed the shoreline. When it ran out at the water's edge, she dropped down, her back against a tree, and gazed blindly at the harbor, half-hidden in the rain.

Oh, Gran, did you know? Is that why you sent me here?

All these people she hadn't even known existed, yet they'd known all about her. Why had Gran never shared any of it with her? Maura felt naked and exposed, yet claustrophobic at the same time, like things were closing in on her, forcing her in directions she wasn't sure she wanted to go. But what *did* she want? She had no idea. Ever since Gran's last illness and her death, she had been running on autopilot. She'd taken care of the funeral. She'd paid all the bills, closed the accounts, given away or thrown out most of the pitifully few possessions she and her grandmother had kept. And she'd honored Gran's last wish, to make what she had thought would be a quick visit here. Maura hadn't even bothered to look past that, because her future was a big blank.

Her face was wet. It had to be rain, right? Because she never cried. She hadn't cried when she knew Gran was failing; she hadn't cried at the funeral, attended by people she only half recognized; she hadn't cried when she walked out of the shabby apartment for the last time. Why would she cry now? Just because she'd been nearly driven into a lake and attacked by a thug, because she'd learned more about her family in a week than she'd learned in all the rest of her life, because some old guy she had never met had just dumped a pub and a house in her lap. Why was she crying?

Because that was what people did when they were sad and hurt and confused and overwhelmed. *Hey, Maura, welcome to the human world — where've you been all this time?*

Time passed. The rain didn't let up, and it grew darker. A few lights appeared in houses she could barely even see on the far side of the harbor. All she could hear was rain and wind. Still, she wasn't surprised when Mick Nolan suddenly dropped down beside her. She swiped at her face.

"You left your jacket behind," he said, draping it over her shoulders. She realized belatedly that she was not only wet but also cold.

"How'd you know where to find me?" Maura asked.

"I saw you go, and there's nowhere else this direction."

"Aren't you going to ask 'How are you doing?' "

"You'll tell me if you want, I've no doubt." He pulled one leg up and wrapped his arms around it, looking at ease in the dark and the rain.

Maura shifted so she could look at him. "Why are you here? Are you worried about your job? Did you know what Old Mick was planning?"

"He never said much about himself or his life, for all that he was a publican for most of it. No, I didn't know, but Old Billy just filled me in. His hearing's surprisingly good, and he heard what the solicitor told you."

"I'm sorry. I had no idea, and now I feel like I'm cheating you and you'll hate me."

"You had no hand in it. Do you want me to work for you?"

She looked up at him and fought a laugh. "That's ridiculous. You want to buy the business from me? I'll give you a really good deal."

He didn't answer immediately. "Don't be hasty, Maura. You don't know this place, and you don't know us, but your gran wanted you to be here. There's no rush to decide anything."

"But . . . I've never owned anything. And now suddenly I've got a pub, and, oh God, a house somewhere. What am I supposed to do?"

"Whatever you want. You're a free woman. You can walk away if you like. You can reject your inheritance or turn it over to all the relatives and let them argue about it."

"What about Jimmy? He seemed to be counting on at least a piece of the pub. You weren't?"

Instead of answering her question, he looked out over the dark water and said, "You never knew Old Mick, I know. I won't tell you he was a grand old man — old, yes, but hardly grand. Set in his ways, he was. Loved the pub, loved talking with the people who came in, friend or stranger. They were his family, the children he never had. And he had a good long time to think about what he wanted to do with it. Sure, he could have left it to me, but he knew full well I'd leave it if a better chance came along, or when my grannie . . . no longer needs me. If he'd left it to Jimmy, it wouldn't have lasted the year. Jimmy would have bought a round for all of County Cork, and that would have been the end of it."

What he was saying made sense to Maura. "That still doesn't explain why he left it to me. He didn't know me."

"He knew your gran, his niece, and she remembered him and wrote him, which is more than most of his other nieces and nephews ever did. Mick told me, in bits and pieces, when there were few patrons in the pub. Maybe he was sounding me out — I don't know. He knew you stuck by your gran, when surely there were other things you might have done. He knew you had very

375

little to your name. I'd wager he gave it a lot of thought and decided that you deserved a chance. He's probably watching you from somewhere, to see what you make of it."

At least she'd stopped crying. "Look, maybe I know how to pull a pint, but that's a long way from running a business. And there's so damn much I don't know — like how laws and licenses here work."

"But those are just *things,* and things you can fix or learn or hire someone to figure out."

"Would Jimmy be willing to work for me? Would you?"

"I'd stay long enough to see you on your feet. After that I can't say." He considered her gravely. "Jimmy'll take the easy course, and that would be to stay, and if he stays, Rose stays."

"About Rose — I don't want her to be stuck in a dead-end job just to take care of her useless father. She needs to a chance to make something of her life. Not like me."

"She can find her own way — maybe faster with you kicking her backside."

"It's an uncertain world, isn't it?" Maura slipped her arms into her jacket and pulled it straight. "So, what now?"

"You'd best start with that solicitor you

left sitting at Sullivan's."

"Did your grandmother know what Old Mick was planning?"

"I couldn't say. Did you not know he lived across the lane from her?"

"Up on the hill, in Knockskagh? So that's where the house is?"

"It is. I can take you through it, although it's better done by daylight."

A house. *Her* house. She tried to remember what she had seen up on the hill, but all she could recall were open fields and the sound of distant cows. "Oh, right, there's the pub to run tonight. Did you leave Rose all alone?"

"Jimmy's there."

"Close enough to alone, then." Maura stood up. "Mick, I need to think about this. I don't want to do or say anything that'll give people the wrong idea. I know Old Mick meant well, but I don't know right now whether I can handle this, or if I want to. Can you understand that?"

"Of course. And I'll say nothing until you're ready, if that's worrying you."

"Thank you. Although maybe I'll take you up on that offer to show me the house. Would your gran be up to going with us?"

"I'm sure she wouldn't miss it."

CHAPTER 31

Maura wasn't sure how she got through the evening, with so much going on in her head. How could a man she'd never even heard of until last week have handed her a livelihood and a place to live, just like that? It was beyond imagining, yet a lawyer had said it was true, and Mick had agreed. In only a few moments, her life had changed — if she wanted it to. She could still say no; she could walk away. But then where would she go, and what would she do?

As Rose had predicted, the pub was well filled, everyone eager to hear the latest news about the arrest of the Skibbereen killer. Maura tried to choose her words carefully, but it appeared that many people already knew much of the story, and she just went along and filled in the blanks, correcting the versions that got it wrong.

As she pulled pints and cleared away empty glasses, though, she also looked at

Sullivan's with a new, more critical eye. She'd seen the inside of plenty of pubs, both good and bad; how did this one stack up? It was cleaner than when she'd first arrived, thanks to her and Rose's efforts, but there was a long way to go. Some of the chairs and tables looked ready to collapse, and the plumbing fixtures were antique. She really hadn't explored the rest of the building, although she knew there was a small kitchen behind the bar, and the other rooms in the back that were used only for private functions. And there must be rooms further along the road — like the one Old Billy lived in — and what was above? She had had no business training back in the States, apart from making sure that her tabs added up, and over here there would be a whole new set of rules and regulations to learn. Who were their suppliers? Were there building codes? And of course, the biggest question was: did she *want* to do this? It was hard to find reasons to say no. There was nothing waiting for her in Boston — no place, no job, no boyfriend. And she'd already agreed to stay for a while, since she had no other plans. But making it a more permanent move? What would it mean to be an American living in Ireland, particularly in a very small village? Even if she had an Irish passport and her name *was* Donovan? Mick had been straight with her: he wasn't prepared to take on Sullivan's for the long term, and Jimmy wasn't a businessman and shouldn't try to run the place even if he wanted to. If she turned down Old Mick's inheritance, Sullivan's would probably close forever. Or some chain would sweep in and convert it to a Quaint Ould Irish Pub for tourists. What would that do to the sleepy character of the place? And if that changed for the worse, she had an uncomfortable feeling that the people here would blame her, even if she wasn't around anymore. Great — she already felt guilty about the local people talking for years about "that Maura Donovan, who came and killed Sullivan's Pub."

She needed time — and space — to think. She needed to see Old Mick's house, to know what the full package was. She'd never given any thought to where and how she wanted to live, but an Irish cottage wouldn't have been on her short list before now. A *free* Irish cottage, she reminded herself. A home of her own, that she didn't have to share with anyone unless she wanted to? That was a luxury she had never expected.

The night wound down slowly, until Mick announced it was closing time, no exceptions — which met with a number of protests, suggesting that he'd been talked into extending the hours plenty of times before. This time he stood firm, and once the last patron had left, he turned to her.

"Maura, you've had a hard day. I'll take care of closing up, and I'll stop by Ellen's in the morning to bring you out to Knockskagh, right?"

"Okay, I guess. You're right — I'm beat. Thanks — for everything."

She stepped out into the night, pulling the door shut behind her. The rain had stopped, and the Keohane house was dark, so she didn't have to worry about explaining anything more to Ellen, although she doubted that she would escape so easily at breakfast. Maura went around to the rear and slipped into her room, undressed quickly, and fell into her bed.

Morning came quickly, and Maura flung open the curtains to find bright sunshine once again. Fluffy clouds raced across the sky, and the resident pair of swans glided by a small islet in the harbor. *Picture-postcard stuff,* Maura thought; the kind of pretty pictures that drew tourists to come over and kiss the Blarney Stone — that was in County Cork, wasn't it? — and buy some Belleek china and Waterford crystal, and tell the people back home that they'd seen Ireland. They'd go on about the friendly people — who really, really needed their American dollars — and how pretty and green it all was.

Maura heard noises upstairs, so she showered quickly, dressed, and headed for the kitchen.

"Ah, Maura, there you are." Ellen greeted her, handing Gráinne in her high chair a piece of bread. "No ill effects from yesterday?"

"No, I'm good. And it's a relief to stop looking over my shoulder all the time."

"I'm sure Detective Hurley's glad to have this one cleared up so quick. Gráinne, stop wriggling — we'll be going in a minute. Maura, will you be needing the room much longer?"

For a moment Maura wondered if Ellen knew about Old Mick's will, then she decided she was going paranoid. "Do you have another booking?"

"No, nothing like that. I was planning to stop in at the market and wondered how much food I should lay in."

"I've got a few things to work out" — *like the rest of my life* — "but I should be able to tell you later today. Say, a couple of days more?"

"That's grand. You take your time — I've got to get moving. Come on, Gráinne *mo chroí,* we're on our way!"

Maura munched her way through breakfast, glad of the peace. She was ready when Mick rapped on the front door.

As he led her to his car, he asked, "Have you had any time to think?"

"None. I slept like a log. Did you order up the sunshine, to make things look better this morning?"

"Sorry, but I can't take the credit. Will it help, though?"

"Can't hurt." As Maura watched the now familiar landscape roll by, she had to admit she was in a good mood. Maybe because she knew no one was chasing her. Or maybe because for the first time that she could remember, she had choices. She could stay and make a go of running an Irish pub, or she could go home and figure out something else. Those two paths were probably equally difficult, but definitely different.

When they neared the top of the Knockskagh hill, Mick pulled into the small lane to let her out.

"What about your gran?" Maura asked.

"I'll go get her now. I'd take you in" — he held up a large, old-fashioned key — "but I thought you might like a bit of time alone with the place before I brought her over."

Mick handed her the key, and she hefted it in her hand. "That's the house?" She pointed.

"The very one. I'll leave you to it."

She walked past the ruined house on the right. Stone, probably covered with stucco once upon a time — and the new houses were built just the same, from what she'd seen. A tumbledown shed on the left, all but covered with last year's dead brambles. Then Mick Sullivan's house, on the right. It was bigger than she had remembered — had she really thought it would be a one-room thatched cottage with roses blooming? *Get real, Maura.* Instead it was a once-proud stucco-clad stone building with chimneys at both ends, its slate roof now sagging just a bit, like a swaybacked horse. Other than a single empty home beyond it, there was nothing to interrupt the view of endless rolling green fields. There were sheep grazing in the grass behind a wire fence, and Maura watched them scurry away at her approach. So somebody was still using the land. Where did Mick's — her? — property start and end?

Working up her courage to try the key in the door, she stood in front of the house and looked up at it. Straight ahead was the central door, painted a cheerful light green fairly recently; there were two flanking windows, and three above. A pair of stucco-clad pillars marked the short walk leading to the door. She had no idea how old the place was, but it looked like it was in solid condition, at least from the outside. She braced herself for whatever she might find inside. Old Mick's ghost, maybe? And what would she say to him?

The key turned easily in the lock, and she pushed the door in and stopped on the threshold. From where she stood, the inside was much like Bridget Nolan's: she could see two rooms downstairs: the big one in front of her, with a huge fireplace at one end, and a smaller but more formal one through a door to her right, its fireplace smaller but fancier. Both had floors made of large slabs of slate. A narrow staircase along the back wall led to the second story, and a door beneath it led to what she hoped was a bathroom. Was it too much to hope for indoor plumbing? There was little furniture: a broad, well-scrubbed pine table took up the middle of the big room, along with four mismatched chairs, and a plain wooden chest under the front window. In the corner next to the fireplace nestled a very small stove with an oven, and an old sink. Maura wondered if the stove worked or if Old Mick had stuck to using the fireplace, where a cast-iron thing she had no name for still held its pot suspended. Shelves over the stove displayed a hodgepodge of pots and china. A row of wooden pegs against the wall next to the front door where she stood was intended for coats — an old tweed cap still hung there. Old Mick's, most likely?

She stepped tentatively into the main room, then walked into the second room. There she found a low single bed that sagged in the middle, where she guessed Mick had slept in his later years. It was stripped of its sheets, down to the mattress. In front of the window toward the lane there was a pair of chairs with a small table between. She looked around for a lamp, but all she could see was an oil lamp, half-filled, sitting on the mantel. Was the house even wired for electricity?

Back in the big room she took the stairs up to the second story, finding them dusty but strong. Upstairs there were two bedrooms, one to either side, and a small room directly over the front door, all their walls clad in tongue-and-groove boards that continued up the slant of the ceiling. The bedrooms each had an old iron and brass bedstead and elderly mattress, and there was the occasional chair or chest placed here and there. Everything was very bare, but at least it was clean. She wondered how often Old Mick had come upstairs in the last decade or two. She looked up and saw no water stains on the boards. That was a good sign: maybe the roof was sound.

She drifted toward one of the bedroom windows that faced the back. The house sat below the crest of the hill to the front, but the hill continued to slope down behind. More fields, with cows and sheep. A few stands of trees. She could see the road below in the distance, and the bog beyond — the bog where Denis McCarthy had lain for close to a century. From here she could see his burial site.

Whose house had this been? Had Mick built it for himself? Someone would know. It didn't really matter anyway. Mick's ghost might still be hanging around, but the odds were good that there were earlier ones here too. Maura wondered briefly if she should try to spend a night in the house before making any decisions. She shut her eyes, listening, trying to sense any of those lost inhabitants. All she noticed was the silence of the country: the distant sounds of animals in the fields, the wind in the trees. Just as it had likely been a century or two centuries before.

And she realized slowly that she felt at home in this place. There was no guarantee that people would accept her as the new owner of Sullivan's, and there were other pubs nearby that customers could choose. Still, she had no doubt there were improvements that she could make at Sullivan's without changing the character of the place, and ways to bring in new customers. And maybe there was something to be done with the rooms over the pub, for tourists, or offices. It would be a shame to let them go to waste.

And this house? Could she really see herself living here? She was surprised to find that the answer was yes. It was a lot more space than she needed, but it could be — it *was* — her own. And suddenly she understood why the Irish felt such a bond with their land: it was a part of their identity, their history. It was their place in the world, however small and precarious. Here she could slip into that place, and it came with its own history — one that was hers too. How could she walk away from that?

She heard the sound of voices outside and went down to meet Mrs. Nolan and Mick. Mrs. Nolan took one look at Maura's face and said, "You're staying." It wasn't a question.

Maura nodded, smiling. "I am. How can I turn down having you as a neighbor?"

Mrs. Nolan nodded, returning her smile. "A pot of tea might be nice." She settled herself in one of the chairs at the table.

Tea? Well, if Old Mick had been dead only a couple of weeks, there were probably still supplies on hand. Maura exchanged a glance with Mick. "I'll do it," he volunteered.

"No, I'll do it," Maura said, spotting an aluminum kettle in the kitchen corner. "Mick, is there water?"

He was leaning against the front wall, watching her with something like amusement. "Of course there is — the tap's just there. And the bath's to the rear. All modern conveniences, only half a century old."

"Mick had the well drilled out and the pipes put in not long before my Michael passed away," Mrs. Nolan volunteered.

So she'd guessed right. At the sink, Maura turned the handle and, reassured that the water wasn't brown, filled the kettle and set it on to boil, remembering to light the burner with a match, as she'd seen Ellen do in her own kitchen, conscious all the while of the twin gazes of Mrs. Nolan and Mick.

389

Now, tea . . . in a canister on the shelf, next to a china teapot; the cups were further along the shelf. Sugar in a jar.

"We'll be needing a bit of milk," Mrs. Nolan said before Maura could open her mouth. "Could you run back to my kitchen and bring some over, Michael?"

"I'll do that," Mick said, and headed out the front door, leaving Maura and Mrs. Nolan alone.

Maura turned to face her. "Did you send him out on purpose?"

"I did. I thought you might have questions about the finding of my father in the bog."

It took a moment for Maura to realize the full meaning of what Mrs. Nolan had just said. "You *knew* about that?"

"I did, though not always — not until lately. Sit you down, Maura — the tea'll keep." Mrs. Nolan gazed over Maura's head, remembering. "Mick Sullivan knew Jeremiah McCarthy, years back. Mick was working in the pub, a young man then, before he came to buy it, and Jeremiah would come in now and then — couldn't stay away, I'd guess. And sometimes he'd get to talking, especially after too much of the drink."

Old Mick had known that Jeremiah Mc-

Carthy was a killer? "If Old Mick knew about Denis McCarthy, why didn't he do anything?" Maura asked.

"What would you have him do? Jeremiah was settled over in Clogagh, and my mother had made a new life for us, and she didn't want to hear any of it, or so Mick said, long after. And times were hard then. Mick couldn't see any good thing coming from telling, so he let it be. But he kept an eye out for me when I came back here, made sure I was comfortably set. Which I was. But he never told me the rest of it until he knew his end was near. For all he knew me da would stay right where he was forever. It was long ago, and I've made my peace with it."

Maura had to stifle a laugh. Mick was trying to protect his grannie, and it turned out that she didn't need protecting at all. "Mick — your Michael, that is — he's been trying to spare you, you know."

"And it's dear of him to try. I'll sort it out with him. But might I ask one thing of you?"

"Of course. What is it?"

"Will you help me see to it that my father is buried right? Seeing as it was you that finally put the name to him?"

"Of course. Thank you, for everything."

They fell silent when they heard footsteps

outside, and Mick finally appeared with the milk. Mrs. Nolan smiled at him. "Did you have to go milk the cow, then?"

Mick set the bottle on the table. "I thought you might like some time to talk, the two of you."

"Ah, you're a good lad, Mick. Maura, your kettle's boiling."

Maura stood up quickly. "Oh, right. I'll take care of it." And Maura made her first pot of tea in her house, to serve to her first guests — and family.

EPILOGUE

The Church of St. Mary was surprisingly well filled, for the funeral of someone that most of the people seated inside could never have known. And maybe there was a sprinkling of gawkers who had read about the body from the bog and wanted to pay their respects or see what the fuss was about. In any case, Maura was happy that the long-dead Denis McCarthy was going to be laid to rest at last, buried in the family plot in Kilmacabea.

They'd held a wake the night before, at Sullivan's. Maura had served at plenty of wakes back in Boston, but this was the first time she'd had a personal connection with the honoree. Mick was a closer relative to Old Denis McCarthy than she was, but he had graciously volunteered to handle the bar, to give her a chance to talk to people. And talk they had! She'd lost count of how many times she'd told the story of tracking down a killer (even if that wasn't what she'd had in mind), and when she'd finished that, they had asked how she'd come to inherit the pub. But the curiosity did not seem intrusive, and she found herself smiling more than she had expected. She'd never remember the names of all the people who had come up and introduced themselves — and their introductions had often been accompanied by a short genealogy and how they too were related to Denis or Old Mick — but she was sure she'd see them again. How many more complicated family relationships could be found in this crowd? It made Maura's head hurt to think about it, but she'd bet she was cousin to about half of the people. If she had wanted to expand her family, here she had done it with a vengeance.

In the church Maura had taken an unobtrusive seat in the third row, and Jimmy and Rose had squeezed in beside her. The current Denis McCarthy sat in the front row with his grandson Jerry beside him — looking uncomfortable in a jacket — but at least he was there, and Jerry was trying to do the right thing. He had met Maura's eye once in passing and had nodded in recognition, then looked away. Bridget Nolan sat next to him, with Mick at her side.

Once the service ended, a group of young, husky pallbearers lined up by the plain wooden coffin and began the slow procession out of the church. Denis McCarthy made his slow and cautious way behind the coffin, followed by Jerry and then Mick escorting his grandmother. Outside the church Old Denis would be carried off to the Kilmacabea cemetery. The lane leading to the site was too narrow for cars, so most of the attendees scattered rather than attend the burial, and Mick had explained that the ground was too rough for his grandmother to manage, and he'd volunteered to stay with her. Others lingered, since Mick Nolan had made it known that there would be food and drink available at Sullivan's after the ceremony. Maura saw Jimmy and Rose head straight down the street, to finish setting up and to open the doors. She drifted toward the cluster of people around Mrs. Nolan and Mick. "You want me to go ahead?" she asked.

"We should go together," Mrs. Nolan said firmly.

"Are we walking?" Mick asked his grandmother.

"What else would we be doing? I think I can still manage a sidewalk, thank you. I've plenty of years left in me," Mrs. Nolan said, and looking at her now, Maura could believe it.

"I'll be along in a few minutes — there's something I want to do first. You go ahead and I'll meet you there," Maura told them. Odds were that it would be another late night, and she wanted to do this one thing before she joined the crowd at Sullivan's.

As Mick led his grannie slowly to Sullivan's, Maura crossed the street and went to her room at the Keohanes' house. There was one loose end left: she had to tell Denis Flaherty in Australia all that his letter had set into motion. She took up a pad of paper and stepped outside her room, finding a seat at one of the tables on the patio. After a moment of gazing at the view, she began:

Dear Mr. Flaherty,
You don't know me, but I'm a distant cousin of yours, formerly from Boston but now living in County Cork. I want to tell you about the family that we share here and how I came to know about it . . .

ABOUT THE AUTHOR

Sheila Connolly is an Agatha Award–nominated author of both the Orchard and Museum Mysteries. She has taught art history, structured and marketed municipal bonds for major cities, worked as a staff member on two statewide political campaigns, and served as a fundraiser for several nonprofit organizations. She also managed her own consulting company, providing genealogical research services. In addition to genealogy, Sheila loves restoring old houses, visiting cemeteries, and traveling. Now a full-time writer, she thinks writing mysteries is a lot more fun than any of her previous occupations. She is married and has one daughter and three cats. Visit her online at www.sheilaconnolly.com

The employees of Thorndike Press hope you have enjoyed this Large Print book. All our Thorndike, Wheeler, and Kennebec Large Print titles are designed for easy reading, and all our books are made to last. Other Thorndike Press Large Print books are available at your library, through selected bookstores, or directly from us.

For information about titles, please call:
  (800) 223-1244

or visit our Web site at:
  http://gale.cengage.com/thorndike

To share your comments, please write:
  Publisher
  Thorndike Press
  10 Water St., Suite 310
  Waterville, ME 04901

CPSIA information can be obtained
at www.ICGtesting.com
Printed in the USA
FFOW03n2043230317